W9-ANU-125

Date: 4/13/12

LP FIC CARIE
Carie, Jamie.
Pirate of my heart

PIRATE OF MY HEART

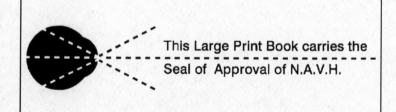

PIRATE OF MY HEART

JAMIE CARIE

THORNDIKE PRESS

A part of Gale, Cengage Learning

GALE
CENGAGE Learning®

Detroit • New York • San Francisco • New Haven, Conn • Waterville, Maine • London

GALE
CENGAGE Learning·

LIBRARY OF CONGRESS CATALOGING-IN-PUBLICATION DATA

Carie, Jamie.
  Pirate of my heart / by Jamie Carie. — Large print ed.
    p. cm. — (Thorndike Press large print Christian historical
fiction)
  ISBN-13: 978-1-4104-4384-7 – ISBN-10: 1-4104-4384-1 1.
Heiresses—Fiction. 2. Nobility—England—Fiction. 3. Ship
captains—Fiction. 4. Large type books. I. Title.
PS3603.A7465P57 2012
813'.6—dc23   2011045645

Published in 2012 by arrangement with Broadman & Holman
Publishers.

Printed in Mexico
1 2 3 4 5 6 7 16 15 14 13 12

To Patricia and Roger Thompson
(Aunt Pat and Uncle Roger)

I didn't realize when I married Tony that he would bring such wonderful people into my life. Your love and support over the years has meant the world to us. We are so blessed to have you in our family. Roger can still be "the duke" but I hope you both like pirates too! This one is for you!

Prologue

Arundel, England — 1777

The gray clouds of dawn shivered against the paned glass of the castle, shrouding the three figures at the side of the four-poster bed in an eerie light. The raging storm of the night before had settled into a dreary misting rain though an occasional jagged flash of lightning flaunted its power, not yet ready to relinquish its right to ravish the leaden sky. Dim light clung to the faces of those inside the bedchamber where the very walls seemed to echo the anguish felt inside the room.

All that could be heard in the chamber was the shallow, labored breathing of the one abed. A frail creature, now, pale and lifeless after the travails of childbirth. The others included the old family doctor, Radley, who hovered beside his patient and friend of many years with a strained look in his eyes. Hovering in the shadows was

Bridget, the lady's long-standing nurse and companion. But their suffering was not to be compared to the tall, handsome gentleman who knelt at the woman's bedside, her hand clasped in his; a haunted look in his eyes that attested to the fact that he, too, feared the end was near for his beloved.

He gazed down at the limp form of his wife. She lay so still, so pale, sunk into the feather mattress as if she'd become a part of it. In a matter of hours she'd become a shallow breathing shell of the bright and glorious woman she had once been. How was he to live without her? His heart spasmed with the thought.

He held his breath as her thin, white eyelids opened to reveal pain-racked eyes the color of bluebells. She exerted a small strength in squeezing his hand while a serene smile played at her lips. Her voice was a weak whisper. "I will not be leaving you forever, my darling. Our daughter will grow strong and always be a symbol of the love we shared."

"No." Edward groaned in anguish, his head falling forward, his hand clasping tight as if to force his strength into her. "I will not let you go."

"Love her, Edward. Love her with all that you are." Lady Eileen closed her eyes seeming to gather what little strength she had to continue speaking. A small, whimpering sound came from the shadows of the room where Bridget held the newborn babe to her bosom. Lady Eileen opened her eyes at the sound. "Please, let me hold my sweet child."

The nurse skirted around the bed with the tiny bundle, her eyes bright with tears. "She's the mos' beautiful of babes, my lady, truly she is." She laid the wee babe in her mother's fragile arms.

His wife stared down at their daughter and then looked up at him. Her voice became fierce but still so quiet Edward had to lean in to catch the words. "This one has a special purpose in life and I expect you all to care for her as I would have."

Edward could only nod, mute and staring, aching with grief.

"I have one more request to ask of you, my love." Her breath rasped in and out causing the panic in Edward's stomach to claw into his chest like a nightmare's hand, but he nodded for her to continue and clung to her hand.

"My greatest joy in life has been you. I want her to find love, someone to share her life with who is as kind, as loving and wonderful as I have had in you." She rested a moment before continuing. "Let her choose, Edward, do not make a match for her. I know it is right." She gasped for a final breath. "I've made provision. In my will . . . no entailments, Edward. Give her the dragonfly brooch as a promise from me that I will be looking down from heaven to keep her safe."

"Of course, my darling, anything you ask I will do."

A small smile touched Eileen's lips as she gazed at their beautiful child for the last time. With a single tear sliding down her cheek, she kissed the light fuzz on the child's head. "I love you." She breathed the words with her last breath, barely audible, and then she went still.

Edward collapsed over her limp hand still clutched in his strong one. "No," he cried with ragged breath. He brought the hand to his cheek, soaking it with his tears, willing her to come back to him.

CHAPTER ONE

Arundel, England — 1796

Kendra stopped halfway down the path that led to the stables, happiness lifting her heart at the autumn scene. The leaves had turned into a crimson, sunny yellow and carroty riot of color, as if a magician had waved a wand during the night and created a new world. She stepped across the lawn, feeling the kind of happiness that burst against the walls of her chest, stopping long enough to turn in slow circles so to watch the waving leaf show. She closed her eyes, still slowly twirling, and smiled up toward heaven, humming a simple song of praise to God. The notes of her song danced around her and made a happy knot form in her throat. There was nothing she loved more than singing praises to God. Her father had instilled his love for God in her since she was a child — always making sure they had a curate in the village residence for weekly

11

services at St. Nicholas Parish Church, praying with her each night before bedtime and teaching her Scriptures and hymns. Most of all, he'd been an example of someone who was temperate, kind, and patient. They had memorized the Scripture about the fruit of the Spirit — love, joy, peace, patience, kindness, goodness, faithfulness, gentleness, and self-control — and often reminded each other of the one they should practice when the occasion called for it. She wished so much to be like him, but sometimes her best intentions went awry and she fell short, far short of her father's shining example.

The sound of wheels crunching over dead leaves gave her pause. She stopped, turned toward the horseshoe drive at the front of the castle, and saw a shiny black post chaise carriage. Who could it be? They had not seen visitors in so long. Kendra hurried toward the entrance to meet their guest, then came to an abrupt stop and clasped her hands in front of her dress. She held her breath as a tall, handsome man sprang from the carriage. He was dressed in a double-breasted waistcoat of navy wool with an intricately knotted necktie at his throat, cream-colored breeches, and matching hose. She lifted her gaze to his face. Her jaw dropped with surprise. The face staring back at her looked like the one in her bedchamber mirror each morning . . . except for the color of his eyes.

Andrew Townsend matched his niece's startled gape as he found himself looking into the younger, female version of himself. Surely this was not Edward's daughter! She could have been his own child. Recovering from his shock with more effort than he'd exerted in months, Andrew questioned the young lady. "And who might this lovely creature be? A relative of mine, perhaps?"

She curtsied and smiled up at him. "I'm Kendra Townsend, sir, and who might you be?" Her smile was soft and contagious, so irresistible that Andrew found himself thawing in her presence.

"I am Andrew Townsend, your uncle, my dear." He held out his hand in greeting. "I am most pleased to finally meet you. It seems we bear a striking resemblance to one another."

"You're very handsome," she stated with bold-faced honesty.

Andrew let out a bark of laughter. "Well. Thank you, I'm sure. Now, would you be so kind as to show me to your father? I have some business to conduct with him."

"Of course, sir," Kendra replied as she reached for his arm. "You're Papa's brother, his twin, aren't you?" Her eyes lit up as she led him through the front door, past an astonished butler, and down the wide corridor, the elegant carpet making silence of their footsteps. Just as well, the surprise element couldn't hurt. It was impossible to gauge how his dear brother was going to react to his request.

"Father will be in his study with his solicitor this time of day." At her knock they heard a preoccupied "come in."

The Earl of Arundel sat behind an ancient desk with stacks of documents in front of him. Facing him was Mr. Walcott, the trusted family solicitor. Andrew hadn't seen him in an age and a half. As they walked into the study, Edward's face lit up with joy. Then, as he looked beyond her, his eyes widened and his mouth dropped open.

"Andrew?"

Andrew put on his best smile and chuckled, walking forward toward his brother. He needed Ed to accept him back into the family fold and that might require some persuasion.

"Great heavens, man, is it really you?" Edward came from behind the desk and greeted him with a handshake and an

14

awkward hug that turned into a haphazard slapping against his shoulder. "You remember Parker Walcott." He motioned to the man who had risen, eyes round behind his spectacles.

"Yes, of course. How's the family, Parker? Dorothy and the children doing well?"

"Oh, very good, my lord, yes indeed. And yourself?"

"After meeting my lovely niece here, I couldn't be in better spirits," Andrew replied. "Ed, why have you failed to mention our likeness in your letters? It nearly frightened us both out of our wits when we clapped eyes on one another." The laughter in his voice was real this time.

"It's been so long since I've seen you." Edward hastened to explain. "Until this moment I didn't realize just how much you resemble each other." He glanced from one to the other, astonishment and something disapproving — consternation perhaps — in his eyes before continuing. "Your eyes are more blue than her unusual shade of violet, but you're quite right, you resemble twins more than you and I ever did. It's remarkable, is it not?"

Edward motioned for Andrew to have a seat. "Please, join us." They both looked up at Kendra to find her staring at Andrew.

15

Andrew winked at her as he plopped down in the chair beside Parker. Edward cleared his throat and frowned at his daughter. Obviously ol' Ed didn't want his daughter fawning over him. Not that Andrew could blame him. He *had* been the rake of the decade and everyone knew it. "Kendra, go down and have Willabee bring up some refreshments, please."

Kendra nodded but clung to Andrew's side before she left. "How long can you stay Uncle Andrew? You should stay at least until the end of the week." Her eyes were bright with excitement.

"And what, pray tell, happens at the end of the week?" Andrew asked with a half grin that he'd been told sent the ladies into a swoon.

"I've persuaded Papa to have a garden party." Her eyes slid to her father before she continued. "He hates to entertain you know, but I've been so forlorn for company my own age since my friend Lucinda moved away that he's feeling guilty and has agreed. Please say you'll stay. Lady Tarlington's girls will be absolutely speechless for once."

"I seem to recall a Lady Tarlington, lives down the way, only other gentry around here?" At Kendra's nod Andrew chuckled with the memory. "A bit of a sourpuss. Are

16

her girls as malicious and backbiting as she and her sisters used to be?"

Kendra put her hand to her mouth in an attempt to suppress a horrified giggle.

"Can't offend them though," Andrew continued with grave mirth, "must do our duty and invite the only other *crème de la crème* in the area, even though it is soured cream. Is that the dilemma you find yourself in, my dear?"

"Papa says I must love them as the Bible says." Kendra raised her brows in beseeching charm that he recognized as one of his own trademark moves. "But if you were there it would be ever so much easier. They will be nice in hopes of an introduction. Please say you'll stay."

Andrew caught his brother's gaze and asked in a soft voice, "Can you deny her anything?"

Edward looked down and cleared his throat, a red flush filling his cheeks. "Very little, I'm afraid."

Swinging back to Kendra's expectant gaze, Andrew mused, "I will have to give you your answer later, moppet, but I promise I'll try."

That seemed to satisfy her as she gave him a happy nod and turned to leave the men to their business.

"You're going to have a devil of a time fighting off all the suitors at your door, Edward. She's amazing," Andrew remarked as he watched the whirl of Kendra's skirts around the door as she left.

Edward sighed. "I've already had my share of offers, but she's just nineteen. I'm not ready to see her betrothed to anyone yet."

"I can understand why, she brightens up the old place." Pausing, Andrew ran his fingers through his blond hair and added, "I was truly sorry about Eileen, Ed. I would have attended the funeral had I not been out of the county."

"I won't pretend I was anything other than devastated. But time has a way of taking the edge off the grief and Kendra has taken care of the rest. I don't know how I would have gone on if she had died with her mother."

Andrew didn't know how to respond to his brother's heart-wrenching revelation. Edward had aged in more than the receding hairline and creases around his mouth, it would seem. Andrew cleared his throat and looked down at the floor.

Edward leaned across the desk, his hands clasped together. "Enough about me, what have you been doing with yourself these last fifteen years?"

"A little of everything, I dare say. Traveled

around a good bit." The rake's smile slid across his lips and he shrugged. "Been enjoying life with good drink, fine horse-flesh, and beautiful women."

Edward shook his head in an older brotherly way. "I know only too well of your love for the worldly passions. It's a life that will never satisfy you, you know. I have to hear of your exploits every time I'm in London. When will you settle down? Start a family of your own?"

A bark of laughter escaped Andrew's throat. Not here ten minutes and he was already getting the lecture. "Now is not a good time for thinking of that, Ed. I . . . uh, seem to have gotten myself into a bit of a jam." Glancing at Parker Walcott, Andrew girded up his courage and rushed out the rest before his nerve failed him. "I was hoping to have a word with you, big brother. I have some business I would like to discuss."

Parker rose and gave a brief bow to both men. "I will bid you both good day, my lord. You and your brother have much catching up to do."

After the door was closed, silence descended upon the room. Andrew braced his elbows on his legs and pressed his sweaty palms together.

Edward broke the silence with a voice

19

both grave and guarded. "What can I do for you, Andrew?"

Shifting in the chair, Andrew ran a well-manicured hand though his blond hair, took a deep breath, and plunged into his story.

It would seem Andrew had heard, through a reputable source, about an investment that was sure to make him a very wealthy man. The Brougham Company had been started to finance several voyages of trade to America with goods the colonists desperately needed. Five great ships had set sail over six months ago to deliver their goods. Andrew had invested all that he had and was given a great deal of credit as he bore the Townsend name.

The first two ships had been attacked by pirates and overtaken. The following ship did not survive a great storm, and of the two that made it to America, one had perishables on it that were ill-packed, causing the contents to spoil, while the other had cheaper goods that even when sold at an exorbitant price did not come close to making up for the expense of the trip. "I've lost everything and my creditors are threatening Newgate Prison if I don't come up with the funds."

Edward listened with sinking despair. It seemed fate would never grant his twin the

20

power he so desperately coveted. "Of course I will help you, Andrew. Have your creditors send me the contracts and I will take care of them." He paused before continuing in a fatherly tone. "I understand you want to handle matters on your own, but please consider consulting me or even Parker Walcott before plunging into a scheme like this in the future." Edward pressed his lips together with that eagle-eyed stare that always made Andrew squirm in his chair. "I could have had the company investigated for you, at the very least."

"Of course." Andrew shook his head, eyes downcast. The act was growing tedious but he pressed on. "It's just that I was so excited. I wanted to surprise you and Mother with my good fortune. I realize the family thinks me a spoiled dandy so I wanted to do something to make you all proud. Instead, I proved what an idiot I am."

"Now don't be too hard on yourself. We've been through worse and we'll come through this together."

"I can't thank you enough, Ed. Just the thought of that prison sent me fleeing here on wings. There is just one more thing," Andrew rushed out, fidgeting with his fingers. "I was wondering if the creditors could go through old Parker instead of you.

21

That way it won't become common knowledge that my brother had to pay off my debts. It's a matter of pride, you see." He raised his brows and gave Edward a shrug of his shoulders.

"Of course. There's no need for our business to become something for the gossip mills."

Andrew stood up, gave his brother a quick, firm hug, and hurried from the room.

Edward gazed at the closed door, sadness and bewilderment weighing down his shoulders like a sodden blanket. He had not seen his brother for years, and then when he finally did come home, it was only because he was in trouble and needed money. Would they ever be close?

Dear God, help me reach him.

He let his thoughts drift back to their childhood, a good and proper upbringing he had always thought, but not without its animosities. Animosities that led all the way back to their birth.

They had heard the tale countless times. Edward had been the firstborn twin, the heir to the earldom, but it had come about by a strange quirk of fate. His mother, who now lived on her own estate miles from Arundel, had pushed for hours with no sign of a baby coming.

The midwife, in an effort to feel the baby's position, placed one hand on the extended abdomen and the other inside the womb. She pulled back in surprise. "Your ladyship, I do believe you are having twins. There's a head and feet near the opening."

His mother gasped and her face whitened. "Twins! I shan't be able to do it."

The contractions continued though, strengthened instead of daunted by the thought of two.

Hours dragged by as they all wondered if Lady Lenora would be able to deliver the babies. In a wondrous moment, a hushed moment between pushes, a tiny foot poked out of the womb. The midwife didn't say anything but knew the importance of the firstborn's place so she tied a scarlet thread around the tiny ankle. Gently slipping the foot back up, she concentrated on delivering the other baby in the head-down position. The child seemed ready to cooperate and after several more minutes emerged from the womb.

"A boy, my lady." One of the servants rushed to take the child to clean him before he was presented to his mother. After another hour, Lady Lenora held two healthy sons. She noticed the thread and looked up at the midwife. "But what's this, Ida?"

The midwife told the story of how that child had poked his little foot out first and thought to tie the thread around his foot in the event that Lord Townsend would regard him the firstborn.

And he had. Lord Albert Townsend named the babe with the string around his ankle Edward Alexander Townsend, and proclaimed him the rightful heir. Lenora named his twin brother Andrew Richard Townsend and privately thought that son was cheated.

Edward's knuckles whitened with the memory as he clenched his hands into fists. They'd been so close when they were boys! Inseparable until the day Andrew heard the story of his birth, bluntly put by a stable hand. Andrew had changed then, pulling away and becoming distant and ever more brooding. After awhile it seemed they had little in common and less to like about each other. And that wasn't even the worst of it. The resentment his mother held destroyed their parents' marriage. Lenora devoted herself to spoiling her younger son which forced the earl to take Edward's causes.

Edward sighed, his head dropping forward, sadness pulling at his heart. They were so different in every way. Andrew was strikingly handsome with his fair hair and pale blue eyes, so much like their mother. Edward supposed he was the epitome of an Englishman with his dark brown hair, aristocratic nose, and hazel eyes. And that was only their outward differences. Inwardly they couldn't be more distant. He, a long-grieving widower, and Andrew, a financially destitute dandy in dire straits. But he was back.

His brother had come home.

Maybe if he loved him enough, if he showed it and gave him all the attention and praise and . . . well, whatever it was that Andrew needed, maybe he could, uptight Englishman that he was, humble himself and shower his brother with love.

Father, help me love him the way he needs it. Help me show him You.

CHAPTER TWO

Boston — 1796

Dorian Colburn stood in the shipyard, eyes squinting against the midafternoon sun, a satisfied smile playing around his lips. She was beautiful, perfect, and he couldn't be more pleased. His gaze roved the sleek lines, the curves and hollows and rich tones of ivory and brown. Fast. The best way to describe her. The speed he anticipated she could produce sent a jolt of excitement through him. She would surpass anything he'd known until now, he was sure of it. And she was all his.

At the sound of steps he turned and let his smile fade a degree as he greeted the ample form of the builder, Don Monteiro. "How much longer?" Dorian asked.

The man's gaze swept from Dorian's face to the huge ship and then back, finally meeting his eyes. "Another two weeks, as I thought." He shrugged. "We're doing our

26

finest work with this one. I'm sure you wouldn't want it rushed."

Dorian gave him a ruthless grin. "There's where you're wrong, Monteiro. I want it within the week and I want it perfect. I have contracts waiting."

Don Monteiro, the most renowned ship designer in the New World, drew up his stocky frame to an impressive five feet and ten inches and, with his thick neck turning a telling shade of red, scowled. "If you hadn't had to have the luxury of a king she'd have been done before schedule. You've had my men at their best." He rocked back on his heels. "As it is, with all those fancy additions of yours, you'll by lucky to get her within a fortnight. You've already cheated me out of her name, my boy. You'll get her when she's done and not a day before."

Dorian's lazy smile at the reminder of the ship's name caused the man's entire face to redden in an angry flush.

Monteiro usually demanded the privilege of naming each of his ships before he sold it, but Dorian had wrenched that particular pleasure from him within weeks of working on this project together. Monteiro's daughter, the beauteous Angelene, had taken to visiting the docks, batting her long dark lashes, and bestowing a besotted gaze on Dorian, taking every opportunity to stroll with him down the quay and touch his arm and laugh at whatever he said as if he were the most charming man she'd ever met. Monteiro hadn't been too happy about that. He'd made it clear that they were to stay away from each other. But Angelene hadn't paid her father any mind and neither had he.

It wasn't as if he had openly courted her. But women always made it so easy! Was it his fault they fell at his feet? He wouldn't be a man if he didn't notice a pretty woman like her flitting about, practically begging for his attention. But then Dorian had come up with a brilliant idea. A way to make them both happy — in return for the *privilege* of naming his own ship as Dorian had put it, he would tell Angelene that he was spoken for and let her down easy.

Monteiro had been outraged at first. It had taken him awhile to realize that Dorian wasn't the typical dandy of the wealthy and affluent, but an intelligent negotiator who knew what he wanted. He'd given in and hadn't mentioned the name of the ship since.

Dorian pushed his annoyance with the famed shipbuilder aside as he studied the

28

sleek lines of the ship. The new gaff sails were up, flapping in the wind, and men were just now testing the headsail. He chuckled and then locked his gaze to Monteiro's and drawled out, "I thought you might like to know I've decided upon a name."

"What is it then?" Monteiro's voice grated gruff and angry.

Dorian blinded him with a dazzling smile. "I'm thinking the *Angelina,* after a certain young lady I know, that is if you don't meet my date. But . . . if she's on time?" He shrugged his broad shoulders and lifted one dark brow. "Who knows what lovely lady I'll meet up with before the week is out."

Monteiro let out a dark expletive and slapped his thigh in vexation. "You wouldn't dare! Why the girl would think you were in love with her if you were to go and do a fool thing like that."

"Precisely. Don't look so glum, Monteiro, we both know you can do it if you want to. Hire some more workers," he shrugged, "whatever it takes." Dorian put out his hand and waited, one brow raised, for the man to capitulate. It didn't take long. He grinned with mock sympathy at Monteiro's harassed features. "I'll see you at the end of the week. Good-day, sir."

■ ■ ■ ■

Monteiro cursed again, turned, and trotted as fast as his stocky legs could carry him back to his office. He had a lot of work to do if he had any prayer of getting the ship done in five days. But then he slowed and paused with his hand on the door handle and let out a laugh. That boy was something else. No one had had him scurrying to do their bidding like this since he was a young man himself. Maybe his daughter couldn't do better. He considered the thought, his brow creasing. Maybe he shouldn't be in such a hurry after all.

Making his way to his hired carriage, Dorian rapped on the side with his knuckles to wake his driver. He shook his head in amused disdain. He'd never encountered a driver who fell asleep if you left him alone for more than ten minutes, but this poor fellow had been doing it all day.

The thin man jerked awake, uncurling into a stiff, upright position. "Pardon, sir. Where to next?"

"The Stag. Time for some dinner, eh?"

The nervous man jerked around in his seat and slapped the reins just as Dorian reached to open the door.

"Whoa!" Dorian yelled after him, letting go of his grasp on the handle of the carriage as it bounded away. The man sawed back on the reins, giving the poor horses a sudden stop, and turned in his seat to see Dorian walking up to the carriage.

"It might be a good idea to wait until I'm safely inside before we travel, don't you think?" Dorian asked with mock gravity, choking back a laugh with a loud cough.

The driver stammered. "Your p-pardon again, s-sir. It's m-my first day with this team."

Well, that explained some of his peculiar behavior. "Just relax, my good man. You'll do fine."

The man stared, speechless at the kind treatment, so Dorian slipped inside and yelled, "Now go!" Dorian leaned back against the worn leather, stretched his legs out to rest upon the empty seat opposite him, crossing them at the ankles, and thought back to his ship. After five long years of working aboard one or another of his father's ships, all brigs, he was finally getting his own. He'd planned and saved and worked for this for the last two years, and in a few more years he hoped to have a small fleet. Yes, Colburn Shipping Company was being born with this three-masted schooner. Trade with England was good, better than good. He already had several contracts for tobacco, rice, and indigo, and those names his man in London had scratched up were promising, very promising. Now if Monteiro believed his bluff about the name, he could expect to have the *Sea Falcon* loaded and taking to the water within seven days.

The sudden halt of the carriage jerked him out of his thoughts and back to his inexperienced driver. With a sigh, Dorian jammed his dove-colored hat upon his head and climbed out to the dusty street. John would be waiting for him. They were to meet for a quick meal in the hotel's dining room. Turning toward his driver, he shouted up, "If you'll go around to the kitchen, I'll have them revive you with some food and drink."

The man nodded his thanks and trotted off toward the back of the building. Dorian couldn't help but grin, it was the fastest he'd seen the fellow move all day.

Dorian made his way through the crowded sea of townsfolk to where John sat waving him over. He was thankful he hadn't had to make this trip alone. There had been a hundred details to attend to with getting the ship ready and hiring a crew. John was going to make an excellent first mate and, more important, Dorian could trust him with his back.

"Well, look who the cat dragged in. I'd about given up. Did you have problems with Monteiro?" John goaded as Dorian sat down across from his friend.

"No, he's agreed to have her ready by the end of the week."

John uttered a soft word and grinned, showing off his white even teeth. "I know your powers of persuasion to be convincing, but would you care to tell me how you managed that?"

Dorian shrugged. "Just a small matter of his daughter and the name of the ship. The *Angelina* has a nice ring to it, don't you think?"

Their boisterous laughter rang out across the dining room, attracting the attention of the patrons. There wasn't a pair of female eyes looking elsewhere.

"So how's the search for able-bodied sailors coming?" Dorian asked after the serving girl set down two plates of meat pie and a variety of colorful vegetables.

"Found three more this morning. That brings us up to, um, seventeen. Two or three more ought to do it, right?"

"Better sign on a few extras. Sailors are

known for getting roaring drunk the night before they sail. We'll be lucky if they all show up."

"Good idea. I know you wanted quality men, Dorian, but it hasn't been easy. Most of the men I've found are a rough lot. I'm glad several men volunteered from your father's ship to help start out your crew. At least that way we know we'll have a few good men."

Dorian nodded, swallowing before he answered. "Father was glad to let us have a few. He said after captaining them for the last few years they were more loyal to me than him anyway." Dorian lifted his broad shoulders in a shrug and grinned. "Too bad I couldn't have taken them all."

John laughed. "From what I heard, your father didn't stop you, it was old Captain Hassock. He said he was taking over the *Endeavor* and he didn't want a bunch of greenheads underneath him."

Dorian leaned back in his chair and pushed the empty plate away. His mother was always complaining he inhaled his food and he supposed he did. John had barely eaten half of his pie. "He never did let me get away with anything. I still remember the first day I set foot aboard his ship. Cabin boy and only sixteen." A grin tugged at

Dorian's mouth as he remembered how frightened he'd been. Hassock was a huge man, over six and a half feet tall and weighing over two hundred and fifty pounds, the crew had nicknamed him The Mountain. "He taught me everything I know." Dorian's voice was soft in remembrance.

"And then you decided it was time to go out on your own." John finished for him. "I'll admit I'm more than a little excited to be going across the pond, but don't you ever get tired of being at sea? I don't think you've been home for more than a few months at a time since those cabin boy days."

Dorian turned his head away, remembering what had really, at first, driven him to life at sea. He'd been running, running away from *her.* But John knew better than to bring that up. Barking out a laugh to chase off the sudden chill in his spine, Dorian mused. "I'm sure your pretty fiancée hopes it doesn't happen to you, but it's in my blood. I feel landlocked if I'm away from it too long." He couldn't really put it into words but when he stepped on the deck of his ship, after being on land awhile, he felt alive again, rejuvenated, home. The sea demanded much of a man. At times, strength and endurance to brave the mighty waves and gale winds. At other times, patience, watching the calm lapping water lick the massive side of the hull, but always a bated expectancy, never knowing from one moment to the next what nature had in store for the small, lowly men in her belly.

Shaking himself from his nostalgic mood, Dorian sat up and drained his mug. "Anyway, we'd better get back to work. There are still a lot of last-minute details before we sail, *first mate*."

Two weeks later the ship took to the water like the gentle landing of a flock of geese on a pond, settling gracefully to the hull's midsection. White water frothed around the bow as the *Angelina* was launched into the Atlantic. Dorian stood with his first mate and best friend at the stern, watching where they could oversee the activity of the men.

"I still can't believe it. The *Angelina*?" John's face had reddened from being out in the wind and sun and new freckles stood out on his cheeks. It was a face Dorian had known as his best friend for as long as he could remember.

"I had no choice. The old fellow took me up on my bluff and I was forced to hold with my word." Dorian answered with no small degree of anger in his voice.

"Are you saying he purposefully delayed

the ship's readiness?"

"So it would appear. I asked for her to be ready in five days, and she was, almost. Monteiro claimed part of the rigging was frayed and he wanted it checked before handing her over."

"But you don't believe that?"

"I checked the rigging myself the day before and it looked sound to me."

"Then why'd he do it?"

Dorian let the corners of his lips raise a notch in self-mockery. "I believe he has reconsidered the prospect of having me as son-in-law."

John let out a whoop of laughter. He clapped Dorian on the shoulder. "Monteiro doesn't know who he's dealing with and neither does the pretty Angelene. You'll find a way out of this scrap, like you always do."

Dorian hoped he was right.

Edward looked up as his solicitor, Parker Walcott, entered the earl's library a fortnight after Andrew's visit. His gray hair poked out in all directions, accenting the deep crevices upon his face and making him appear more and more a loony old man than a respected barrister. He'd never seen Parker look so pale. "Parker, is something wrong? You look as if your daughter just ran off with a servant."

"I only wish it was something akin to that, my lord." Parker's hand shook as he reached out to steady himself into the chair facing the desk. "You may wish you hadn't rejected all of Lady Kendra's suitors after I tell you this. I'm afraid no one will have her now, after what I'm about to show you."

Edward felt the man's panic come over him in an alarming wave. "Well, what is it, Parker? Stop rambling riddles and tell me."

"I just received the contracts from your brother's creditors. My lord . . . did your brother give you any indication of the amount of the notes?" His voice shook.

"Well, no, but it doesn't matter, I can't have my brother sent to Newgate. Are they much more than we expected?" Edward raised his brows in consternation. Of course Andrew didn't tell him the amount. Why had he not thought to ask before blithely agreeing to cover them?

"Here, take a look, my lord." Parker thrust a stack of dog-eared papers across his desk.

Edward thumbed through the papers, the numbers jumping out at him as if alive. His stomach quivered as he made the calculations. Outrageous. Preposterous. How could Andrew have rang up such a mountain of debt? And how could he have been so dishonest when he'd hinted at the amount? Andrew had not even come close to being honest with him. Besides the enormous sums due from the creditors of the Brougham Company, there were several thousand pounds worth of bills from various gambling debts.

"You'll be ruined, my lord." Parker's eyes pulsated with the bleak truth. "These men played your brother for a fool. If you pay them off, there will be nothing left, not even a decent dowry for Lady Kendra."

A strange deadness had come over him but at the reminder of Kendra's dowry he perked up. "Eileen left a small estate for Kendra to receive on her betrothal as a dowry. It's from her side of the family and is untouchable." Edward's voice lowered. "At least she'll always have that to fall back on."

Parker nodded. "Ah, yes, the lack of entailments stating that only the male heir can inherit. Lady Eileen, God rest her soul, was wise to insist on the matter. I had forgotten about that."

Edward dropped his head in his hands. "But how are we going to pay all of these debts, Parker?"

"You could always change your mind about paying them and let Andrew take his own chances." From the tone in his voice it sounded like the course Parker recommended. Maybe he should. Andrew would never learn his lessons if he was always bailed out of his scrapes. But the thought of his golden-haired brother being tossed in the horror of Newgate made his stomach turn.

"No." Edward shook his head in his hands. He would rather become a pauper than let his twin brother suffer such an end.

"Well, in that case, you can pay a large portion of the debt with your available funds and the sales from this year's harvest. After that I'm afraid you will have to sell your partnership in the shipping business. And then you may have to sell some land, the more valuable paintings and furnishings," Parker paused with a look of despair, "possibly everything of value that you own. You should be able to retain the castle and some Arundel land to make a small living, but that is all."

Anger expanded from the pit of Edward's stomach, spreading to his throbbing temples. How could his brother have been so ignorant as to gamble such a large fortune when he was already in debt from past gambling failures? "I want a summons sent to Andrew immediately. I vow, he will sell his worldly possessions down to the clothes on his back and be here to witness his family's ruin." He wanted to add "may the devil take him" or "may he rot" but stopped the thought. *God help us,* he cried out in silent helplessness instead.

It took Andrew two days to arrive in his fancy black carriage. Edward watched it swing into the Townsend drive from an upstairs window and ground his teeth. That carriage would be the first thing to go. His gaze roved over the matched team of grays and his brother's fashionable clothes, calculating their cost in his head. Fury hummed through his veins as he realized his brother didn't seem to care that he flaunted the picture of a wealthy gentleman while his family became paupers. This had gone too far, beyond sin to some sort of evil. Never in his wildest dreams had Edward imagined his brother could get himself into so much trouble. Didn't he have any sense?

A scratching at the door announced his butler.

"Come in."

"Sir, Lord Andrew has arrived." The butler's cheek gave a nervous twitch as he looked across the expanse of the sparse room toward Edward. And well he should

41

be nervous. After serving the Townsend family for over three decades the man wouldn't have a job for much longer!

"Bring him in." Edward walked forward and crossed his arms in front of his chest.

A few moments later, Andrew slunk into the room, his head down, shaking his head at the carpet like a sorry little boy.

A tirade of insults sprang to Edward's mind like he had never imagined, but he pushed them aside. "Do you realize what you've done?" His voice held the despairing rage that he felt.

No answer.

"You've ruined your family! Ruined us all, you fool."

Andrew remained looking shamefaced at the carpet.

Edward walked up to his brother, standing only inches away. "Look at me, Andrew. Look into my eyes and see the devastation."

Andrew looked up, those pale blue eyes glassy with unshed tears. "Ed, I —"

"Everything I've worked for is gone. Not just for Kendra and myself but for you too, the future Townsends." Pointing back toward the window, he whispered in a hiss, "Then you pull up in that fancy carriage with horses that must have cost a small fortune." He poked Andrew in the chest.

"While I've been paying off your debts, you've been living life on the scale of the haute ton." He reached out and gripped one of Andrew's shoulders. "That's going to end, Andrew. You are going to sell everything you own down to your extra pair of stockings and live here while we, *together,* work like beasts to keep what little we have left. Do you understand me, Andrew?"

Andrew nodded his head. "Ed, does this mean I actually have to move home? You're not going to work me like an animal around this old pile of stone, are you? Won't I even get a small allowance?"

The whining tone put Edward in a new state of anger he had never experienced before. "Allowance!" he thundered. "Even if there was money to give you one, I would not! It's time you took responsibility for your actions and became a man. Your carousing days are over. Your gambling days are over. You are going to stay right here and pick up your responsibilities." Edward backed away, afraid he would strike him. He took a deep breath and lowered his voice to that of a stern father. "You've been coddled and spoiled far too long and it shows. It's partly Mother's and my fault, you've been left to yourself all your life and had too much time and income to get into this mess. You need discipline, not an allowance. I see our mistake now, but it's too late. The damage is done."

Andrew waited, standing silent and still, head hanging, face in shock, like the golden boy who had just been sentenced to prison.

"I don't want to see any more of you now, leave me." Edward pointed toward the door. "And don't bother my daughter!"

CHAPTER THREE

An ominous thunderstorm slashed the night sky as Dr. Radley hunched deeper into his cloak, rain pouring in a steady stream off his hat and down his back. He tried to hurry through the shards of sleet but his horse trembled beneath him and started with every flash of lightning, making progress difficult. His gaze rose to the swirling dark clouds as his face contorted in agony, wishing to be well away from this night, this news he must impart. It was eerie — the similarity between this night and the other, over nineteen years ago, when he had been to the Arundel castle and helped deliver the lovely woman he raced to see.

Minutes later he rode through the gate, yelling to the guard to fetch a stable hand for his horse. He rushed through the castle, the cold clinging to him like his news. There she was, in the main salon, looking out a window toward the direction her father would arrive home, even though it was too dark to see. Doctor Radley stood there, dripping all over the floor, his sodden hat limp in his hand. She turned as he walked further into the room. "Lady Kendra." He held out an arm toward her. "I have terrible news. I'm sorry, my lady. There's been a terrible accident. I'm so sorry."

Kendra shook her head slowly back and forth, a sensation of falling making her sick and dizzy. "What?" But he didn't have to say it. She saw it on his ravished face. She turned away from the doctor, the news, and buried her head into her hands. "No, no. It cannot be." She shook her head, a small move of disbelief, the anguish pulling her under. He was dead? Her father? The only person in her life who had always loved her? Her knees gave way and she collapsed to the threadbare settee, numb, dazed with the shock. Her fingernails dug into the ragged cloth of the arm.

"It was a terrible accident." Doctor Radley's voice seemed to come from very far away. "The only carriage that remained in the earl's possession this past year wasn't in good shape. Lord Edward shouldn't have taken it out."

"How? How did it happen?" Kendra managed to make herself look up into his pain-racked eyes.

"My dear, mayhap we should discuss the details after you've had a chance to, ah, calm down."

"Calm down? Calm down," she repeated, her hands reaching up to either side of her head. She rocked back and forth, pressing on her head. "My father is dead and I'm to calm down." Her voice dropped to a whisper as if all the strength had pooled out of her. "I have nothing now. Nothing. Tell me what happened."

"The horses must have been frightened, the lightning you know. It's a devil of a storm out there." He rushed on, "The carriage plunged over a cliff, there was nothing but scraps of wood left of it."

Her father had driven out to an old family friend to ask for a loan. It had taken the last of his pride, Kendra knew, but they needed the money if they were to even consider spring planting. He had been gone two days and had likely wanted to return home to Kendra despite the storm. She had watched from the window all evening.

"Where is he?" Kendra whispered, her hands pressed to her heart as if to keep it from breaking in two. "I have to see him."

"I don't think that would be wise, my

dear. It was such a great fall. You would not recognize him —" He took a step toward her but she jerked away.

The doctor stopped and then turned toward his black bag. Reaching inside, he pulled out a bottle and poured some of the liquid into a cup of tea that was sitting on a small, round table and had grown cold. "Come, Lady Kendra, drink this. It will help calm you." He coaxed her into a sitting position and pressed the cup into her hands. She lifted it to her lips, not caring what it was. After a few moments a lethargic weakness came over her. Her arms grew tired and leaden, her legs too shaky to stand upon. Doctor Radley took her arm and helped her up to her bedchamber. He tucked the blanket under her chin and promised, "I will come back and check on you soon. Try and get some rest."

Kendra closed her eyes as silent tears rushed, one after the other, down her temples and into her hair. After a while, the numbness settled over her entire body and she was left with a barren emptiness that reached to her soul. The grief pitted in her stomach like iron to a lodestone but a languid tiredness overcame her body as the doctor's sleeping draught took full effect. She allowed her heavy, swollen eyelids to drop and she slept.

The days following the funeral blurred together in a numb stupor. The whole village had turned out at St. Nicholas Parish Church to say farewell to their kind master. Kendra wandered about the estate in a lost way, with the vacant hole in her heart deadening the blue of her eyes. Her uncle Andrew took up his place as the new Earl of Arundel, but she rarely saw him, even at dinner time. He was locked away in her father's library. Doing what, she did not know.

Months after that horrible day, Andrew called Kendra into the library and bade her to sit down. Her uncle took the seat behind her father's massive desk. She could hardly look at him there, where her father should be. When she did look up, Andrew's gaze was impassive while her father's had been kind and so full of love for her.

"You must have something terrible to tell me since I've barely had the comfort of your presence," she said in a dead voice. She was so tired, nothing seemed to matter anymore.

"Not terrible, my dear, and I'm sorry I've been so absent. I miss him too, you know."

"You do?" It didn't seem so.

"Of course I do. Now, I have had to decide

upon your future and we need to discuss a few things." Andrew cleared his throat and took on a lecturing mien. "After giving the matter a great deal of thought, I've concluded that it is time you marry. This has been too hard on you, hard on us all as you know, and I believe the best way to put your father's death behind you and move forward with your life would be to have a family of your own." He stared down at her. "No, don't give me that look. A husband with some little ones along the way is the obvious answer." He paused here and looked down at the papers on his desk, shuffling them around a bit. "As you know we cannot afford a London season and all the fripperies that it would entail, so we must proceed in a quieter manner. I assure you, my dear, I will do my best to find someone suitable to your station."

"And what does 'proceeding in a quieter manner' consist of?" Kendra asked. She could hardly endure the thought of men calling on her.

"I have put forth word, in an offhanded way of course, that I am seeking a suitor for my niece. I'm rather hoping that some of your past suitors come up to scratch."

"My past suitors?" Kendra exclaimed. "What suitors?"

"Your father must have failed to tell you of the offers he had for your hand. In his foolish attempt to keep you with him as long as possible, he turned them all down. Now, considering our present, er, situation, a suitor will be more difficult to find."

Kendra paled. Her father *had* wanted her to marry. Maybe what Uncle Andrew said made a certain amount of sense. She had little desire to stay in the empty loneliness of the castle with an uncle that didn't seem to care for her company. Maybe a family of her own was the best solution. "How soon should you know something?"

Andrew smiled brightly, a little too bright for Kendra's peace of mind. "You should be pleased to know that I have been fortunate enough to already have an interested party."

Kendra disliked the way he spoke of the whole ordeal like she was something to be rid of rather than considering that this would be the most important decision of her life. "And who would that be?"

"His name is Lord Randall Barrymore. He owns a grand estate in Wilfortshire and a respectable fortune. Furthermore, he is coming to dinner tonight. If all goes as expected, we can sign the betrothal agreement and have you married before the summer is out."

"Before the summer is out?" Kendra rose to her feet. "How will I decide in such a short space as that? I'll need time to meet these, these suitors and if, and only if, one of them is acceptable to me, then I will need further time to get to know him. I'll not marry a total stranger."

Her uncle's handsome face turned red as he set his teeth. It was not a pleasant look on him.

"Your father raised you to be entirely too independent, my dear," he grumbled in a low voice. "At any rate, thus far there hasn't been a very great response to my hints, actually next to none, so you will have to make the most of the situation and make yourself as pleasing as possible to those who have responded. Lord Barrymore is a fine catch and I assure you that you will have plenty of time to get to know the old man once you're married." He must have realized his slip of the tongue as he reddened further.

"Old man!" Kendra cried. "Surely you could find someone closer to my age."

"As I said before, the pickings have been slim." Her uncle's tone rapped sharp and impatient. "Wear a nice gown, not the black mourning frocks you've been moping about in and be on your best behavior for dinner."

Kendra gasped. "But I am in mourning. It

would be scandalous to wear anything but black before a year is out."

Andrew leaned in and impaled her with his flashing blue eyes. "We do not have the time nor the resources to wait until a year is out. You will do as you are told, Kendra!"

Kendra's eyes widened at the rebuke. She had never been spoken to in such a harsh manner and felt a rush of shame as tears threatened her eyes.

Her uncle gentled his tone. "Kendra, please. I'm only doing what I think best. We do not have the most ideal circumstances and will have to make the most of it."

Kendra stood and curtsied but her soft answer parried like a sword. "Yes, but don't *you* ever forget who brought about those circumstances." The thrust rang true as Andrew's face blanched white. Kendra turned and stormed from the room, slamming the door behind her.

Of all the low down, horrid, mean spirited. . . . ugh! Kendra muttered to herself the entire way to her room. There weren't words in her vocabulary to heap onto her uncle's character. How had he turned out to be such an insensitive clod who hadn't a care for her feelings? Her father would have never allowed the situation to come to this. The gall, asking total strangers to come and look her over as if she were some prized mare. She had no doubts about what tonight was really about, however her uncle tried to disguise it. Oh! It was intolerable. Unbearable. She had to think of something.

She rushed into her room and rang for Tess, the kitchen maid who was good at arranging hair. Eyes narrowed, she sat down at her dressing table and scowled at her reflection. She had a couple of hours to come up with a plan. She wanted to hide until the old coot gave up and went home, but that wasn't really an option. Her uncle would only drag him back and she would have to face him sooner or later. She needed something more subtle.

Rummaging through her wardrobe she chose her plainest gown. All of her everyday dresses were getting a well-worn look to them, but she still had some formal gowns remade from her mother's clothes and she dared not be so blatant as to appear in anything else. She remembered how her father had insisted she keep her mother's things when over a year ago they sold most of their belongings to pay Uncle Andrew's debts. A kinder, dearer father never lived. The thought brought a lump of tears to her throat.

Tess arrived and rushed to her side.

"Here, now, my lady. Let me help button your gown." After finishing that task she led Kendra to the seat at her dressing table and started fussing over her hair. As she reached for a pair of pretty combs, Kendra shook her head and handed her plain ones. "Won't you at least let me run some ribbon in your hair?"

"No, Tess, I want to look my worst." She sighed as she contemplated her reflection. The gown was a dull gray, but it only seemed to enhance her violet-blue eyes. It had an unfashionably high neckline with small ruffles around the collar edged in lace. The sleeves were long, tight fitting with matching ruffles at the wrists. The cinched waist made her figure curvier than she liked. Her blonde hair was caught up in a severe bun at the nape of her neck, but a tiny wisp had already escaped to frame her face in a softening way. Kendra stuck out her tongue at her reflection and stood. Oh, well, she would just have to be as unpleasant as she could manage.

Tess threw up her hands. "Well, I've not seen you look worse."

"That's excellent news, Tess. Thank you."

Tess only shook her head and rushed out of the room to help prepare the meal.

A short time later Kendra was summoned

to the green salon, one of the few rooms with furniture left in it. The dread in the pit of her stomach caused a strange churning sound. She hoped she wouldn't need to carry a chamber pot on her arm throughout the evening. She smiled at the thought, what an entrance that would make! Mayhap she should go back to her room and fetch it. With a shake of her head, she inched down the curving stairway and stopped just inside the door to survey the scene.

Her uncle looked up at her and frowned. Kendra held back the bubble of laughter that threatened to explode from her chest. He probably hadn't known Kendra owned anything so distasteful. He composed his angry expression, though, and came forward to lend his arm.

He led her over to a man who must be at least seventy if he was a day. His beady eyes surveyed her from the top of her head to the toes of her shoes peeping from beneath her gown. She stared back, chin up, looking down her nose at him in exaggerated distaste. He finally looked away, mopping his forehead with a lacy handkerchief. A cloying smell clung to him and made her want to gag. She didn't know if she should burst out laughing or crying. Lord Randall Barrymore was a terribly thin, slavering man with beady, darting eyes set in a red, splotchy face. *Dear God, please get me out of this!*

He took Kendra's hand, leaving it with a sloppy kiss, and stated in a nasal voice, "I am most pleased to meet you, Lady Townsend."

Kendra jerked her hand away and wiped it on her skirt. She turned her head away, ignoring his greeting, which caused Andrew to jab her in the ribs with his elbow. "The pleasure is mine, I'm sure." She didn't try to cover the sarcastic tone in her voice.

Andrew gulped down the drink in his hand as a servant announced that dinner was ready to be served. Her uncle hesitated and then offered Kendra his arm once again. He must have known she would ignore Lord Barrymore's arm, had he extended it.

"Shall we?" Uncle Andrew glared at her behind Lord Barrymore's back, despite his tight smile and jolly voice.

During the dinner, between tiny bites of food, Lord Barrymore boasted of his wealth, describing in detail his penny-pinching methods of keeping his estate intact.

So, he was a miser along with being too old for her. When he started to expound on his manly abilities and how she was not to worry that age had slowed him down, she knew she had to do something. It was time to act.

"Not to worry, Lord Barrymore, for I have no desire for children. We need not even consider them, really." She looked up into his face and gave him a sunny, innocent smile. "I always sleep with my door bolted and a gun under my pillow."

Andrew sucked in a breath at the blatant lie and glared at her, his face turning red.

"Well, there will be no more of that!" Lord Barrymore wiped his thin lips with a cloth and widened his eyes at her.

Kendra floundered for a second in despair and then plunged forward. "Oh, you'll not want to see me as a mother. Why, I've taken such poor care of my pets that they never lasted over a year." She laughed with a fake, hollow sound. "My greatest talent is, of course, shopping. I must have a new wardrobe every season, and I seem to go through jewels like water. Why, just the other day I misplaced my favorite diamond and emerald necklace. We must replace it with a better one, dear uncle," she added sweetly, nodding to Andrew, knowing he couldn't disagree with her without giving away their dreadful state of finances.

Andrew gave her a look that said he would like to wrap his hands around her throat but only smiled a smile so bland that Kendra had to shove down the laughter.

"Of course, my dear," he choked out.

Lord Barrymore gaped at her, looking properly appalled with the vision of his wealth slipping through his fingers.

By dessert Kendra had countered everything important to Lord Barrymore until, by the end of the meal, he made his apologies, saying he had suddenly taken on a headache, and fled as fast as his legs could speed him out the door.

Andrew burst into a fit of rage as soon as the door slammed shut, while Kendra let out the laughter she'd been suppressing all night.

"What do you think you're doing, you ungrateful brat?" He stormed around the room. "He was the only one that responded to my offer!"

Kendra looked him square in the eyes and replied in a calm and serene voice. "I wouldn't marry that skinny old goat if he were the last man on earth. We will not suit and you know it."

Andrew's eyes turned dark as he glared at her. He took a deep breath and made another circle around the room and then faced her with his hands extended. "My dear, don't you see, with no dowry we are limited . . . I'm only trying to do what is best for you."

"A lecherous old man is in my best interest? Uncle, how could you think such a thing?"

Andrew turned away with a great sigh. "Well, if you won't wed a man of my choosing then I have only one option left. You will go to America to live with your mother's sister." There was a hint of certain victory in his voice that made Kendra sit up straighter and grip the arms of her chair so that her knuckles turned white.

"You would send me away from my home?" Her anger grew apace with despair at the thought of leaving England. "You would ship me off halfway across the world just to rid yourself of me? You despise me that much?" Her voice dropped into confusion mixed with the pain. "What have I done to make you hate me so?"

"Kendra, I'm only trying to do what is best. You shouldn't live here the rest of your life. It's time to make a future of your own. If you can't find it here in England, then mayhap you will find happiness in America."

America or Lord Barrymore. She could hardly fathom either possibility. "If those are my choices, I will need time to consider. I will give you my answer in the morning,

Andrew." She had deliberately left out the "uncle" title that she had always called him with such pride and joy. She knew it was wrong, but she wanted to hurt him as he was hurting her.

Andrew seemed not to notice the slight as he nodded his head.

Kendra picked up her skirts and ran, tears blinding her, to her room. Once inside her bedchamber she paced back and forth. *Father, why did you have to leave me like this? What do I do?* She could either resign herself to a miserable marriage or take her chances in America where she would at least have some say in her life. She hoped she would, in any case.

Kendra tried to remember everything her father had told her about her aunt and uncle. It wasn't much, she decided, plopping back on the bed and staring at the ceiling. Why had her relatives left their homeland to travel to a new world? She knew that some of the aristocracy had been appointed posts in America when they were England's colonies and many had stayed on after the war. Maybe that was it. She contemplated appealing to her grandmother for help, but soon realized the folly of that plan. Her grandmother only had eyes for Andrew and was sure to agree with him.

Dear Lord, please help me make the right decision. The image of Lord Barrymore popped into her head. She thought of the marriage bed, what would happen if she married him, and knew her answer. She would leave her home and take her chances in a strange new land.

When dawn finally peaked its head above the horizon it found Kendra dressed and ready for her future. She wanted as much of the time she had left to see her favorite places around the estate. There were the tenants to say good-bye to and the wooded creek she had played beside as a child that had been her secret haven. Her uncle was inclined to rise late, so she would have time to spare before the dreaded confrontation.

Just before noon Kendra strolled into the hall. The butler, Hobbs, seemed nervous as he said with a shaky voice, his hands twisting together, "Oh, thank goodness it's you, Lady Kendra. The earl has had us searching high and low for you. I believe he thought you had run off."

"Ran off?" If only she had somewhere to run off to. She made her way down the corridor to the library and knocked.

A gruff voice answered. "Yes, what is it?" Kendra recognized her uncle's black mood and sighed.

She entered the room to a thundering lecture as to the fright she had caused everyone. *Patience!* She repeated the reminder to herself, remembering her father's teachings. Finally, Andrew paused for a breath and she was able to make her announcement. "I have made a decision, Andrew."

He stopped and stared at her. "I hope you've come to your senses."

"I'm going to America."

For the first time ever, her uncle's face blanched with genuine shock. "You would rather leave your country than marry Lord Barrymore?"

"Yes." Kendra stared hard into his eyes.

"Well, in that case, be prepared to leave within a fortnight. I will write a letter of introduction for you to take to your aunt. They will be forced to do their duty by you with you on their doorstep, all the way from England."

Kendra's heart sank. He was really going to send her away. She bolted for the door as fresh tears sprang to her eyes. *Love. Love your enemies.* She heard the words but couldn't imagine how to do that when all she wanted was to have her father back.

Chapter Four

Kendra stepped out onto the stone terrace and blinked back tears. The dawn of a beautiful day, a most perfect day, and her last day in Arundel. The sky was turning blue as the pale pink shades of a sunrise seemed to dissolve in a million tiny faded particles, leaving the world bathed in a warm yellow glow. The lush greens and brilliant colors of the garden with its white daisies, lavender, rows of primroses, and dotted clumps of red and pink carnations that she had painstakingly tended bloomed and waved at her with the early summer breeze. Pots of purple pansies were scattered along a stone path that led to a row of hedges and a low bench where she had spent many a summer's day reading or just daydreaming while sitting in her garden.

Shakespeare's *A Midsummer Night's Dream* and the fairy king Oberon leapt to her mind and made her smile. Furious with his queen over a baby, the king laid crushed pansy petals on his wife's eyelids while she slept as he believed the special properties from the pansies would make Titania fall in love with the first thing she saw upon waking. In this case he planned that she see a man with a donkey head. Kendra smiled and then a crushing sadness swept over her. She would never sit here and read again.

Lord, am I making a mistake? I feel as if I'm leaping from a cliff. She turned down a winding path that led into a leafy bower bordered by rose bushes. She stopped under a sunny spot, closed her eyes, and lifted her face into the warmth. *Please, don't let me make a mistake.*

A whirring sound and something tickling her nose made her eyes fly open. There, darting around her, were two dragonflies. She gasped, reaching for the brooch that she had placed on the bodice of her dress that morning. It had been her mother's gift to her at her birth and she only wore it on the most special occasions or on days like today, when she needed the extra courage and to feel close to her parents. The dragonflies flitted about her, zigging and zagging, swooping near her head and then away. A smile spread across her face as joy flooded her chest. It was a sign. Her parents were with her, watching over her and telling her everything would be okay.

She twirled slowly around with her arms outstretched. *Joy. Thank You, Father. I needed that today.*

"Lady Kendra!" One of the servants called her name.

She turned and hurried back toward the house. "Coming."

Her trunks had been loaded onto a new carriage and she knew her uncle was waiting for her, no doubt pacing and slapping a riding crop against his thigh. She walked through a back door and gave a last look around the drawing room where she and her father had spent many evenings together playing chess or dominoes, drinking hot chocolate while he told her stories of their ancestors' plights throughout the centuries. The ache of missing him flared into a sharp piercing pain as if someone had just stabbed her. Her throat worked as she swallowed it back, pressing one hand against her chest.

Joy. The joy of the Lord is my strength. She remembered the dancing dragonflies and allowed God's peace to return to her heart. Her parents may have been taken from her, but God would never forsake her, not even in a place as far away as America. With that thought bolstering her flagging spirits she forced her chin up a notch and walked from the room, closing the door with a soft click behind her.

The few servants they still had were gathered outside, standing in two short lines on either side of the door in their faded red and gold livery.

She'd heard Andrew trying to discourage them earlier that morning, saying it would make Kendra's parting harder, but they had flatly disobeyed him. They didn't treat her uncle with the same respect born out of love that they had given her father. As Kendra walked down the steps they bowed or curtsied, one after another, several with tears shining from their faithful eyes.

Kendra smiled at their tribute and bit her quivering lower lip. She wanted them to be proud of her and this was no time to be weeping. Several stopped her progress and whispered oaths of loyalty. "You will be sorely missed, my lady," and "We won't forget yer lovely self," among many good-bye hugs. The cook, Mildred, was beside herself, tears racing down her full cheeks as she stammered out with a quivering chin, "It j-just w-won't be the s-s-same without you in the k-kitchen, my lady." At first cook had been appalled when Kendra had rolled up her sleeves to help, but after a time she'd gotten used to the idea of a lady in the kitchen and enjoyed teaching Kendra how to make tasty meals from simple ingredients.

"I shall miss you too, Mildred." Kendra patted her arm. She glanced up and saw Andrew picking invisible lint from his sleeve between heavy sighs and some eye-rolling. Kendra turned to look once more at the visage of her home and the good people who were like family to her and said in a loud voice for all to hear. "On behalf of my father and myself, I would like to thank each and every one of you for the wonderful care you have taken of our family. Please do not think of this as a final good-bye, for one day I plan to return and I expect this place to be in excellent shape." She bobbed a quick curtsy and turned away before they saw the trembling of her bottom lip. Refusing her uncle's outreached hand, she climbed into the carriage and waved one last time. Her uncle ignored the slight with a careless flick of his hand and climbed in beside her.

Three days trapped in this tight space with him. Kendra stared out the window at the rolling farmland that had been her home and wondered how she would endure it.

"You didn't. Tell me you're joking." Dorian could not believe his firstmate had made such a decision. After hearing the story of how some English earl had cornered him at a tavern the night before and how John had been goaded into taking on a passenger, a *female* passenger, he squeezed his hands into fists, hardly able to contain his anger.

"I told him no at first." John slung his hands into his pockets and grimaced, looking away.

"Don't you see, the man was trying to force you into giving in."

"But I raised the fee by a hundred pounds! I couldn't believe he met my price and figured it would make our trip more profitable."

"Did you also figure on all the trouble a woman is going to give us? Confound it, man, what could you have been thinking?"

"Sorry, Captain. I won't make a decision like that without consulting you again."

Dorian stopped pacing and took a deep breath. "Well, the damage has been done so we may as well make the best of it." Even as he said it the damage was moving toward him like the lit string of a firecracker.

"There he is." John pointed toward a tall, blond man walking up the dock toward them. Beside him was a stunning creature, decked out in a plum traveling costume with an enormous hat that bordered on being comical. Huge ostrich feathers drooped and waved over a mass of purple, orange, and white flowers on the brim. No doubt the ridiculous monstrosity was the height of fashion. Dorian groaned. They looked to be London's finest.

"You'll be responsible for her, as you got us into this mess."

John paled beside him. "What do I do with her? She's — ah, she's —"

Dorian laughed. "Move her into my cabin and tell her to stay there. I'll bunk with you."

"What makes you think she will listen to me? I mean, look at her!"

"Just keep her away from my men."

As the elegant couple drew closer, Dorian sucked in his breath. She was tall by standard, her head reaching just above his shoulder. Her golden hair was swept up into the monstrous hat, a hat that matched the most arresting bluish violet eyes he had ever seen. He felt as if he had been punched in the stomach and had to order himself to breathe again.

She soon came to be standing in front of him. She tilted her head back to see his face from under the wide brim. As her gaze met his it seemed a sparking electricity, the kind of which the famed Benjamin Franklin told about with his kite, passed between them, jolting him with its suddenness and strength. She blinked, surprise filling her brilliant gaze as if she too felt it and then quickly lowered her eyes. Dorian noted the small nose with two tiny freckles on it and then his gaze became fixed on a pair of cherry-colored lips, the color of his mother's prized roses back home. He wanted to lean in and kiss them. Absurd. And stupid to even let the thought cross his mind. What was wrong with him? His mind screamed the question while his body stood as taunt as a mainmast in the wind. She was going to be a whole new kind of trouble. He looked down at her and scowled.

Kendra's glimpse of the man had only lasted a few seconds but his image burned in her mind. She'd never met an American before and he looked as wild as she'd heard them to be, handsome in a rugged way that she was unaccustomed to. His face was tan, so different from the milky white complexions she was used to seeing. He had rather long, dark hair that had been brushed back from chiseled features and waved in the breeze. His eyes were a cerulean blue with silver flecks in them and filled with piercing intensity and . . . disdain. Thick black brows arched almost wickedly over his eyes. His chin was square with a small cleft and she sensed he may have a dimple in his left cheek when he smiled. Small lines stood on either side of his well-molded mouth. His lips were slightly wide with even white teeth peering behind them. Kendra peeked up through her lashes and saw broad shoulders and a wide chest. He looked like a pirate she'd once read about. *Goodness Lord, I didn't know You made such men for real!*

Peeking up at his face she saw him frown with such a look of disapproval in his eyes that it took her aback. What had she done to cause him to give her such a look?

Her eyes widened as she realized the turn of her thoughts. What did she care if this captain didn't like her? Heathen, blackguard, thieving pirate most likely! But she did care and that made her all the angrier. Of all the injustices, first she was being thrown out of her home and then there was this, this, man whom she would be forced to spend the next few weeks with, maybe even alone with . . . Oh goodness, she had to get these wandering thoughts under control. *Goodness! Self-control!*

The other man rushed to make the introductions. "Lord Townsend, this is Captain Colburn and I am John Lucas. And this must be your niece?"

Andrew nodded, peering down his nose at Kendra. "This is the Lady Townsend."

Kendra dipped her head toward John but ignored the captain as Andrew continued. "I have the payment we agreed upon and instructions for some overland travel once you've reached America. As your fee is exorbitant, you will see to it that she is safely delivered?" Andrew pulled out a clinking purse and pressed it into John's hand.

Kendra frowned. Where had her uncle come up with so much money?

"Of course, sir." John assured her uncle. "We will see her safely delivered."

The captain cleared his throat and John rushed to correct the statement. "That is, I will see that she finds her destination, sir."

Well at least this John fellow seemed decent enough. The captain obviously didn't want anything to do with her.

Andrew turned to Kendra, gave her an awkward pat and a peck on the back of her hand, which she wrenched out of his grasp, then spun about on his heel and left. Kendra raised her chin a notch, trying to still the traitorous quiver of her bottom lip. She ignored the captain and looked at the kind face of the other man. "I'm ready to board, sir." When she glanced at the captain she saw that he was glowering in the direction of her uncle's back. Well, let him scowl! She was on her way to America and meant to make the most of her new life.

John offered Kendra his arm and saluted the captain with a secretive smile. "I'll just be about my duties to the lady, sir. As you directed."

Kendra looked from the gleeful, teasing eyes of John to the thunderous gaze of the captain, as he replied, "See that you do."

John turned to her and flashed a bright smile. "After you're settled, I'd be happy to show you around the ship."

"Why thank you, sir. It is so good to see that some Americans have gracious manners."

John made a choking sound as he hurried them away, leaving the *pirate,* as she chose to think of him, to follow behind with the trunks.

"I do believe I've upset the captain. He has been looking daggers at me since the moment we met, but I can't fathom what I've done," Kendra confessed to John when they were out of his hearing distance.

John only shot her a knowing smile and murmured, "So I noticed. I do believe, my dear lady, that this voyage is going to be very interesting."

■ ■ ■ ■

Kendra paced the short breadth of the cabin she had so impulsively confined herself to. She did hope that the nice man, John Lucas, would come back for the promised tour of the ship. And where were her trunks? For goodness sake, the captain was right behind them when she boarded. They held all of her belongings in the world and she wasn't about to let the ship sail without them.

Peeping out the door, she looked down the narrow passageway. A man was just going out of sight around a corner.

"Excuse me, sir," she called out, waving her arm.

The man turned around and then gaped at her with slack-jawed astonishment.

"I'm looking for my trunks. Could you be so kind as to check with the captain as to their whereabouts?"

"Three big trunks? We just carried them up to the first mate's bunk. But I'll let the captain know you're wantin' them, ma'am."

"Thank you." Well, if she didn't quite have the nerve to search the ship for the elusive captain, at least she could get a message to him, and she felt better just knowing her things were on board. Kendra shut the door and studied the room. It was something of a surprise — elegant and well appointed, complete with a high feather bed and satin counterpane the color of thick cream. There was a mahogany writing desk and chair in the corner and a rectangular table made of a peculiar light-colored wood with two matching chairs that looked as if it had come from some exotic island. The cabin would be well-lit at night with plenty of candles in elegant silver candlesticks and an oil lamp of modern design on the desk. Bookshelves lined the walls where, after a quick perusal, she found a few novels such as *Robinson Crusoe,* a book of fables, and poetic titles roaming between volumes on natural history and nautical interests.

Walking to the lamp, Kendra lit the wick to better illuminate the room. She was surprised to find that the furniture was secured to the floor, but as the ship rocked to one side, nearly knocking her off balance, she realized the wisdom in this. She carried the lantern to a table beside the most lavish piece of furniture in the room, a deep-shelved armoire. She opened it, her hand gliding across the enameled brown and gold doors to find it full of the captain's clothes.

Before she had time to stop and think what she was doing she had pulled out a crisp, white shirt. It unfolded itself in a neat motion and hung from her fingertips. She held it closer, closed her eyes, and breathed in the captain's scent — brine and wind, the sea, male — her insides slid and a melting feeling washed over her.

Goodness gracious! She balled the shirt up, threw it toward the back of the armoire, and slammed the door shut. What had gotten into her? She must, at all costs, avoid this captain of the *Angelina*!

Kendra woke early the next morning and wandered out onto the deck of the ship. She stood at the railing letting the gentle breeze soothe her rattled mind and body. Yesterday she had stubbornly remained in the cabin and missed their departure, which she regretted now. It could have been her last view of her homeland and she had let that infuriating captain keep her hibernated in the stuffy cabin. Well, that wouldn't happen again.

She looked down at the endless lapping waves of the sea against the hull of the ship and breathed deeply of the salt-laden air, but her calm was unsettled due to the prickling sensation that she was being gawked at. Kendra glanced around and couldn't help but notice all the stares she was receiving from the men who stood in various positions of pretending to work behind her.

Dorian watched, transfixed, as Lady Townsend approached the railing of his ship, *his ship,* with a mixture of awe and anxiety churning in his stomach. The sun shone bright on her uncovered head. She was wearing the plum dress but this time her hat dangled from her hand, feathers trailing the wood boards of the deck that had been scoured with sand until they were almost white. She raised her hand to her eyes and looked out over the endless gray waves to the sunrise. The light was rosy on her face, making her hair come alive with glints of gold.

He expelled a breath and then clenched his jaw closed as he realized he'd been holding it in. His view couldn't be better, directly above her on the quarterdeck. It also afforded him a bird's-eye view of his crew. As reality returned to him, the commotion she was causing with his men became evident. Anger flared into his cheeks. *Get control, man. And get control of this ship!*

His booted steps rang out on the wooden stairs as he marched down to her side. He came up behind her, leaned in, and rasped out in a quick staccato in a voice that never failed to cause his men to pale with fear and rush to obey. "I remember ordering you to remain in your cabin." He took a firm grasp on her elbow.

She swung toward him, her violet gaze a rapier's thrust. The nearness of her, the touch of the silky skin of her upper arm left him rolling, reeling, like a rowboat in the midst of rising thirty-foot waves. Her gaze narrowed at his tone. "But my dear captain, since you ignored my message last night I was forced to search you out myself and find the whereabouts of the mysterious disappearance of my trunks." Her voice lowered to a soft purr. "It seems you only deem yourself worthy of their care."

Dorian bit his tongue, shoved what he wanted to say back down inside, and took a step back. The woman was enough to make a saint curse. "If it's only trunks that you seek, then by all means, we will fetch them this instant."

He turned away to order the trunks delivered to her.

She stopped him with a hand on his arm. It was a mere brush of a touch but it seared his skin and his muscles jumped where her fingertips encountered his upper arm. It took him a moment to be able to concentrate on her tirade.

"Captain, let us come to an understanding. I will not be locked up in a stuffy cabin during the entire voyage. You cannot treat me like a prisoner. I am a paid passenger and expect a passenger's rights."

Dorian found himself gazing at her fast-moving lips, thinking how he would like to take her into his arms and kiss her silent. He shook his head, trying to rid himself of the sensation that someone had stuffed his mind with wool. "This, Lady Townsend, is not a passenger ship. Therefore you have no rights. I am captain of this ship and you will obey my orders like the rest of this crew." When she opened her mouth to argue, Dorian cut her off. "This is for your own good. Don't tell me you didn't notice the attention you are receiving from my men." Her stunning eyes widened at the statement but he didn't believe her. She must be aware of her feminine charms. "I will not have my men distracted from their duties to satisfy the vanity of a spoiled English *lady*."

Kendra gasped as if she'd been slapped. "Your opinion is formed from your vast experience with the ton, I presume? Why, I'm quite certain a man like yourself" — she allowed her glance to flick down to his feet and then back up to his furious gaze with all the condescension she'd seen her uncle Andrew flay someone alive with — "has attended any number of social events with the aristocracy. Next, you'll be telling me you are on excellent terms with the king. Ha. You're little but a heathen and a-a *American* pirate!" As soon as the words flew from her mouth she stopped, eyes widening as shame filled her. *Lord, forgive me. I don't know what's come over me!*

It's not My forgiveness that you need to seek. The words thundered in her ears as her face filled with heat. Taking a step back she bit her lower lip and peeked up at the captain's face, which had turned ashen with shock and anger. "I'm sorry. That was ill played of me." Kendra looked at the floor, at his boots, and thought she quite deserved to have to polish them. Maybe if she offered . . .

When he didn't say anything, just stood there as one frozen with the shock of her audacity, she began to babble. "Of course I don't want to cause any trouble, and I had no idea that I was, uh, doing that, you must believe me. But really, I cannot possibly be confined to that cabin all of the time. Isn't there some arrangement we can make so that I can go above to get some fresh air, properly escorted, of course?"

81

"I keep a sparse crew. There is no one aboard this ship who can give you a *proper* escort," the captain said with a dry note lacing his deep voice.

"Not even yourself?"

"I am quite busy running this ship and I don't have time to escort a woman on strolls." But he sounded uncertain. The captain took a step toward her and searched her eyes. Kendra met his gaze and held it, waiting, knowing he was battling with the decision of what to do with her. His face changed from stiff and stoic to resigned. "As I can see that you are trying to be reasonable and compromise, I would be willing to escort you above in the early morning and after dinner when most of my men are not on deck. That is, if you don't sleep well into the morning as most English ladies are apt to do."

Oh! Had there ever been a man more provoking? *Patience!* She took a deep breath and said in as calm a voice as she could manage, "I will have you know that I am up before the servants and will be dressed and ready at any time you wish."

The captain gave her an assessing look then turned to leave.

"What about my trunks?" Kendra asked after him.

He paused but did not turn to look at her. "Go to your cabin, Lady Townsend. I will have them brought to you immediately."

Her heart pounded as she hurried to the cabin. As soon as the door closed Kendra fell back on the bed with a groan. Had she really called him a heathen pirate to his face? She grimaced at the outrageousness of her insult, remembering how those silver-blue eyes held her caught and confused. The power he had to make her angry and giddy, hot and cold at the same time, was distressing. He was like no one she'd ever met.

Shaking her head, she tried to put some sense to her thoughts. She needed to be planning her future not daydreaming about an arrogant captain. He was part of her problem anyway. If he hadn't been so eager to take her as a passenger aboard this ship, she might have had more time to try and convince Andrew to let her stay home and stay unmarried. Why had Andrew been so stubborn and determined to get her out of his life? That was a question she had no answer for.

She rolled over and curled into a ball, grasping the elegant coverlet with one hand. If only she had someone to talk to about these rollicking emotions. The gaping hole in her chest expanded and ached as she thought of her father. She had always been able to talk to him about anything.

A psalm came to her mind: *"A father of the fatherless, and a judge of the widows, is God in his holy habitation." Oh Lord, I need that right now. Please be my Father and guide me. Help me control my tongue around that man. Help me behave in a way pleasing to You. I've never felt this way before. He makes me so . . . mad and frustrated and . . . thrilled and excited, all at the same time. What is happening to me?*

CHAPTER FIVE

Dorian hurried through his dinner in anticipation of his duties as escort. He watched
himself with self-loathing as he shoveled in
the food on his plate at record pace but he
couldn't seem to help it. There was a growing anticipation, like when dark clouds
swirled and the waves began to heave, at the
thought of seeing her again that he had
never had with a woman before. What was
it about her that held him captive, like moth
to flame? He'd never been the moth; he had
always been the flame. Women had tried to
ensnare him for years, using every trick in
the book. But none of them had ever made
his heart pound as it did when he was spar-
ring with the sharp-witted Lady Townsend.

Minutes later Dorian stood outside her
door, *his* door, he corrected with a flash of
irritation, took a short breath, and knocked.

"Come in," her sweet voice called.

He opened the door, feeling large and

clumsy as he entered the cabin. His voice came out in gruff disharmony to hers, "Are you ready for your fresh air?"

"Oh, I wasn't expecting you to come tonight, but I would love to get out of this cabin for a little while. Do you think we shall see the sunset? I do imagine that the best parts of sailing are the sunrise and sunset." She flashed him a brilliant smile that gave his knees a strange weakness. He barely heard her feminine chatter.

He cleared his throat, noticing the simple blue gown and low-scooped neckline. He couldn't seem to tear his gaze from her rising and falling bosom. He cleared his throat again and turned his head toward the wall. "The wind is a bit cool tonight, you should take a cloak."

"Yes, of course. I imagine the wind blowing off the cold Atlantic can be quite chilly at night, even in the summertime. I have so much to learn about ship life. Have you been sailing long?" It would seem she wanted to start anew and had forgiven his earlier comments. She reached for a blue satin cloak that was hanging on one of the hooks beside his bed as the stream of chatter continued.

Dorian stepped forward to fasten it for her, a movement of habit, as he would have done with his mother or sisters. He didn't consider the differences of what he was doing until he was near enough to smell the light scent of some floral fragrance she must have applied. He didn't usually care a jot about perfume, thinking it more a nuisance than an attraction, but something about the mix of lavender and mint perhaps, he wasn't sure what it was, was pleasing to his senses. "Here, let me help you with that."

Lady Townsend hesitated for a second, her gaze assessing, and then gave him a thoughtful smile and handed him the cloak. She turned, her hands reaching up by the slim column of her neck to grasp for it. Dorian's hands just brushed across the cool skin of her neck before she grasped the ties and took a step away, but he was certain he'd heard a tight gasp when he touched her. She turned toward him, her face becoming pink, her gaze darting about the room, roving on anything but him.

Dorian held out his arm. "Shall we, my lady?"

Lady Townsend bit her lower lip with little white teeth and then took his arm, her prattle ceasing with the tension.

Minutes later they had traversed the narrow hall, climbed the stairs to the top deck of the ship, and were standing side by side at the railing. Dorian searched for a topic of conversation to get her mind off what had happened in the cabin and restore some semblance of normalcy to their outing. "Was the man who was with you when you boarded really your uncle?"

"Yes, he was my father's twin brother."

"Was?"

"My father died over a year ago." As she said it a great heaviness seemed to fall upon her. Her slim shoulders drooped; she looked down and gazed into the lapping gray water.

She appeared so forlorn, standing there rubbing the backs of her arms as if to ward off the chill her words had caused. He fought the astounding urge that filled him — to take her into his arms and comfort her. Instead, he murmured, "I'm sorry, my lady. I am very close to my parents and can't imagine the day when they will no longer be with me. It must be difficult for you."

She looked up at him with a small, sad smile. There was a look of honesty and vulnerability in her face, glowing with the last rays of the sun, that took his breath away.

"Yes, it is. Thank you. And Captain. Please, call me Kendra. I find the phrase 'my lady' coming from you sounds more an insult than an honored title."

She said it with soft humor, causing Dorian to look down and laugh. "Thank you, Kendra, I am honored. You, of course, must call me Captain, as I like hearing that word in your lilting English accent."

Kendra smiled back at him with compressed lips and sparkling eyes. "That hardly seems fair, sir. Am I not to be included as a friend and an equal?"

"An equal? Why, my dear Kendra, no one is equal to the captain. If they were, chaos and anarchy would rule the high seas."

The little minx flashed white teeth at him and bowed her head in acquiescence. "I see your point. Let us hope we don't run into each other on land, as then I will expect to be told your given name."

"Ah, yes. You travel to the countryside beyond Yorktown to nurse your aunt back to health?"

Kendra's gaze snapped to his, confusion evident in her eyes. "To my knowledge, sir, my aunt is in perfect health."

Dorian's brows came together as he explained, "But your uncle told John that she is ill and in need of your care. We assumed that was the reason for your hasty departure and one of the reasons John agreed to taking on a passenger."

Kendra looked away, but Dorian could

see her rapidly batting lashes. That she was trying not to cry made him want to drive his fist into her uncle's handsome face. "My uncle lied." Her voice was shaky but angry too. "After my father died he tried to marry me off, and when that plan proved unsuccessful he made arrangements to ship me to my aunt, whom I have never met and know next to nothing about. You can see how badly he wanted rid of me." A hiccup of sound came from her throat as she stared at something off in the distance.

Dorian's arm strained to reach for her, but instead he kept it tight to his side. "The brute deserves to walk the plank," he said in his best pirate voice, trying to distract her.

She made a choked little laugh and turned to look at him. Had anyone held her since her father's death? Had anyone helped her with her grief? He thought of his large, happy family and found himself overcome with feelings of profound thankfulness and chagrin. He had so much love from family and friends, people who cared and doted on him . . . and he took it very much for granted. This brave, impish young woman seemed to have no one.

He took a step toward her, staring at the sunset with her. Her skirt brushed against his legs as he turned and looked down into her eyes. He smiled a slow smile. She was holding her breath and he could see her pulse throb at her throat. He lifted one hand and brushed his fingers against her cheek.

She swallowed hard, eyes wide. "Pirate." She whispered.

Dorian's grin deepened. "I can assure you, madam, that my business dealings are all above board. I've had fights with true pirates, though." He lifted one brow and pressed his lips together in a grim smile. "Stories that would curl your toes."

The motion of the waves caused the ship to dip. Kendra tumbled into his chest where his automatic response was to wrap his arms around her to keep her from falling. "Oh!" she yelped, and then sprang back with a gasp. She looked up at him with wide eyes, yanked her arms from his grasp. "I think I should retire now," she rushed out. "Thank you for the walk, Captain." She turned and fled from the deck, skirts swaying in her effort to take herself back to the cabin.

Dorian stood where she left him for a long time, gripping the rail and allowing the night air to cool his heated blood. She'd bewitched him. He barked out a laugh and turned to stare out at the cresting waves of endless sea. He'd been wrong to withhold his name from her.

After this night, perhaps he should be calling *her* captain.

CHAPTER SIX

Perhaps avoiding her would help him regain his sanity.

At least that's what he'd thought when he came up with the brilliant plan of commanding John to take over the duty of escorting Kendra on her twice daily turn around deck.

Dorian leaned over the quarterdeck rail and watched the two of them laughing as they came around the corner, Kendra's hand tucked in the crook of John's arm. She didn't seem to miss *him* at all. No, she seemed perfectly happy to have John's company. More happy and comfortable than with him. Jealousy, he decided, was a very unpleasant emotion. Not that John had any intentions toward her. John had been engaged for over a year and planned to marry Victoria at the end of the summer. Still, the more he tried to appear uninterested in his passenger, the more she haunted his mind.

And worse still, the crew was noticing something was amiss with their captain. He'd caught more than one hastily turned gaze or stopped conversation when he entered a room. And he'd barked orders in a tone that spoke of the raw edge to his nerves. It was astounding. How could a mere slip of a woman turn him into someone he didn't know? For the first time in his life, he felt like he didn't belong in his own skin.

The object of his thoughts laughed, causing his gaze to snap back down to her. John was leaning down and saying something close to Kendra's ear. She looked up at his first mate with another laugh and joyous sparkle in her eyes. Dorian gripped the railing under his hands until his knuckles turned white. Why did he want to march down there and jerk her from John's arm? Maybe he would.

Before he had time to talk himself out of the madness he had reached the couple. Kendra jerked her head up and took a step back. Dorian realized he was breathing with a harsh sound coming from between his teeth. *Get control, man!* He unclenched his fists and demanded his body to relax. John watched him approach with raised brows and the quivering mouth of a suppressed smile.

"Something amiss, Captain?" John looked at him as if to say, *what in the world is wrong with you?*

Dorian pasted a smile on his face and attempted a light tone. "Nothing wrong, John. I just forgot that Smythe has the grippe and has taken to his bed. I'll need you in the crow's nest this evening."

John ducked his head and Dorian could swear his shoulders shook for a moment. When he looked back up he had his features back under control. "Yes, sir. Funny though, saw Smythe a little while ago and he seemed as healthy as a horse to me." The corner of John's mouth quivered.

Dorian set his teeth. "It came on suddenly."

"Of course, Captain." John looked down at Kendra. "If you will excuse me, my lady, duty calls."

Kendra's gaze settled on Dorian with a perplexed crease on her brow, as if she knew something was not quite right but couldn't put her finger on what it was. "Thank you, John. I always have a lovely time with you as my escort. And I am looking forward to meeting Victoria. She's sounds wonderful."

John bowed his head at her then turned to

Dorian and saluted. Dorian frowned at him. He never demanded his men salute and they knew it.

Kendra sighed. "I suppose you are much too busy to play nursemaid to me, Captain, and I will have to return to my cabin."

Dorian had achieved his goal of getting her away from John, but found the idea of confining her to the cabin on such a nice evening unfair. It wasn't her fault he couldn't seem to behave as a person with a morsel of sanity. "Actually, I have a little time. It is such a fine evening. Would you care to allow me to escort you?" He held out his arm and found to his further discomfort that his heart was pounding with the fear that she would reject it. She stood there looking at him for a moment too long. He was just about to pull his arm back to his side where it belonged, when she reached out and clasped his arm, taking a step closer to him. "Why Captain, I apologize for the hesitation, it is just that you surprise me so. I was under the impression that you couldn't abide the sight of me."

Couldn't abide the sight of her? Was she daft? He couldn't get the image of her from his mind. Of course, when he looked at the situation from her perspective it might appear he wanted nothing to do with her.

Dorian put his other hand on top of her hand, the one resting on his arm, and turned them toward the bow. Determined to regain his legendary charm, he took a small breath and gave her the smile that usually had the fair sex looking at him with doe eyes. "My dear Lady Townsend, don't think it, I beg you. As captain of this ship, I have duties — I am the eyes and ears at all times. But if you've missed me so much, I will try and prioritize my time better. You are my first passenger and I'm afraid I don't quite know what to do with you."

Wrong thing to say. Very wrong.

Kendra's eyes flashed violet-hazed heat. "Oh dear," she pursed her lips, "I had no idea I have been such a weight on your mind. Why, all I asked for was a little fresh air when the weather allows. I do apologize for my . . . neediness."

Dorian stopped them and gazed down into her rueful orbs. She dimpled at him. Where had those come from? He hadn't realized when she smiled a particular kind of smile — more a smirk — that she had two adorable dimples on each cheek. Their effect on him ruined any verbal thrust he could come up with, instead causing him to stare at her lips. There wasn't much he wouldn't give to kiss those lips.

■ ■ ■ ■

Kendra took a step back and inhaled. The sun was glinting off the water and shining on his face. His eyes were smoldering as they locked with hers. She could hear her heart beat in her ears. *Oh, dear. Lord, get me out of this or I'm going to let him kiss me right here in front of all and sundry.* The prayer sounded funny, and she smiled, breaking the tension. "Captain, are you a believer?"

Dorian's gaze snapped awake. "Believer? Of what, my lady?"

"Of the Christian faith, of course. I find prayer helps at times like these." She raised her brows, hoping he knew to what she was referring.

He seemed to take the question seriously and looked off into the distance at the low summer clouds. "It's been some time since I last prayed, I admit, but I am a man of faith. My mother, she made sure we all attended church every Sunday."

"I shall miss my church," Kendra admitted in a soft and wistful tone. She thought back on the little chapel on their property. All the neighbors gathered there every Sunday and the magistrate, Pastor Timms, gave such sincere messages. Then there was her work with the poor and sickly parishioners. Bringing them baskets of muffins, bathing fevered brows, and tidying up, it was a work she had been glad to do. "I do hope to find a church in America."

Dorian stared at her with a thoughtful gaze, his humor seemingly restored. "I shall make it my mission to see that you visit mine. I do believe your aunt and uncle live close enough."

"Oh? Do you know where they live? I had thought to have to discover that on my own upon our arrival."

Dorian took her arm again and led her further down the deck. "It is just north of Yorktown, I believe. According to the description your uncle gave me."

"Is that close to where you live?"

The captain gave a short nod. "Close enough."

He didn't sound very pleased by the prospect of having her so near, which was confusing, seeing that he was offering to help her find a church. Kendra felt as if her feathers had been ruffled. She sniffed, crossing her arms across her chest.

"Are you cold?" He was the very picture of concerned care. Gracious, how the man made her emotions swing to and fro like a child's swing.

"No," but she shivered, belying her words. The breeze was rather chilly by the rail.

"Here, we can't have you catching a chill." The captain shrugged out of his coat and placed it around her shoulders. He stood in a white, full-sleeved shirt, dark breeches, and tall Hessian boots. The wind plastered the fabric of the shirt against his wide chest. Kendra averted her eyes but couldn't stop the scent from his coat wafting to her nose. It was the same scent she'd smelled on his shirt earlier, when she'd practically ransacked his armoire. Her cheeks grew warm with the memory. "Thank you," she choked out.

Thinking to turn the conversation to safer ground, she clutched the coat under her chin and asked, "Why haven't you prayed in so long?"

The captain shifted against the side of the ship and shrugged. "I guess I haven't found the need."

Kendra's eyes widened. How could anyone not need to communicate with God?

"I see I've shocked you. It's just that life has been busy and . . . well . . . taking care of itself, I suppose."

"Don't you miss Him? God, I mean?"

He was quiet for a long moment. Then he looked at her with a flash of revelation in his eyes. "Now that you mention it, I guess I do." His eyes turned teasing. "You will have me a reformed man, my lady. Indeed, I will say my bedtime prayers from hence forth."

Kendra wasn't sure if he was making sport of her or not. She was just about to launch into the benefits of a prayerful life when they heard a shout. It was John's voice, up in the crow's next.

"Ship to starboard!"

The captain straightened, turned, and started to go, then turned back toward her. "Go to your cabin and lock the door. Do not let anyone in or come out until I come for you."

Fear and an excited panic jolted through Kendra. "Are they pirates?"

Dorian shook his head at her with a small grin. "You have been reading too many novels, my lady. Let us hope not. But to be safe you must stay in your cabin. Understood?"

Kendra nodded and hurried to obey.

The ship turned out to be an American merchant ship. Dorian commanded his crew send out a longboat with the message that the captain was welcome to board the *Angelina* to exchange news if he had the time to spare. Instead of sending a message back, Captain Joseph Moore, booming with laughter and clutching a bottle of rum, arrived a few moments later.

Dorian soon realized he was in a quandary. He usually entertained guests in his captain's cabin where there was plenty of room and privacy. John's first mate's bunk was small, even more so since he had moved in with him. And the deck was growing chilly with the night air and the feel of rain coming. The only solution seemed to be to ask Lady Townsend if she minded hosting them.

It wasn't as if they would be unchaperoned with an old sea-salt like Captain Moore with them, but after his conversation with Kendra tonight, he wasn't sure she would accept such a suggestion. And he wasn't sure how he felt about their conversation on faith. Thankfully, Captain Moore had interrupted that line of talk, giving him time to dwell on the matter.

Dorian sent John to make the request while he gave Captain Moore a tour of the ship. It was something he usually enjoyed, showing off the brigantine to like-minded men who appreciated the fine workmanship, but now he was anxious, tapping his toe against the freshly scrubbed deck boards, awaiting her reply.

He took a breath of relief as John's nodding face came into view at the stairwell. "Lady Townsend said she would be happy to host dinner for you, sir. Shall I have Tipper prepare a special supper for you?"

Dorian nodded to his first mate, turning to Captain Moore. "Sir, allow me to introduce you to my passenger, Lady Townsend of Arundel."

Captain Moore gave him a wolfish smile. "A real English lady, eh? I can't say that I've met a lady of the nobility. What's she like?"

Dorian swung out his arm toward the stairs leading down to the cabins. "If you care to follow me, sir, I will try and satisfy your curiosity."

The old captain chuckled and followed Dorian to the cabin.

Kendra rushed about the cabin putting everything to rights and smoothing her hair in the looking glass. She was just pinching color into her cheeks as a knock sounded on the door. Oh, if only she'd had more time! She turned from her reflection thinking she looked as good as three minutes of primping could accomplish and strode to the door. She had not entertained in a long time. Hopefully, she would be able to keep the conversation flowing with the captain's melting smile facing her from the other side of the table.

She opened the door to find Captain Colburn and a white-whiskered, rotund gentlemen in a dark blue uniform with elaborate golden epaulettes standing beside him. He whipped off his hat in an elaborate gesture and bowed toward Kendra. She gestured toward the room, liking him instantly. "Good evening, Captain. And you must be Captain Moore, won't you please come in?"

The cabin seemed small as the two big men entered. As soon as the door was closed, her captain, as she now thought of him to distinguish between the two, made the introductions. "Captain Moore, may I present Lady Kendra Townsend." Kendra bobbed a small curtsy. "Lady Townsend, this is the captain of an American merchant ship out of Boston."

"I was so relieved to hear you weren't pirates," Kendra teased, allowing Captain Moore to take her hand and plant a big, dry kiss on the back of it. "I've heard so many stories of pirate ships while on board the *Angelina* that I was quite certain I would hear the clashing of swords above my head.

Had the furniture not been nailed down, I was contemplating how best to barricade the door. It is fortunate now that I was unable to rearrange the cabin."

Captain Moore leaned back his head, placed his hands on his hips, and boomed with laughter. He glanced at Captain Colburn with a mischievous sparkle in his eyes, "Pirates! Why, I haven't seen a pirate ship in years. You haven't been trying to frighten the young lady, have you, sir?"

Dorian winked. "Well, perhaps a little. She did seem to enjoy the stories."

"Please, won't you be seated? I asked the cook to bring tea and it just arrived."

Captain Moore took a longing look at the bottle of spirits in his hand and then set it aside on the desk. Kendra poured the tea and seated herself across from Dorian.

"Captain Moore, are you returning to Boston or departing from it?" Kendra asked, thinking to start the conversation. Captain Colburn was staring at her from across the table with a small smile tipping up the corners of his mouth, making normal thought a challenge. She frowned at him and locked her attention to the old captain's face. "I'm off to your city, my lady. London, with a cargo full of grain." He nodded his head at her. "And you, ma'am? There must be a story behind such a lovely lady as yourself sailing on a cargo ship. Making haste to see America?"

Heat infused her cheeks as Kendra realized she would be asked this question again and again once she arrived on American soil. What was she to say? Her uncle had taken a sudden dislike to her and booted her from her home? Before she had time to think of something, Dorian spoke for her. "Lady Townsend is going to visit her relatives north of Yorktown. Her aunt is doing poorly and Lady Townsend is kind enough to stay with them until she recovers."

"Oh, sorry to hear that, but very kind of you indeed. I have family near Yorktown. What is your aunt's name?"

Kendra's gaze flew to Dorian's face in a panic. He would know them, and Captain Colburn would have to prevaricate the story. "Franklin and Amelia Rutherford."

The captain paused, cleared his throat, and took a sip of his tea. "You don't say." His gaze flickered to Kendra's and then away as if uncomfortable.

"Do you know them, sir?"

"I have heard of the Rutherfords, yes, yes, from England. Must be them." He rubbed his large hands together and glanced back over his shoulder at the bottle on the desk.

A knock sounded at the door, stopping the conversation. Dorian stood, opened it, and took the large tray where steaming dishes resided. He helped the cook, a reed-thin fellow with a toothy grin, set down the food and then nodded for him to leave. Kendra passed out the plates and the silver utensils while Dorian took the covers off the food. Fish in a creamed gravy, salt pork, roasted potatoes, ears of golden corn, and thick slices of buttered bread made up the simple meal. There was a bottle of sherry, which Dorian poured for the captain and himself, and cranberry tarts for dessert.

Conversation turned away from Kendra's family, to the relief of all, as Captain Moore told his own tales about life at sea. The hour passed in a pleasant way, both of the men growing more comfortable as they enjoyed each other's company. She looked across the table at her captain and felt a tenderness well up in her heart for him. He was relaxed, smiling and laughing, his tanned hands crossed upon one knee. He had wonderful hands, she thought on a whim. Strong, perfectly formed hands. The thought of them touching her . . . her face, her hair . . . gliding down her back . . .

"Lady Townsend, are you quite alright?"

Kendra's gaze jerked up from the captain's hands to his eyes, eyes that had turned a shade darker. Heat filled her cheeks and she cleared her throat to make space around the lump so that she could speak. Still, her voice squeaked. "Oh, sorry. Wool-gathering, I suppose."

That he saw through her lie was obvious by the small smile and knowing mirth in his eyes. "Anything interesting? Perhaps you would like to share it with us?"

"Oh, um. No, that is . . . it was nothing, just silly, flirting, uh, *flitting* thoughts." She narrowed her eyes at him, daring him to gainsay her. His slow grin sent a wave of excited nervousness through her stomach. She cast a pleading glance toward Captain Moore for rescue. The good man jumped in to save her by patting his round stomach and announcing he should be on his way. "As much as I would like to stay, I'll not make it to London on time to meet my contact if I dally here any longer," he said in a wistful voice.

They all stood and Captain Moore took Kendra's hand in his big one and gave it another kiss. "A pleasure, my lady. A true pleasure you are."

"Why thank you, Captain. It has been a very enjoyable evening."

He leaned in and whispered in her ear, "Be strong now, remember that. America isn't a place for the faint of heart, but I have a feeling you will do quite well there if you set your mind to it."

The words made her feel proud somehow. Like he believed in her. "Thank you, Captain. I will remember that."

After he left, Captain Colburn helped Kendra clear the dishes. They were both silent, but it was a companionable silence, working side-by-side, a brush of Kendra's skirts against his shoes, a reach for the same plate, both pausing, then one of them backing quickly away. After the tray had been taken away and the last crumb brushed from the floor, they stood facing each other for a long moment.

"Thank you, Kendra. You were wonderful tonight."

A pleased feeling expanded inside her. She smiled and glanced away. "It was rather fun. I haven't entertained in so long. I had forgotten what a pleasure it is. Thank you for including me."

It was absurd really. How good he made her feel. How they both knew he didn't want to leave but that he must and how they were both prolonging the moment as long as possible, straining toward each other.

"Well" — Dorian bowed his head toward her — "I suppose all good things must come to an end. Good-night."

Kendra stood rooted to the floor, demanding her feet stay put when all she wanted to do was take a step or two toward him. "Good-night."

He hesitated, started to turn away and then turned back, taking the necessary steps to stand right in front of her, his face inches away. He reached for her hand, a naughty twinkle in his eyes as he reminded her in a low voice. "You allowed the other captain to kiss you —"

"My hand!" Kendra interrupted.

"As I was saying . . . Captain Moore kissed you . . . here . . ." Dorian took up her hand, raised it to his lips, and closed his eyes. Her heartbeat doubled as he paused, his breath fanning across the back of her hand. Finally, he lowered his lips, her palm turning clammy, and planted the faintest of a soft kiss on her knuckles. She shivered, rooted to the floor. *Oh, heavens! I mean God! Whatever am I to do now?*

Dorian pulled her hand toward his chest. She could feel his heart pounding against her palm. The loud thudding made it all too real. This man was not playing games with her. If he were, he would not be as affected by her, the evidence too strong and sure under her hand. There was something happening here, something real that quite possibly didn't happen very often. It was thrilling and terrifying at the same time.

What if they were falling in love?

CHAPTER SEVEN

The clang of a bell and the shout of "ship approaching starboard side" caused Dorian to jerk upright from his study of the account book as he stood in his makeshift office on the quarterdeck. Horrace, the man presently on lookout at the fore masthead, sounded the alarm.

John's booted steps rang out as he climbed the steps to the quarterdeck. "Come quick, Captain. I don't like the looks of this." They had to shout to be heard above the unrelenting north westerly wind.

"What kind of ship?"

"Square rigged, large, standing toward us."

Dorian strode to starboard, raised the spyglass to his eye, and agreed. He could see the huge lugsails, flattened like boards in the stiff wind, coming right for them. "It's a lugger. One of the fastest ships built. They're notorious for pirating, better ready the men."

"All men to their stations!" John shouted above the combined roar of gale and activity. The crew recognized the threat, readied their weapons, and scurried to their respective posts. They had been drilled for this event.

The crew's excited tension matched the rapid pumping in his own veins. With the *Angelina* barely a year old this crew was yet green, but Dorian knew he had prepared them as best he could. This might be the test which would prove their mettle.

Turning to John, Dorian commanded, "Tell Lady Townsend to lock herself in the cabin and not open the door for anyone save you or me. Warn her that this might be the pirate fight she's been asking for." It had been two days since their dinner with Captain Moore, two days of stormy weather that had kept him occupied with the ship, without a chance to see her.

John nodded, face grim as he turned to obey.

As the ship came closer into view Dorian saw an ominous sight. A huge, sleek vessel with scores of men on deck, some stood at the rail, shouting and waving their arms above their heads, others were occupied with sails and rigging bringing the great beast ever closer to them. A soft curse escaped Dorian, still peering through his spyglass. The sixth sense Dorian had cultivated from years of experience told him what he was watching was different. These were not the ordinary pirates he had confronted in the past. There was no stealth in their manner, nor cunning, only a show of reckless confidence, giving away any element of surprise. They appeared well-organized despite their bold frenzy, turning into the headwind to fight perpendicular to the *Angelina.* He took a deep breath of determination. *God have mercy.*

The *Angelina* was well armed with thirty-nine guns: long eighteen-pounders on the main deck, and thirty-two-pound carronades on the quarterdeck and forecastle. The men awaited their opponent's first move, a mixture of fear and fight on their faces. As expected a fiery blast came forward, flying straight above the bow of the ship, demanding that the *Angelina* stop.

The men cheered for the pirate ship's bad shot and fired back with their ready cannons. Grapeshot peppered the pirate ship's midsection but did not seem to penetrate and do the damage expected. As they drifted closer still, their various guns came into range. Smoke and the smell of gunpowder made Dorian's eyes burn, and the shots of the enemy cannons splintered the wood of the deck like bombs going off. Shards and needle-sharp splinters flew through the air to imbed themselves in his men and rip through the sails, leaving little more than white, flapping tatters attached to the masts.

Suddenly, the ship shuddered and a loud groaning sounded with a sharp crack. Dorian spun around, his heart sinking in dread as a main mast snapped in half and fell across the quarterdeck with a horrible crash. Grapeshot peppered the deck with more splintering wood as the pirate ship came within shouting distance. *God help us.* Dorian ducked for cover, all the while shouting orders to his men. The pirate ship was within boarding distance.

Dorian knew the pirates would not want to sink them yet, wanting to keep their precious loot from sinking into the depths of the Atlantic, which gave them a little more time to try and disable the pirate ship. While the pirates abandoned the heavy artillery in favor of muskets to continue the attack, Dorian had no such reservations, ordering his men to reload and fire the cannons. After several attempts the crew cheered as the bow of the lugger caught fire.

Dorian only had time for a quick assessment of his men before the lugger moved alongside the *Angelina* to board. A few of the men had been hit and Dorian's stomach quivered in anger and fear. He was responsible to keep his men alive, to keep them safe. There must be more he could do. Dorian stood on the quarterdeck, watching with a sense of helpless frustration as the lugger moved along the *Angelina*'s side.

"Stand ready, men! To arms! To arms!" Dorian and John shouted the phrase as the men reached for their muskets, blunderbuss, pistols, and swords. The thwack of boarding hooks sank into the wood of the *Angelina*'s side, marring her beauty all the more. Minutes later pirates leapt over the railing, whooping and wild, with boarding axes swinging and all sorts of firing weapons. Dorian's men leapt into the fray and a moment of pride filled him at their courage. *Dear God, give us courage and strength,* his whole being cried out the silent prayer.

The booming of muskets gave way to the clashing of cutlasses which appeared as a silvery light in the dying light of the sun. The night echoed with groans of men falling to their death. Dorian no longer had time to assess the losses on board his ship, he was much too busy forcing down one hellion after another. He could feel his muscles shudder and ache from the weight

116

of his sword.

There were so many of them.

Suddenly Dorian was rushed by a huge opponent. He had long scraggly black hair, the top of his head wrapped in a piece of brightly colored cloth. A golden ring swung from one ear, and a long, black beard, thinly braided in the middle, hid most of his face except for the evil glint of his eyes.

Dorian dodged the powerful swing of the curved cutlass while trying to push the man closer to the edge of the deck. Their blades made wide arcs accented by loud clangs as they met and held. The man was strong. Quite possibly too strong to hold off. Trickles of sweat ran down the center of Dorian's back. His chest heaved with exertion and his muscled arms strained to their limit.

Dorian barely felt the pirate's blade slice his forward thigh, but soon felt the effect as his leg gave a little beneath his weight. Desperate not to show his weakness, he gritted his teeth and redoubled his efforts. Taking fortifying breaths, he forced his foe closer and closer to the railing. A grin widened upon Dorian's face when he saw a glimmer of uncertainty enter his opponent's eyes. Confidence gave Dorian a new burst of strength. His thrusts became harder, more accurate. One step forward, then two more, he gradually pushed the man toward the edge. As the pirate's back brushed the rail Dorian bit out, "You'll not win this day." With one final push of the mighty steel he twisted the blade around and used the dagger in his other hand to plunge it into the pirate's chest. A look of surprise gripped the man's face and then he was pushed overboard into a watery grave.

Dorian had no time to revel in his victory, for when he turned around he was confronted with another opponent. Blades clashed for several more agonizing minutes, until a shrill whistle stopped the pirates mid-swing. It was amazing to see. Each pirate disengaged himself from battle and fled for the pirate ship. With amazing speed the ship turned and, before Dorian could gather his men to fire much upon them, they had sailed out of range. It wasn't long before they were just a dot on the horizon.

Dorian turned to survey the damage. His men! God, what had happened? He strode over to the surgeon who was busy attending the injured. Blood smeared the white boards of the deck and coated their boots. He stood above a bloody body of a man that the surgeon, McCally, was working on. Dorian didn't at first recognize the man as the wounds to his head were so profuse.

"It's Sam Edwards, Captain." The surgeon gave a sad shake of his head. "He's not going to make it, I'm afraid."

Sorrow filled his chest as he saw that it was indeed his quartermaster, Sam Edwards. Kneeling down beside the man's body he lifted his limp, bloody hand in a tight grasp and promised, "They'll pay for this, Sam. I'll find out who they were and they'll pay."

The dead were being prepared for their sea-burial when one of the men strode up to Dorian and called out in a tight voice, "Sir, the most valuable of the cargo is gone. Silks, teas, the spices, and even furniture."

Turning back to the bodies strewn across the deck, Dorian clenched his eyes shut. The cargo was gone. How had the enemy seized it while fighting a battle with his men? No wonder they had stopped fighting at the sound of that shrill whistle. It was a signal. A signal that the cargo was aboard their ship and they could abandon the fight. Dorian's hands clenched into fists on either side of his legs, the one cut burning with pain and dripping blood. These weren't ordinary pirates. They were too skilled at their operation and they had known the *Angelina* too well. Whoever ran this operation was a mastermind at thieving, and Dorian was determined to find out who it was.

And then there was Kendra. If the pirates had reached the cargo deep in the hold, had they found her too? She could have been spirited away to the pirate ship while he was fighting and he wouldn't even know. His heart leaping at the thought, he ignored his injury, turned, and ran to the steps leading down to the cabins.

The door was still shut and locked. A good sign. He banged on the door with all his strength. "Kendra, it's me. Open up!"

No answer. No sound came from the room.

In rising panic, Dorian backed up, ran toward the door, and plowed his shoulder into the wood, causing it to crack and splinter. "Kendra!" He yelled through the hole. "It's okay. Open the door."

Still no sound. Was she injured? Was she even there? He again plowed into the door, this time rendering enough of a hole that he reached inside and unlatched the door. Pushing against the splintered wood, he opened the door and sprang inside.

Kendra stood in the far corner of the room, her back to a pirate, a knife to her throat.

Dorian reached for his pistol.

"Don't cha be thinkin' o' using your gun, Captain. Or else, this here lady'll be sliced up real pretty. Put yur weapons down on the floor, real easy like."

Kendra's eyes bulged with fear and her breathing rasped quick and loud across the room. Dorian nodded his head. "Don't hurt her. I will let you go unmolested. You have my word." With slow, deliberate moves he took his gun from his belt and lowered it to the floor.

The pirate — a thin, filthy man — chuckled, showing several missing teeth. "That ain't my instructions."

Dorian felt his knife that he always kept shoved in the back of his waistband burn against his back. If he could only distract him long enough to reach for it. He glanced at Kendra. She looked ready to faint; not much help there. "Instructions? Did your plan include being the only one left on board my ship? It would seem your plan has gone awry as your ship has sailed away without you."

The man blanched but tightened his grip on the knife hilt.

"So this is a suicide mission, is it? Once your deed is done there will be nowhere for you to go. My men will see that you pay if

121

you harm her." Not that he was getting a chance at that. Dorian took a couple of steps closer.

"Stop right there." The man pressed the knife into Kendra's throat, causing a muffled scream to escape her.

Dorian held up his hands in surrender. "The path you are on will mean certain death for you. Let me give you another option."

The man scowled. "Enough talk. I'm to kill the lady with you watchin', so take a seat."

With a move so quick no one had time to react, Dorian simultaneously pulled out his knife and plowed into the man's free shoulder. Kendra screamed and stomped down on the man's foot, further loosening his hold on her. Dorian grasped the man's arm that was holding the knife, but not before he made a desperate swipe, cutting Dorian across his cheek. Dorian swung around, kneed the man in the groin as hard as he could, and grasped the pirate by the hair. With a tremendous swing of his arm, he punched the skinny man in the temple and watched with satisfaction as the man's eyes rolled into the back of his head. The pirate went limp, hanging by his hair from Dorian's hand.

Dorian turned a celebratory grin on Kendra but she was too terror stricken to respond. Wide eyed and gripping her throat, she could only stare at him. Oh no. She looked ready to faint any second.

"Get me something to tie him up with, will you?" Dorian barked out the command, knowing that action might help her regain her ability to function.

Kendra swallowed hard, nodding. Her eyes were glassy with unshed tears as she tottered over to the armoire.

"There should be some rope in the bottom drawer."

Kendra nodded and opened the drawer. Dorian dropped the pirate to the floor while she dragged the rope over to him. "Now, go and get help. Find John or any of the men and call them down here."

Kendra nodded, turning to go. In a quick move, Dorian stood and swung her into his arms. "It's okay now." His voice gentled as he held her close. "I wouldn't let anything happen to you."

Her stiff body melted into his as a hiccup of a sob broke from her throat. "But your cheek is bleeding!" she cried out in an hysterical wail.

Dorian chuckled and pulled his head back to look at her. With one arm still around her waist supporting her, he took the other hand, and with his thumb, caught a tear racing down her cheek. "Is that what's bothering you? I thought this scoundrel had scared the wits out of you."

She sniffed, blinking out more tears. "I knew you'd come."

Her faith in him caused a feeling of protective love to sweep through him. He grasped her tight to him again, whispering near her ear, "My cheek is only a scratch, my lady. My leg, however, will need some tending though. You can nurse me back to health if you'd like."

She looked down at his bleeding thigh and took a deep, shuddering inhale. "Oh no. You must sit down. Was the fight terrible? It sounded so terrible."

Being reminded of the seriousness of the battle was like having a bucket of cold water thrown into his face. "Bad enough. I've lost a few men and several are injured." He gave her a hard, sudden kiss then stood her away from him. "Go and get help, my lady. As soon as this man awakens, I intend to find out who is behind this."

"But your leg!"

"Is not as bad as it appears. I'll let you doctor me after I've dealt with this man."

Kendra nodded and ran from the cabin.

Dorian hoped the sight of the deck wouldn't send her into a swoon. The *Angelina* and her men were going to need a long recovery time.

Moments later John entered the cabin with two seamen. "Captain, you've captured one of them?" John's face was white with tension lines standing out on either side of his mouth.

Dorian stood, equally grim. "So I thought. It seems I've hit him too hard." He looked down at the inert body. "He's gone and died on us."

Kendra gasped, pressing her hand against her mouth.

John shook his head.

"Well, throw him overboard. We'll have to investigate this matter on our own once we get to Yorktown."

"Aye, Captain." The two seamen lifted the pirate by the arms and legs and carried him from the room.

CHAPTER EIGHT

Yorktown, VA — Summer 1798

"Land!" The shout came from above.

Kendra glanced up from the book she had been reading, and then, as the word sank in, she sat up, gripping the book to her chest. Had someone really said *land?*

"Land ho!"

They had! She tossed the book aside and leapt from the bed. Taking up her cloak, she dashed out the door and down the narrow corridor, shivers of excitement racing through her.

"Land ho!" she heard again. She fairly flew up to the deck where several of the sailors had gathered at the western rail, gazing out at the dark line of coast just visible on the horizon. Kendra joined them, a mixture of excitement and anxiety battling in her stomach. What if her aunt and uncle didn't want her? What would she do then?

Dorian saw her the minute she came up on deck, a sunny spot of yellow against the gray-green water. He started toward her, grinning at the way she clapped down another monstrous hat, this time a wide-brimmed yellow straw trimmed in black ribbons with some kind of enormous bunch of yellow feathers in the front and a single, long black feather sticking out in the back. The feathers looked ready to make use of their original design and give the hat flight in the stiff wind. Once he reached her side he asked on a cheerful note, "Are you happy to see the end of our voyage is in sight, Lady Kendra?"

"Oh, yes," she breathed, looking at up him with excited eyes. "I will be most happy to plant my feet upon solid ground."

Dorian took in the sparkle in her violet-hued eyes as he jested, "I'm afraid you will have to endure another day or two of my company as I am bound to escort you to your new home."

Her eyes widened and a hint of surprise flashed across her face. "You are personally seeing me to my aunt's?"

"Would you rather John saw to it? He is the one who assured your uncle that he would see you safely home."

"Oh. Whatever is most convenient, of

course." She worried her lower lip between her teeth for a moment and turned toward the spot of land in the distant. In a voice almost too low to hear she admitted, "I should welcome your company, though. I am a bit nervous as to my reception when I first meet my aunt and uncle."

"You have never met these relatives before?" His regard for Lord Townsend slipped another notch.

"No, they left for America soon after they were married. I hadn't been born."

"I see." But he didn't really. The protective urge he felt for her surged to the fore. "What else do you know of this aunt and uncle of yours?"

"Not much," Kendra replied with a shrug. "Aunt Amelia was my mother's younger sister. She married Lord Rutherford and they soon left for America." Kendra looked up at him with such innocent eyes. The thought of dropping her off at a stranger's house made his stomach churn. He tried to focus on her speculations as she continued. "I thought perhaps he had been assigned there by the king, before the war, or some circumstance like that."

"Hmmm." Dorian didn't want to upset Kendra with his reservations so he merely nodded. If this aunt and uncle were unsuitable he would take her to his home.

His home? The thought, so strong and sudden, gave him pause. He looked away from her open face to suppress a groan. What would he do with her then? Marry her? His first marriage had been a sham, a disaster, and he'd vowed never to make that mistake again. Molly's face flashed through his mind. A pretty brown-haired girl with curves beyond her years. He'd only been eighteen. Young, intemperate, and foolish. Molly was two years younger and knew something about batting eyelashes and leaning close enough that he could feel her body against his arm. He'd gotten her pregnant. At least that's what Molly and her mother had told them after their one time together. His parents had urged Dorian to do the right thing and marry the girl. Something they never spoke of now, something they all regretted. As soon as she'd moved in with them, Molly had turned from a demure innocent who'd unwittingly been lured into Dorian's arms to a selfish girl who took every opportunity to demand and complain. She'd insisted on her own maid, had no interest in learning the duties of a wife or helping Hannah, Dorian's mother. She spent all of her time parading about town in the Colburn carriage and begging Dorian to take her places and buy her things.

Driven by despair, Dorian threw himself into work and it paid off. Within a few months and with a little help from his father, he had bought his first ship and sailed away from his problems — leaving them in the hands of his family. But Molly had tricked them all.

When he arrived home, six months after his wedding, he discovered that Molly wasn't really pregnant, never had been. It was all a ruse. Dorian turned his back on her and never looked her in the eyes again. He left again and again, leaving his parents to deal with her, never home, always sailing, always free on the wide-open sea. He'd grown hard, he could feel it inside, a hardening that only cared for his ships and the sea and this form of freedom.

A couple of years later his unuttered prayer was answered, leaving him mired in another level of wretchedness. While Dorian was away on one of the ships, Molly went to visit her mother and contracted small pox. She had been forced to stay at her mother's for fear of contaminating the Colburns, something that couldn't have pleased her. In less than two weeks she had died. Dorian hadn't even been there for the funeral and when he finally did find out, it was as if a great burden had been lifted from him. He was almost happy about it, and for that he couldn't forgive himself or Molly.

He'd drifted then. Free but not. Building his fortune and turning his back on any kind of depth in relationships. Women were off limits except to flirt and dally. The more he pulled away from them the more willing they became. He found himself having to use his wits to escape their entrapping tactics. Like Angelene. No one understood that he knew she and women like her had been playing their game to his advantage for years. He'd never thought to have a different life.

He needed to remember all of this, keep it in the forefront of his mind when the lovely earl's daughter flashed her brilliant violet-hued eyes at him and turned his stomach into mush. He? Husband and father? Tied to the land and a woman he would struggle to trust? The idea struck him as a blow while a constricting feeling tightened around his neck, making him struggle to drag in the next breath.

"Are you alright, Captain?" She looked up at him with that open, heart-shaped face and big, tilted eyes. She placed her gloved hand on his arm, all concerned loveliness. He found he couldn't answer. He was certainly *not* alright. Before true panic could set in, he bowed in a short jerk and muttered, "I had better get back to my duties," and turned and walked away.

Kendra's brows came together as she watched him leave. Whatever had she done to send him scurrying off like that, as if his very life was in danger? She exhaled with a loud humph and turned back toward the growing dark line on the horizon. America. Land of the free, they said. She could only hope the adage proved true for her, an Englishwoman, who didn't know the first thing about freedom and what her life here might become.

The next twenty-four hours brought them up to the shores of a new republic. The late afternoon sun glinted off the gray-green water of the York River as the *Angelina* wound her way across the choppy waters of the Chesapeake Bay toward Yorktown. Kendra stood at the railing, watching the lush landscape go by either side of the ship. The water narrowed and narrowed from wide-open sea to a sliver of river waves cutting through wild land. Heavily wooded forests flanked the river's edge — greens, browns, and the tawny colors of scrub and bush.

Kendra took a great, long breath of the moss-damp air and tried as best she could to tamp down the rising anxiety this wilderness brought to her chest.

An hour slid by as they turned toward a bend in the river. Kendra felt her heart rise in hope and wonder as the beginnings of a town came into view. Various-sized storehouses dotted the wharf where men scurried about loading and unloading ships. The sailors aboard the *Angelina* were soon busy docking the great ship as if it were no more than a toy. Kendra marveled at their skill as they slid with ease into their moorings. They were soon bobbing alongside other sea craft of various shapes and sizes, waiting to disembark.

She was just wondering what she should do next when the captain tore himself away from his duties long enough to stride over to her.

"I've asked John to escort you ashore, my lady. I have many duties to attend to as yet, but if you will allow him to take you to The Swan, he will see that you have some dinner and a room for the night. In the morning I will procure a carriage and see you to your new home."

Kendra kept her voice steady even though her throat was as dry as parchment with nerves. "That is very kind of you. Thank you, sir."

Captain Colburn gave her a small bow and a wink and then hurried off to his duties. John came up from behind him, grinned at her, and offered his arm. "Shall we, Lady Townsend?"

Kendra's legs shook as she walked down the gangplank, leaning on John's arm for support. When they stepped off the ship onto dry land, her knees buckled beneath her. John chuckled and hauled her upright. "It might take awhile to regain your land legs, my lady."

She clung tighter to his arm and laughed in return. "I feel like a babe just learning to walk. How long will it take, do you think?"

John patted her hand. "Not long."

They took a few more steps and then stopped for Kendra to better gain her balance. Her gaze swept up and down the street, taking in her first look at town life on American soil. There were several townsfolk milling around in fashionable dress, but compared to the mayhem of London, America seemed sparsely inhabited and a bit wild. As they walked along the road that ran along the shore, Kendra had an urge to stretch out her arms and embrace the clean, fresh air. She grinned at the thought as restless energy and excitement filled her. John looked down at her exuberance. "What do you think of America so far?"

"I think I shall like it very much," she said with a happy tone and a flashing smile. Tucking her hand in his arm, John led her up a long hill and around a bend to Main Street, where the lodging house sat among various shops. Kendra chuckled as they walked down the quaint, cobblestoned street.

"What is it?" John asked.

Kendra looked up into his dark brown eyes with a self-deprecating smile. "I'm laughing at myself, I suppose. I had thought, well imagined, America to be rough log cabins and Indians lurking behind every tree. And here I find myself in this quaint, little town. The houses are two-storied and many of them are made of brick. I hadn't imagined it so . . . civilized."

John patted her hand on his arm, eyes alight with humor. "I think you shall find us Americans to be a resourceful sort. York-town is becoming rich as a seaport and the folks here are flourishing. Wait until you see some of the plantations. Our own captain's family has a plantation that boasts an enormous three-storied house that I would wager would rival any of your manor houses in England."

"You're proud to be an American, aren't you? How long has it been since you won your freedom from England?"

"Yes, I am very proud. We have been Americans for just fifteen years. The final battle was right here in Yorktown. Cornwallis surrendered on October nineteenth in 1781."

"To George Washington? His fame has spread wide and far across England."

"Yes, I can't imagine we would have won the war without him." John was silent for a moment but there was a look of intense purpose in his eyes that caused Kendra's heart to swell. Had she ever felt anything like that for England?

"Do you . . ." she hesitated, and John paused in their walk to look down at her.

"Yes?"

"Well, it's just that I'm so very English. Do you think these Americans you speak so highly of will accept me? Shall they despise me because I am a titled Englishwoman?"

John shook his head. "Lady Townsend, I do believe you could melt the heart of the devil himself. Have no fear. I predict your charm and grace will make you most popular."

Kendra let out a held-in breath. "I am

glad to know you and Captain Colburn." Her smile turned impish. "I may even become an American myself someday."

"I can think of only one sure way to do that."

Kendra quirked a brow at him and cocked her head to one side. "And what, pray tell is that? Shall I have to memorize your constitution? Swear on the Holy Bible to uphold your American ideals of freedom and liberty?"

John's chuckle was low and full of mischief. "No, my lady. Much easier than all that, I think. All you have to do is marry an American."

Kendra's cheeks grew warm and she looked down but she couldn't help her next question. "And would you know of someone worthy of such a title, sir?"

John laughed out loud. "Oh, I don't know that he's worthy. But I do know of *someone.*"

They both laughed and continued down the narrow street.

They stopped when they came to a white painted, plank building. The sign hanging from an iron bracket read, The Swan Tavern.

"Come along, Lady Townsend." John hurried her up the steps. "I'm famished and The Swan has the best shepherd's pie this

137

side of the Atlantic."

Dorian entered The Swan with an eager energy to his steps. It was always good to be back home after a successful shipping journey, but he recognized that he'd not been thinking of home so much as a certain Englishwoman he had yet to convey across the countryside. It would be interesting to discover their footing when he wasn't playing the role of captain of a ship.

He stopped just inside the door, his gaze searching the common room. It was crowded with patrons, many of them his crew, sitting at tables or at the long bar in the back of the room. A familiar, tinkling laugh caused him to turn. There. With John, enjoying a meal as expected. It only took a few steps to reach their table.

Kendra looked up upon his arrival and locked her sparkling gaze with his. "Captain, have you finished your duties? Won't you join us?"

Dorian scooted out the empty chair, nodded to John, and then turned back to the woman he couldn't seem to erase from his mind. "Yes and yes, Kendra. And as I am no longer your captain, I give you leave to call me by my given name."

"I am honored, sir," — Kendra's right

eyebrow arched over one of her brilliant eyes — "but I'm afraid I cannot."

Dorian frowned. Why was she forever taunting him? "You wound me, my lady. And why can you not?"

Kendra laughed, the sound filling his ears and then his heart with a light, floating feeling. "Because, dear sir, you have never told me what it is!"

Dorian cleared his throat, choking back a laugh. "I shall remedy the omission at once." He stood up, bowed a slight bow, and grinned wickedly at her. "Dorian Colburn, at your service, my lady."

She allowed him to take her hand and press a kiss onto the silky skin. He held onto it for a moment too long, gauging his limits. She must have realized his game as she snatched her hand from his grasp and clasped her hands together under the table.

"John and I were just discussing your home." Kendra gave him a pointed look as she returned them to the conversation at hand. "Your family owns a plantation?"

Dorian reseated himself and ordered food from the hovering serving woman while answering, "Yes, my father started out as a sailor, saved his money, and bought his first ship when he was twenty. He then turned that ship into four, and by the time he was twenty-six, he owned a thriving shipping company. He married my mother a few years later, which led to the plantation. Mother didn't like him away from home so he hired captains to take over and became a gentleman farmer."

"Does he miss the sea? I should think being landlocked a challenge to a true sailing man."

Her intuitive grasp of the situation surprised him, but he supposed it shouldn't have. Kendra may be a striking woman but she was also perceptive of the thoughts and feelings of those around her. "I suppose he missed it at first but now I believe he's grown used to it. With seven children, we gave him plenty to take his mind off his seafaring days, I suppose."

"Seven children? You have six brothers and sisters?"

John chuckled and joined the conversation. "And Dorian is the baby of the family. Rather spoiled, I always thought."

"Ha! With two elder brothers who were always bigger and stronger and four bossy sisters, I was far from spoiled. It's a wonder I'm still alive."

Kendra and John laughed together. There was a pause and then Kendra spoke in a wistful voice, "There must have never been

140

a dull moment in your home."

"Have you no siblings?" John asked.

Kendra shook her head. "My mother died giving birth to me. My father never remarried."

An odd constriction tightened around Dorian's heart as he imagined her as a little girl. Those big violet-hued eyes in a sweet little face. How lonely she must have been living in some enormous manor house with only her father. Wanting to banish the sadness from her eyes, he teased, "I shall introduce you to my mother. She is forever complaining that she has no one to mother anymore and not enough grandchildren to suit her. Though I believe the count is at fourteen now." He shook his head and took another bite of shepherd's pie. "Her heart will be quite taken with you, I vow, and will distract her from smothering me."

Kendra laughed, but the sheen of tears in her rapidly blinking eyes told him she was touched by the thought.

After dinner, John bowed toward Kendra and gave Dorian a jaunty salute. "I shall bid you both good-bye as am most eager to continue home before night falls."

"Eager to see a certain young lady?" Dorian asked, clapping him on the shoulder.

"As you say, Captain. If I hurry, I can be

at Willow's Hill before dark. I believe Victoria's mother will put me up for the night and then we can inspect our house together in the morning."

"That's right. Your new home should be finished, should it not?"

John turned toward Kendra to explain. "Victoria promised to set the wedding date as soon as our house was built. I plan to be a married man before the summer is out."

"That is wonderful, John. Congratulations. And give Victoria my regards. I am so looking forward to meeting her."

John agreed, slapping his hat onto his head and hurrying out The Swan's door. After he left, Dorian turned to Kendra and held out an arm. "Would you like to go for an evening walk to see the town, my lady?" She didn't look tired despite the long voyage and Dorian was too restless to turn in for the night.

Kendra took his arm. "That would be lovely, thank you. I should so like to hear about the town."

They took a turn down Main Street and then crossed over to Water Street, making a big rectangular tour of the progression. Dorian pointed out the Nelson House, which still sported a cannonball lodged in the bricks between two upper-story windows from the last battle of the Revolutionary War. The owner, Thomas Nelson, had served as governor of Virginia. Then there was the Custom House where Dorian paid his port charges, several mid-sized brick homes, another inn, Grace Episcopal Church, the medical shop, the courthouse, and even a pottery factory.

By the time they returned to The Swan the sun was setting behind low, silvery pink clouds.

"Pink sky at night, sailor's delight; pink sky in the morning, sailor's warning," Dorian gave voice to the old wives' tale as they gazed at the sunset.

"Is it true?" Kendra asked.

"Much of the time. Looks like we shall have a fair day for our journey tomorrow."

Kendra peeked up at him. "Thank you for seeing me all the way to my aunt and uncle's home. I own to being a bit nervous about my reception."

Dorian wanted to reassure her that everything would be alright, but he had spoken with Tom Winkler at the Custom House and a few other men in town and what he had learned about Franklin and Amelia Rutherford had not been encouraging. They had fallen far from their state of nobility. Dirt farmers, and not very successful ones at that. If only there was another option, but what? She wasn't his responsibility. He needed to remember that.

Reminding himself of the fact didn't help when he was gazing down into those big, anxious eyes though. He found himself reaching out and touching her cheek, a mere brush of a touch, saying the words he knew he shouldn't, "They are fools if they don't welcome you. You have nothing to fear. Everything will be alright."

She clasped her hands together in front of her gown. "I must trust God to guide me, sir. I have a feeling that everyone is hiding the fact they are quite sorry for me that I am related to the Rutherfords."

"If only there was something —" He paused and shook his head. No use promising something he couldn't deliver. "I won't allow them to harm you. Know that, at least."

Kendra's eyes widened. "Harm me? Could it come to that?"

"No, of course not. I beg your pardon. I am trying to make you feel more comfortable and instead I'm adding fire to the flames of your worry. As you say, God will guide you and I will do what I can to make certain they are agreeable."

"Will I see you again, then?"

Dorian forced his back to stiffen and his arms to stay at his sides. He wanted, more than anything, to take her into his arms and comfort her, but he resisted. "Of course. I'll lay odds that I live within two or three hours from your relatives. The Colburn Plantation is known for miles around. You shouldn't have any trouble finding me should the need arise."

"Let us hope it does not." Then she stopped as if realizing what she'd said. "At least not in that sense." Her eyes widened as Dorian burst out with laughter. "Oh! I mean, I hope to see you from time to time, of course, and there is that promise of meeting your mother."

"Ah, yes. I shall see to that after you are settled."

They turned to walk back into the lodging house, side by side, arms swinging close together.

Just before reaching the door, Dorian grasped hold of Kendra's hand and squeezed it.

"I will meet you in the common room for breakfast at eight o'clock."

Kendra looked up at him with sweet innocence, the starlight heightening the contrasts of dark brows against her pale skin, lashes that made fluttering shadows against her cheeks, and rosy lips turned pale and shimmering. He had to remind himself to breathe. "Thank you, for everything, Captain."

"Captain?"

She blushed rosy beneath the silvery light reminding Dorian of the sunset. *Pink at night, captain's delight . . .* ah, how she brought delight.

"Dorian," she corrected in breathy softness. She stood beneath his riveted gaze with a shy upturn to the corners of her lips and before he knew what he was about, he leaned down and touched their petal-softness with his.

She stood still, trembling as their breath intermingled. He should stop. For heaven's sake they were right outside the door and anyone, at any moment, could come out of it. The thought slid away as a deep wash of desire spread like wildfire through his veins. He'd kissed more than a few women before, but it was nothing like this. *Dear God, what is it about this woman? Help me stop this madness . . .*

Pulling away, he chuckled and groaned at the same time.

Finally reaching out to God and it was a plea about kisses.

CHAPTER NINE

When Kendra came downstairs the next morning she was surprised to find John standing near the door in the common room.

"Why, John! I thought you left last night."

John shook his head. "By the time I found a decent mount that looked capable of making the journey, it was too late. As eager as I am to see Victoria, I knew it would be prudent to wait until morning."

Kendra gave him a kind smile. "While I'm sorry for your delay, I would love the company. Will you be traveling with us?" She had stayed up many hours into the night thinking about being alone with Dorian for the journey. The thought had brought both worry and excitement. And the excited part of her was all the more reason to worry. She had prayed God would help her act as she ought, and it would appear God had answered her prayer with the presence of John.

"I can travel with you most of the way." He nodded toward the kitchen, "I've asked Lottie to fix up a luncheon basket for the three of us."

Kendra turned and saw Lottie, the serving woman, totter from the back with a heavy basket on her arm. John rushed forward to grasp it from her.

"The hired carriage is outside. Dorian has gone to take care of some last-minute details but said he would return shortly. Shall we load the carriage and await him outdoors?"

"Yes, but I fear I don't know where my trunks are. I haven't seen them since we landed." She didn't add that she had borrowed a shift from the innkeeper's wife to sleep in last night. It was not the fine quality she was accustomed to and she found herself rubbed red from the coarse material.

"I believe Dorian has already loaded them onto the carriage. Shall we go and see?"

Kendra nodded and followed John out to the street where an open, black carriage stood shining in the sun. There were two horses, one brown with a black tail, the other lighter brown with cream-colored tail, hitched to the front.

When they reached the conveyance, Kendra turned a corner and saw a striking, raven-haired woman standing behind the carriage.

"Well, hello, Miss Monteiro. I wasn't expecting to see you here. Are you waiting for someone?" John's arm had tightened under Kendra's hand.

"I'm not waiting for you, though you are a handsome devil, John," she drawled in a husky voice from rosy lips. "Where is your captain?" Her tone turned snappish as she surveyed Kendra's face and plum traveling costume.

"He's taking care of some business. He'll be along soon."

Kendra regarded the woman, curious despite herself. She was wearing a beautiful evening gown of emerald-green silk, which pushed her bosom past the propriety of daytime wear. Her black curls were becomingly draped around a round, sensual face and her wide, red lips snarled ever so slightly as she returned the gaze through slitted green eyes.

John looked back and forth between them with darting eyes, like a cornered animal ready to bolt. Kendra suppressed a laugh. After too long a silence, John jumped in to make the introductions. "Kendra, may I introduce Miss Angelene Monteiro, a, er, friend of ours, and this," he said, motioning his head toward Kendra, "is Lady Kendra Townsend, our passenger from London."

Kendra saw the woman stiffen at the title and was, for the first time in her life, glad of it. Satisfaction was replaced with despair, however, when she realized the beauty's name. Angelene — the *Angelina* — the two had to be connected, didn't they?

"Friend?" Angelene slanted John a coy look, batting her thick lashes. "Why John, you know Dorian and I have been closer than mere friends this past year."

Kendra's questioning gaze flew to John's. Could it be true? Why, that meant that Dorian was exactly the arrogant colonial she'd first thought him! All this time, while he had been trying to . . . to seduce her on board his ship, he had this woman waiting for him at home. Kendra stared at John, brows lifted, waiting for some explanation why this was the first she had heard of her.

John's face grew redder by the minute. "Um . . ."

He was saved an explanation as Dorian came walking up the street toward them. Angelene's face turned from smug to adoring, a sensual smile on her lips as she strolled, hips swaying in a provocative roll, over to meet him.

"Dorian," she cooed, "I'm so glad you're home. I've missed you so." Her boldness knew no bounds as she threw her arms around his neck in an amorous embrace.

Kendra gasped despite herself. Thus far these Americans were as she'd always heard — unmannered, brash, bold-faced, liars! A wave of embarrassed chagrin washed over her as she remembered their kiss. How had she allowed herself to be so duped?

Kendra stared, brows furrowed together, as Dorian attempted to untwine Angelene's arms from his neck. He glanced up and caught the heated stare that Kendra was trying to burn into his very soul.

"Angelene, I'm surprised to see you. You didn't come all this way just to welcome me home, did you?" The emphasis was on "me" as he looked at Kendra with pleading in his eyes.

Kendra realized she was acting like a jealous fool, and no doubt giving him a certain amount of satisfaction. Oh! She just wanted to be rid of this man, and the only way to accomplish that was by beginning their journey. *"Dorian"* — she wasn't about to call him captain now — "I am anxious to reach our destination. Could we make haste?"

"What is your destination, Lady Townsend?" Angelene asked, tense anxiety underlying the bland, questioning expression on her face.

Not knowing why she answered the way she did, Kendra heard herself saying, "Why, I believe you were going to introduce me to your mother." She directed the statement to Dorian, whose lips were quivering in what appeared to be a manly attempt at pressing back a laugh at the clever jibe she was giving Angelene. Oh, dear! There she went again, speaking before thinking. She would have plenty to repent for before this day was over. Kendra balled her hands into fists and determined to be better, sending up a silent plea for help.

Angelene's cat eyes darted toward Dorian, panic showing on her face as she awaited his answer.

"Yes, I am most eager for you to meet her."

Oh, this was even worse! Now he was playing along with her game, which made Kendra feel just wretched.

Angelene's eyes flashed hatred toward Kendra. She took a step closer to Dorian and purred up at him as if he hadn't just insinuated that he had feelings for Kendra. "Dorian, so much has happened since you've been away. Father took a house here in Yorktown and I've befriended your sister

Faith. I've offered to help your mother and sisters with the details of your father's birthday ball so," she glanced sideways at Kendra and smiled, "I will be staying at your home for the next several days." She paused, looking up at him with her dark, slanting eyes. "When I heard your ship had arrived, I realized how fortuitous it was! I needn't bother Father with driving me. I can travel with you to Colburn Plantation."

Dorian's jaw clenched as the trap snapped neatly around him. Kendra tried not to groan aloud. There would be no reason Dorian could refuse her if what she said was true. Kendra shot John a glance and saw that the corners of his mouth were twitching as he looked down at his shoes.

Dorian bowed his head at Angelene in defeat. "I suppose if John is riding that sorry excuse for a horse, there will be room in the carriage."

John rubbed his hands together and chuckled. "She may not be the quickest mare, but better than such a crowded carriage."

Dorian gave John a look that said he would like to throttle him and then asked Angelene, "Your things?"

"Oh, I've already had them loaded in the back." She looked down at Kendra's trunks sitting on the ground next to the carriage. "I do hope there will be room for more."

Dorian went around the back of the carriage and peered into the small storage space. "For goodness sake, Angelene, must you really have two trunks for a few days' travel? Lady Townsend's things must be transported."

"Oh, but I must have it all." She batted her lashes up at him. "I've promised Faith we would have lots of gowns to try on for the ball. She will be so disappointed if I don't bring them."

Bring the sister into it, Kendra thought, her mouth pressing into a tight line. This woman was not one to underestimate. "Dorian, could we not fit the smaller of the two in the seat with us?" Kendra had already thought through the seating arrangements on the small, single seat of the carriage and suspected Angelene had too. It wouldn't be at all surprising if the woman didn't manage to wrangle to sit in the middle, next to Dorian. Maybe a trunk squeezed between them would be just the thing.

"That is so kind, Lady Townsend. Yes, let's try that." Angelene's bright smile could have melted the lacquer right off the carriage.

Dorian gave Kendra a considering look as if trying to discover what she was about and then shrugged and lashed down all of Kendra's trunks to the back with one of Angelene's and carried Angeline's smaller one over to the seat. He started to reach for Kendra's hand to help her up, when Angelene edged in front of her and took a firm grasp on Dorian's forearm. "Do let me sit in the middle, Dorian. I get dizzy if I sit on the edge, the trees whizzing by so fast and all."

John made a choking sound that turned into a cough while Dorian took a deep breath and gritted his teeth. Kendra saw that Angelene was now sitting beside the trunk and that it would be between her and the driver, but then Angelene surprised them all by heaving up the article by herself and moving it to the other side. She didn't say a word, just faced forward and waited.

Kendra walked to the other side of the carriage and allowed Dorian to take her hand and help her up. He squeezed her hand with gentle pressure as she seated herself. Kendra glanced down at him and saw him mouth, "I'm sorry," with a pained expression. Kendra faced forward, the hard edge of the trunk pressing into her side, and took her own resigned breath. What had started out as a delightful, sunny day had turned into an endurance race. *Love, joy, peace, patience, kindness, goodness, faithfulness, gentleness, and self-control.* She ticked off the nine fruits of the Spirit with a silent groan. She had no one to blame but herself. This should teach her to plot and scheme as if she had some rights to this man. She was no better than Angelene.

With fresh determination to do right, she turned to Angelene, smiled with some measure of genuine warmth, and asked, "Won't you tell me about your life in America, Miss Monteiro? I have so much to learn."

A look of surprised suspicion flashed across Angelene's face but then she settled back, her shoulder pressing against Dorian's, and launched into a stream of feminine chatter that lasted for the entire next hour.

The sun moved across the sky above them with agonizing slowness. The trunk pressed into Kendra's ribs, making each bump feel as if a new bruise was forming. The jostling from the rutted road made her whole body ache. But worst was Angelene's outrageous flirting. She cooed and batted her lashes like a strumpet. When a wheel dipped into an especially deep rut, she squealed and clung to Dorian's bulging upper arm. Kendra bit her tongue and stared out at the countryside of rolling hills and forest land. Once in a great while they passed a farm, but for most of the journey it felt as if the four of them were alone in the world.

As the long afternoon waned into evening the wind quickened and turned cool. Looking up she noticed the weather and said with concern furrowing her brow, "It looks as if a storm is brewing."

Dorian followed her gaze toward the western sky that was swirling with dark clouds. "Yes, it does look as if we're in for a big one."

"Oh, no!" Angelene moaned. "We'll get soaked in this open carriage. Isn't there any place we can go?"

"How far *do* we have to go?" Kendra asked.

"From the directions I received, your aunt and uncle have a small farm just southeast of Williamsburg. I'm afraid it will take us another day to reach their farm. I had planned that we stay at an inn tonight as there is one on the way."

"And your home? Is it further away?" She did want to meet Dorian's family but not with Angelene hovering over them.

Dorian propped his foot on the dash in front of them and edged away from Angelene's side, peering around her to look at Kendra. "It would be out of the way to take you there first, but I did promise to introduce you to my mother." He winked at her.

"I don't want to cause you any trouble. Perhaps I can meet her another day."

John trotted next to the carriage on his horse and entered the conversation. "What about that ball Miss Monteiro mentioned? You could make sure she gets an invitation and introduce her to the family then." John gave Kendra a big grin and conspirator's wink. Kendra couldn't help but smile back at him.

Angelene stiffened beside her, crossing her arms over her ample bosom and elbowing Kendra in the arm.

Dorian frowned at her and then cast a glance at John. "That is an excellent plan, John. I shall see that Kendra and her aunt and uncle are invited." He looked over at Kendra. "That is, if you would care to go?"

The thought of a ball made an excited feeling bloom in Kendra's chest. "That would be lovely. Mayhap I can meet some of our neighbors there."

A sudden gust of wind tore at the carriage and caused Kendra's hat brim to press around her face like a fluttering veil.

Angelene shrieked and grasped Dorian's

upper arm, clinging to him.

Gazing at the sky, Kendra's brows knitted together in concern. The clouds were whipping up into a frenzy and headed right for them. She clung to the side rail as the carriage swayed back and forth with the wind. After a few more minutes, huge drops of rain began to pelt the carriage. Dorian slapped the reins, trying to keep the frightened team under control as the rain began to come down in earnest.

"Lady Townsend, grab the side of the top and help me pull it up!" Together they tugged on the leather cover but the sides of the carriage were open so the flimsy covering did little good. Within minutes they were all drenched and the road, as rough as it had been, grew muddy and slippery. "This may be worse than I thought!" Dorian yelled. "We may have to stop and take cover."

Kendra nodded her head, fear rising in her throat. This night reminded her of the thunderstorm that had taken her father from her. And they were in a carriage with unfamiliar horses.

A strike of jagged lightning, close by, and the boom of thunder caused Angelene to scream and cover her face with her hands.

"Look, do you see that?" Doran pointed

to a weathered gray building in the distance.

Kendra nodded, shivering so much that she didn't think she could speak.

They struggled through, taking only minutes but what seemed like hours to reach the building. One of the horses jumped with fright, the other reared, as the lightning zigzagged across the sky. Kendra had never felt so cold and soaked through as they pulled up into the yard of a ramshackle, abandoned barn.

There was no door so Kendra rushed from the carriage, Angelene just behind her, and ran into the dark, leaky building. Dorian and John unhitched the horses and led them one by one to the stalls on the far side of the barn. Dorian shouted in delight at finding some hay that wasn't too damp and then walked over to where Kendra was scouting through the dim light for a lantern or candles.

Kendra found a nub of a candle on the floor and rubbed the dirt off with the corner of her skirt. "You wouldn't happen to have flint, would you?"

Dorian reached into his pocket, showed her the flint and stone, and gave her an admiring look that made a happy thrill rise in her chest. "Gather anything that looks worthy of making a fire and I'll have one warming us in minutes."

Kendra was shivering so hard her teeth were chattering as she gathered scraps of wood that had fallen from the walls and roof. Water dripped from the ceiling, making mud puddles on the dirt floor and increasing the smell of musty hay. There was an ancient-looking cookstove in one corner. After some pushing and pulling she managed to get the door open and shove the wood inside. "I think I have enough for a decent fire." She looked over her shoulder toward Dorian. He came over, squatted in front of the open door, and struck the stone to the flint. After a couple of tries, he had a nice little flame eating through the rough, dry wood. "I hope the stovepipe works. If it's clogged, we'll be in for a heap of smoke."

Angelene stood in front of the fire complaining. "What a mess this is! I'm so cold. We need to get out of these wet clothes before we catch our deaths!"

Kendra stood as close as she dared and held out her hands to the growing flame. Her clothing began to steam as the wet cloth warmed. She shot Angelene a startled look at her comment. What did the woman propose they do? Strip down to their shifts in front of the men? They would just have to stay close to the fire until they dried out.

Her stomach made a loud rumbling noise. Dorian looked up and grinned, ignoring Angelene. "Hungry?"

Kendra bit down on the side of her lower lip and nodded. "I'm afraid so."

John ran inside, his back hunched over a basket of food to keep it dry. He motioned toward the three of them. "Good thing I thought to bring this along in case we didn't make it to the inn in time for supper."

Dorian clapped him on the shoulder. "You have always had a knack for taking care of our stomachs. Let's have a picnic, shall we?" He opened the basket and pulled out a large loaf of corn bread, a pot of ham and beans, and an apple pie. "A feast, John. Thank you."

"How long will we have to stay here?" Angelene wailed, not appearing the least grateful for the food.

"The roads will be impassable after this storm and I won't have light enough to drive around the dangers. We will leave first thing in the morning, I promise. Kendra will be home before tomorrow is out."

"But, we can't possibly spend the night here! Where will we sleep?" Angelene's pout was almost comical.

Dorian's face was grim. "We have no other choice, Angelene. Let's just make the best of it, shall we?"

Kendra looked away. An image of herself curled up next to Dorian, he holding her in his arms flashed through her mind as bright as the lightning outside. She took a big bite of the corn bread and forced the image away. Tomorrow she would be home.

Her new home.

That was the only thing she needed to be concentrating on right now.

CHAPTER TEN

The yellow streaks of morning spilled through the roof's cracks and onto Kendra's face, awakening her. She rose, stretching, feeling as if she hadn't slept at all, and smoothed the wrinkled plum traveling dress. Sleeping on the hard ground had left her body feeling like a stiff old lady.

There was the leftover half of apple pie for breakfast, which they washed down from Dorian's water canteen, each taking it up, wiping it off with a sleeve, and taking a single swig, except for Angelene, of course, who drew long draughts on the spout. Kendra tried to ignore the wretched feeling that slashed through her every time Angelene took an opportunity to touch Dorian, which was often, and the even more painful jab when he didn't rebuff her. Kendra was the first to climb onto the carriage seat and didn't even bother to try and sit in the middle. They obviously had a fondness for one another.

After two long hours of creeping through the muck-filled roads, they came to a Y in the road.

"This is where I'll be leaving you," John said with a tip of his hat. He looked into Kendra's eyes with a kindness that brought a well of emotion to her throat. It was as if he was saying what he couldn't out loud. *Have courage. Everything is going to be okay.*

Dorian stopped the carriage and looked at his friend with a thoughtful wrinkle in his brow. "You know, if Miss Monteiro can manage a horse . . . I could give her one of mine and you could see her home first. It is on your way to Victoria's —"

John's eyes widened and Angelene gasped. Dorian turned to her and said in quick staccato, "I do so admire a woman who can sit a horse." His black brows rose in challenge as he stared her down.

"Well, of course I can ride a horse. It's just that, it's so . . . so —"

Dorian chuckled. "You'll be with my sister all the sooner. Isn't that why you've come?"

Kendra pressed her hands together to keep them from clapping. Dorian was as adept at this game as Angelene it seemed, and the knowledge that he could take care of himself around the forward woman made

165

Kendra feel giddy with relief.

John, though, had a tight, pained expression on his face. "Oh, very well. Let's unhitch one of them. Do you have a saddle?"

"Oh yes" — Angelene jumped on the statement — "I must have a sidesaddle."

"Really?" Kendra joined in the fray. "At home I often rode bareback."

"Bareback! Like the Indians? You must be jesting." Angelene's face registered genuine shock.

"Oh, yes. My father, Lord Townsend, encouraged it. I became quite adept."

"There is no need to panic, Angelene," Dorian interjected. "I have a saddle lashed to the back with the trunks. Just in case we had difficulties with the carriage."

Angelene huffed but couldn't seem to come up with a good argument why she shouldn't go with John. She took Dorian's proffered hand and climbed down from the carriage. While they were readying the horse, Kendra hefted the trunk and moved it to her other side. It was past time she was sitting next to Dorian.

Angelene did not miss the maneuver.

"That was neatly done," Kendra observed as Dorian started the horse and John and

Angelene rode off down the other road.

"Do you think so?" Dorian cast her a glance full of mischief.

Kendra laughed. "She's very beautiful."

"I suppose so, if one is attracted to dark temptresses."

"Are you saying that you are not? I should think most men would be flattered by so much blatant attention."

"I am not most men."

"No. I can see that you aren't." Kendra looked at his strong, rugged profile. "So what type of woman *are* you attracted to?"

"Oh, damsels in distress have always been appealing." He shot her a grin and Kendra huffed.

"Those are plentiful, I'm sure."

"Yes, I have run into a few over the years but none have held my attention for very long."

"Just long enough to rush in for the rescue? The adventure and all of that?"

"That's about right." He furrowed his brow as if in deep thought. "I suppose I need a woman who is always getting herself into scrapes." He cocked one brow at her. "Do you know anyone like that?"

Kendra huffed, looked away, and said in an irritated mumble, "Insufferable, churlish, colonial rogue."

Dorian threw back his head and laughed.

The next hour was spent in companionable silence until they neared what appeared to be a farm, hacked out of the rough wilderness of this country. Dorian turned the horse toward the front door and Kendra began to feel as if she might be ill. Her stomach rolled as her thoughts sunk from bad to worse. What if they didn't want her? What would she do? She turned her head to the side and blinked back tears. Stop it. She would not let her mind run wild like this. Surely they would be glad to see her.

The carriage came to a stop. "I think this is it."

They sat there for a few minutes looking out over the disheartening view. There was a log cabin, small and drab, with two smaller outbuildings behind it. The land to the west had been cleared, showing rows of short green plants that Kendra didn't know the name of. To a woman who had only lived in a castle with famed manicured gardens all of her life, the reality of her aunt and uncle's existence made her heart pound with anxiety. How was it they were so sadly situated? They were still of England's nobility, still had titles, and should have had some wealth, should they not? But then her own family had lost so much, so it didn't stand to reason to judge them. She would treat them with love and respect, no matter what.

"It's worse than I expected," Dorian ground out, his mouth set in a grim line.

"Something of a shock, yes. But the land is nice." She pointed to a meadow with forest surrounding it to the north. Wildflowers grew in abundance, creating a yellow and purple carpet all around the clearing. Rich black dirt of the fields could be seen behind the house and off to one side, and behind and around it all was thick woodland, filled with leafy trees and the sweet smells of long grass. She took heart in the woods and rocky ledges that met her gaze.

Dorian turned toward her with a startled look of respect. A small, gentle smile formed on his lips as his eyes turned proud. "As you say, my lady, the land is quite nice." He sprung down from the carriage, went to her side and extended his hand. "Shall we?"

She took it, the tight hold giving her a measure of courage.

They walked arm in arm to the front door, pausing in front of it for just a minute, and then Dorian reached out and knocked. They waited for several moments until a worn-out looking woman opened the door. She stood in a faded blue skirt and yellowed bodice, bare feet poking out from the hem. She looked back and forth at them as if they'd come from another world. "Yes?"

Kendra tried to say something but found herself tongue-tied. Dorian spoke for her. "Madam, we are trying to locate the residence of a Lord and Lady Rutherford, Amelia and Franklin. Is this their home?"

"You're looking at her," she said in an unpleasant whine, eyes narrowing. "What do you want?"

Kendra's knees started to shake as she surveyed her aunt. The woman was of medium height, with a rounded figure, faded blonde hair with streaks of gray, and a wan and wrinkled face. The one reminder of her youthful beauty were eyes of clover green, which now only made her look like a frantic cat.

"Aunt Amelia?" Kendra took a step toward the woman. "I am Kendra Townsend, your sister's daughter." She saw a look of startled disbelief change her aunt's face. "My uncle, Lord Andrew Townsend, wrote a letter of introduction, explaining my need to come and stay with you awhile." Kendra pulled the sealed letter from her pocket and held it out to her aunt. Her heart pounded as the woman wrinkled her brow, staring at it.

"A letter, you say. Stay with us?" She sounded as appalled by the idea as she looked.

Kendra felt she might faint, although the urge had never occurred to her before. *Oh heavenly Father, what will I do?* "Please. Won't you just read it?"

"Well, come in," she backed away, giving them room to enter, "and maybe we can straighten this out. I'll call my husband. He will have something to say about this." She turned from them then, leaving them just inside the door as she wandered off to find her husband.

Kendra glanced around the large room filled with mismatched furniture, some English styles mixed with rough-hewn, homemade pieces. A faded, shabby rug covered part of the rough boards of the floor. The walls were bare except for the fireplace. It boasted a spindly mantel with a few knick-knacks — a glass vase, two candlesticks covered in old drippings of wax, and a few small portraits hanging above it. One of the paintings looked to be her aunt, she recognized the green eyes. The painting hanging beside it was of another young blonde woman with piercing blue eyes. Kendra walked closer and sucked in her breath as she realized this smiling woman was her mother. She'd only seen one painting of her mother. It had hung in the blue and gold drawing room back home. Her father told her it was commissioned shortly after their marriage. As a child, Kendra had studied the painting, wondering what kind of woman her mother had been. This aunt, Aunt Amelia, could help answer some of those questions, she realized with a wave of peace coming over her. Aunt Amelia could tell her stories of her mother that her father hadn't known. Stories of their childhood. Coming here, no matter how dismal it looked, must be the right decision. A sudden excitement and determination filled her chest.

Dorian walked up to join her. "Do you recognize any of these people?"

"Yes" — she nodded toward the painting she was studying — "that was my mother. I've only seen one other portrait of her, but I'm sure it is her."

"She was a beautiful woman. You have her nose and her exact shade of hair."

Before she could answer that, her aunt entered the room with a tall, slim man. He was still handsome by English standards with fair skin and the aristocratic features of dark brown hair and amber eyes, eyes that were chilling as he looked from Kendra to

Dorian and back again. His chin was held at a haughty angle that was familiar to Kendra and, for some strange reason, he actually made her feel more at home.

"Your niece? A letter, you say?" His voice boomed with the familiar English accent. He took the letter from Kendra and broke the seal. He took out a pair of round spectacles from a desk drawer, adjusted them to his eyes, and peered at the letter.

Aunt Amelia edged closer, craning her neck to read over his arm and pulling on his sleeve for a better look. He finally looked down at her long enough to bark, "Cease woman," upon which she momentarily stopped. At long last he looked up. "Seems she's told the truth," he muttered to his wife. "Lord Townsend has shipped his troubles to us."

"I'll not be any trouble, Uncle," Kendra rushed to assure him. She took a step closer. "May I read the letter?" She wanted to know what Andrew had said about her and her reasons for coming to America.

"No need for that." Her uncle refolded the paper and pushed the wax seal back down. Kendra dropped her arm, determined to keep her face blank, but sank on the inside. She would just have to hope Uncle Andrew had not painted her in a bad light.

Her aunt's eyes were glittering with resentment as she looked Kendra up and down, studying her face. "You don't look like your mother. How do we know you are truly our niece?"

"Oh, but I am. I —"

"What was my sister's name?" Her aunt interrupted in a stern tone.

Kendra embarked on the family history as she knew it. "Eileen Bentford. She married my father, Lord Edward Alexander Townsend, the Earl of Arundel, when she was twenty. She was married six years before she died, giving birth to me. I never knew her, but I did have a painting and it resembles the one above your mantle."

Amelia cocked her head to one side, her mouth a flat, grim line. "Why have you come here?"

Andrew must have been vague indeed in his letter. The desire to slip through one of the wide cracks in the floor surged through her but she had to tell them the truth. "My uncle attempted to wed me to an unsuitable man. When I protested the match, he decided I would fare better in America with you than with him in England."

"So you were difficult, were you, and he thought to pack his trouble off on us?" Her aunt's voice was little more than a sneer.

Her uncle intervened, shooting his wife a quelling look which seemed to momentarily silence her. "My dear" — he held out his hand to Kendra — "I must apologize for our behavior. The shock, you know."

Kendra smiled back at him, trying to keep up with their changing behavior. Was there ever a more strange set of relatives? *Lord, give me courage to know what to do.*

"Let us begin again, shall we?" Her uncle looked at Dorian and gave him a small nod.

Dorian held out a hand as he introduced himself. "I'm Captain Dorian Colburn, sir. I gave Lady Townsend passage here from England."

At her uncle's nudging, Aunt Amelia gave Dorian a stiff nod as if she was too lofty to acknowledge a mere captain.

Dorian gave her a bow in return and shot an encouraging smile to Kendra. "I must be getting home, would you walk me back to the carriage while I retrieve your trunks?"

Fear lanced through her at the thought of being alone with her relatives. "Certainly" — she glanced at her aunt — "that is, if I am to stay. Might I stay, Aunt? I won't be any trouble."

"Oh, I doubt that, but there seems to be no help for it. Franklin, help the captain there with her trunks."

The silence was heavy on the way back to the carriage. Dorian and Franklin carried the trunks into the parlor while Kendra stood by the carriage. She wanted more than anything to jump back inside and ride away, but she could not. She must make the best of the cards she had been dealt.

Dorian came back alone. He walked up to her and took her hands into his, giving them a firm squeeze. "If you need me . . . I live a few miles to the north. Go back the way we came and take the other road. Someone would give you directions from there."

"Thank you." She slipped her hands from his grasp, thinking that her aunt might be watching them from the window, and took a step backward toward the house. With her best attempt at a confident smile she whispered, "I shall win them over."

Dorian took a deep breath and looked down at his boots for a moment and then, in a sudden way, with his blue eyes alive and blazing, with his lips pressed together, he nodded agreement. He stared into Kendra's eyes for a long moment and she felt his faith in her, his belief that she could make something of this situation when everything said there was no hope. A gentle smile lit his eyes and curved his lips. "That, my lady, is a surety." He placed his hat back on his dark hair and climbed up into the carriage seat. He nodded to her again and said in a steady voice, "Remember the ball. I will see that an invitation is delivered for you in the next few days."

Kendra waved, fighting the tears in her throat. "Good-bye." Would she really see him again? His rugged face and tender voice. His teasing and cajoling, his playful banter that made her heart flutter. On the ship — so many emotions she'd seen cross the handsome planes of his cheeks, his forehead, in his eyes. She would miss him so much, she realized as an aching loneliness filled her. Giant-sized tears squeezed from her eyes and rolled down her cheeks as she watched the carriage roll away.

What now?

Shaking herself, she wiped her wet cheeks with her sleeve, lifted her chin, and turned toward the house.

Be strong and full of faith, for I am with you. The words made her heart lift as if stones had been plucked from it. *Thank You, Father.* But the tears were still close to overfilling her eyes.

Kendra entered the sitting room to find her aunt and uncle abruptly ending their conversation. They turned and smiled at her as if they'd had a change of heart and were happy she was there. "My dear, you must be tired after your long journey. We have a spare room that we've never had much need of as we are childless. Let's tidy it up for you, shall we?"

Kendra followed her aunt to a small room that held a bed, a broken-down table, and some other odds and ends, while her uncle followed behind with her trunks. Aunt Amelia busied herself fetching blankets for the bed and dusting the furniture while Kendra put away her belongings on the hooks on the wall. "We'll put a curtain up to make a closet," Amelia assured her, busy propping up the table leg. With so few belongings, it didn't take long to have her installed in her new room.

"Why don't you lie down for a rest, dear. We can get better acquainted at dinner."

Kendra nodded, already feeling her eyelids grow heavy at the invitation. But as she lay across the crinkling straw ticking and closed her eyes, a feeling of foreboding crept through her tired limbs.

They were being so nice now. Too nice.

Something was not quite right about her relatives.

CHAPTER ELEVEN

It was good to be home.

Dorian drove up the lush tree-lined drive toward the three-storied, white plantation house with the sun warm on his face and the familiar contentment of home settling over him. The house looked quiet, a fact that his mother despaired over. The few times he had mentioned the idea of getting a house of his own she'd vacillated between stony silences and spoiling him with favorite meals and anything she could think of to make him never want to leave home. He chuckled, thinking of how excited she would be when he walked through the door. The plight of being the baby of the family.

As if thinking of her had conjured her up, his mother flew out the door as Dorian stopped the carriage. She must have heard from Angelene that he was soon to come and had probably been watching for him through the window. She was always so relieved to find him still in one piece.

Dorian sprang down from the carriage while a servant rushed forward to take the horse to the stable.

"You're finally home!" His mother threw her arms around him, her head coming just to his shoulder.

Dorian laughed and gave her a tight squeeze, kissing the top of her head. "How are you, Mother? You are looking well!"

"Happiness takes years off, you know!" she said back to him, turning him toward the house with her arm around his waist. She had always been an affectionate mother, and Dorian had not realized how rare that was compared to the staid mannerisms of most of his friends' parents. It was something he had taken for granted as a child but was now thankful for.

As they walked through the door, his sister Faith, the only other sibling still unmarried and living at home, and his father came toward them. Faith laughed with a joyous sparkle in her eyes and gave him a big hug. "I'm so glad you're home!" His father clapped him several times on the shoulder. "Son, it's so good to see you. Seems like years instead of months."

"And it seems longer each time," his mother added. "Do come into the parlor and let's get you something to eat. We must hear all about your travels. Angelene tells us you had a passenger and had to escort *her* home! Whatever is that all about?"

At the reminder of Angelene, Dorian looked up at the wide, curving staircase and saw her standing at the railing that overlooked the entrance hall. She hesitated, which made Dorian feel a little sorry for her in the awkward moment, but he didn't know what to say so he only bowed his head in a miniscule nod and said nothing. She wasn't his guest and he did not want to encourage her attention.

Faith followed his gaze up and motioned for Angelene to come down, which she did, with a haughty tilt to her chin and an exaggerated sway to her hips.

The five of them settled into the formal drawing room that was decorated in tones of greens and creams. His mother directed the housekeeper to bring in a tea tray and saw that they were all comfortably settled before seating herself.

"So tell us, dear brother, how were you persuaded to take on a passenger? You've always said you never would," his sister asked, picking up the teapot to pour.

"That would be John's doing. He was distracted by the grandeur of an English aristocrat, and his money. He made the deal without consulting me." Dorian made a groaning sound and looked toward the ceiling. "I wanted to throttle him to be sure, but aside from abandoning the woman on the docks, there was little I could do."

Faith laughed. "I doubt that. Is she very beautiful? Angelene says she is an earl's daughter."

Dorian sat down his teacup a little too hard. "Her father was the Earl of Arundel, but he died and her uncle, the new earl, wanted to wash his hands of her. She's come to America to live with her mother's sister and her husband."

"What became of her mother?" Hannah asked.

"She died giving birth to Kendra, er, Lady Townsend. She has no siblings and is rather alone in the world."

"That is so sad." His mother then belied the words by shooting a speculative but happy glance at his father.

Dorian cleared his throat. "As to her beauty, I will withhold judgment and allow you all to make up your own minds. I've promised her an introduction."

Dorian looked over toward Angelene for the first time and noted that her gaze was dagger drawn. He looked quickly away.

"You should invite her to your father's birthday party," his mother interjected with a satisfied smile. "We must introduce her to local society so that she can make some new friends."

"Oh, yes. I would love to meet her," Faith agreed.

"She's nothing special, just because she is English and has a title," Angelene muttered.

"No, she is special in that she knows no one, dear, and we must be charitable and kind. We must help her find friends in what must seem a new world for her," his mother corrected in a soft voice.

Dorian's gaze flew to his mother's. It was rare that she would correct a guest. Angelene must have overstepped her bounds on more than this occasion to have made an adversary of her.

"I keep telling them to forget this business of a birthday party," his father turned their attention back to neutral ground. "A man my age doesn't want a big fuss over it."

His mother and Faith laughed. "But you'll be sixty-five, Father! That is such a grand old age. We must celebrate," Faith teased as their father mock-frowned at her.

"My point exactly, Faith. How's a man supposed to forget he's getting old when everyone keeps reminding him of it."

Dorian chuckled. "You'll not win against the women united. Might as well decide to enjoy all the attention."

The conversation turned to other things and it was over an hour later when Dorian excused himself to freshen up before dinner.

Angelene closed the guest bedchamber door with a soft click and surveyed the room with a frown. *Lady Townsend this and Lady Townsend that!* Her brows snapped together so hard she was beginning to feel a headache coming on. "Oh!" She stomped her foot and placed her hands on her hips. Why did that woman have to show up now, just when she had Dorian almost up to scratch? It wasn't fair!

She walked over to the chair and threw herself into it, staring at the wall. The vision of Lady Kendra crystallized on the white plaster. Her laughing face, those enormous violet eyes that were shocking in such a pale face, and worst of all, the fact that she was so genuine and kind. Why, she might have even liked her had Dorian not obviously liked her so much. It just wasn't fair at all.

A scratching sound at the door had her standing up and flipping a long, black curl over her shoulder. She rose, hope beating in her heart that it might be Dorian. Taking a breath, she held it in and opened the door. "Yes?"

One of the Colburn maids stood there with a timid trembling on her lips. She clutched something in her hand. "Oh, it's you. What do you want?" Angelene's shoulders slumped as she turned away.

"I've come to dress your hair, ma'am."

"Don't call me ma'am," Angelene snapped. "I'm Miss Monteiro to you."

"Yes, ma — um . . . Miss Monteiro."

"Well, don't just stand there like a ninny. Get in here and help me dress." Angelene took a step toward her as the maid scurried into the room. Why did the girl have to be so timid? It grated on Angelene's nerves like fingernails on a chalkboard. Her own nanny had been of the fire-breathing sort and it had taken someone like that to keep a handle on her rambunctiousness. With her mother gone and her father rarely home, Angelene had developed a fierce love and respect for her nanny but she had run roughshod over every other servant in her path. "What's that in your hand?" Angelene eyed the girl's clenched fist.

The girl looked down at it and gasped. "Oh, I forgot I had that. It's nothin', Miss Monteiro." She swung her hand around to her back and looked up with wide eyes.

Angelene walked over, took her arm in a tight grip, and wrenched it around to the front. "Give it to me."

The girl's bottom lip started to quiver as she opened her fist and dropped a short stick into Angelene's waiting palm.

"What is this?" Angelene's voice rose in pitch.

"Just a stick. It isn't anything."

"It is too something. A short stick." Angelene sucked in her breath. "You drew the shortest stick, didn't you! You've been gambling with the other servants about who is to wait upon me, haven't you? Just you wait until Mrs. Colburn hears about this."

"Oh, please, Miss Monteiro, I beg you! Don't tell her! It's j-just that we're all so, so busy. I'm happy to do your hair, truly I am."

Angelene narrowed her eyes and leaned in until their noses were only inches away. "We'll just see about that, won't we? I expect my hair to be perfect tonight."

"Oh, yes ma'am — uh, that is, Miss Monteiro. Thank you." Her head bobbed up and down. "Have you picked out a gown yet? You have so many beautiful gowns."

Somewhat mollified, Angelene turned to the armoire and flung open the doors. She sighed with a happy smile as she gazed at all the colorful silks and satins. "I do, don't

I? I think the watered silk tonight; it's turquoise, which looks perfect on my complexion."

Millie clasped her hands together under her chin, eyes big and round as Angelene pulled out the heavy silk. "Oh, yes, I see. It'll make your skin fairly glow." She rushed over to help Angelene out of her day dress and into the gown.

"Don't forget to tighten my laces first," Angelene snapped as she stepped out of the dress and kicked it to the side. She turned and waited, her foot tapping with impatience as the maid untied the knot and hauled back on the laces. The breath whooshed out of her at the young woman's strength but she didn't care. Her waist lost an inch as the girl pulled and her bosom swelled over the top of the corset in a delightfully fetching manner.

Millie guided the gown over Angelene's head, buttoned the back, and smoothed down the skirt over the petticoat. Perfect. Angelene sat down at the dressing table and glared at the young maid in the mirror to begin on her hair. If Dorian Colburn could take his eyes off her this night she would eat her hat.

Kendra walked out to the backyard and

sank down on the wooden step next to a bowl of potatoes. She spread her apron wide across her simple day dress of sprigged muslin, reached for the peeling knife, and picked up a dusty potato. The scents of flowers wafted with the soft breeze as she turned the small potato round and round in her hands, wondering if she was peeling the last of their winter's store. She knew from the worried, whispered conversations her aunt and uncle tried to hide from her that their food stores were almost gone and harvesting anything edible was weeks away. Kendra wasn't sure, but she thought it possible that there was no money to tide them over.

Guilt washed over her and weighed upon her heart like a heavy stone. Her relatives could not afford to care for her. She was only adding to their burden even though she ate as little as possible and helped out as much as she could in the house with Aunt Amelia. She had all but taken over the caring of the vegetable garden, something she had some experience with from the flower gardens back home. But it wasn't enough. There must be something else she could do. But what?

Kendra turned her head at the sound of the back door opening. Her aunt walked over to a short stool carrying a milking churn. She sat down with a sigh, pushed some straggling gray hair back from her face, and began to churn.

"It's a beautiful day, is it not, Aunt?"

The woman looked up at the scene around her as if just noticing they were outdoors. "I suppose so." She looked like she was about to say something else and then she clamped her lips down into a straight line.

Kendra looked back down at the potato she was peeling, the feeling of sorrow for her aunt welling up into her eyes and filling her chest with an aching weight. "Why did you and Uncle Franklin leave England?"

"Humph. No one ever told you?"

Kendra shook her head and waited for the explanation.

The sound of the churning stopped. "Franklin has a hand for gambling. It didn't take long to run through my dowry, which is why he married me in the first place. After we lost Greenbrier Manor, we tried living in London for a time, but it was . . . too costly. One night Franklin came home bragging about a tract of land he'd won in a card game. I was a mite hopeful until he told me it was here." The churning noise started back up as Kendra picked up another potato. "And there you have it. We spent our last coin on coming to this godforsaken place and trying to make a living off the dirt."

Kendra looked into her aunt's tired eyes. Lines of bitterness stood out on either side of her mouth as she pressed her lips down together. "My uncle Andrew also acquired huge gambling debts. My father had to pay them off to keep him out of prison. That is why we lost everything and I was sent here." She took a long breath and hoped the feeling of shared sorrow, the feeling of love she had for her aunt, showed in her eyes. "We share similar pasts, don't we? I promise you . . . I'm going to do everything I can to help —"

She didn't know how to finish the thought but her aunt turned her head and looked off into the distance, blinking rapidly, her face softened for the first time. In that brief moment, Kendra saw the vulnerability of her disappointments. She had finally cracked the wall of her aunt's defenses and had seen a peek into her heart.

CHAPTER TWELVE

Franklin tied his horse to the hitching post at The Swan in Yorktown and made his way into the taproom. His gaze scanned the throng until it lit upon the man he was looking for. Excellent. He was here.

Making his way through the crowded room, he sat down at the table next to his longtime friend, Martin Saunderson. Martin looked up from his cards and gave Franklin a nod, but he didn't focus on Franklin for long. Leaning back in his chair, his long legs extended in front of him, he kept his gaze on the cards in his hand. A plump barmaid came by and Franklin ordered an ale, waiting for Martin to finish his game. He was in high spirits, thinking of the plan that had come to him shortly after reading the letter. It had been a stroke of luck, that letter, and once he'd explained it to Amelia she had come around and seen it too.

Martin glanced over at Franklin and frowned. His friend's eyes were alight with excitement and he was tapping the table in an impatient way that was distracting. The game was going well and he didn't need the interruption tonight. Confound the man, playing havoc with his concentration. After two more hands, he finally gave up and quit the game. "I must join you another time, gentlemen." He rose and scraped his winnings into his hat.

"You'll give us a chance to win back our blunt, won't you Saunderson?" a rough-looking man from Williamsburg asked.

"Of course. I'm staying here for at least a fortnight." He smoothed down his mustache and gave them a vacant smile. "Plenty of opportunities to best me, I assure you."

The men seemed placated so he turned toward Franklin, who had arisen and was standing close behind him. Martin motioned his friend toward the back of the room. As soon as they were seated, Franklin whispered, "You'll never believe the good fortune that walked through my door a few days ago."

Martin lifted a dark brow in mild interest.

He'd met Franklin years ago at gaming tables in various towns and they'd struck up a strange sort of friendship. Luck was something Franklin had little of, and good sense even less. This should be entertaining.

Franklin leaned in, his eyes overly bright, his hand slapping the table as if trying to get Martin's undivided attention. "My wife's niece arrived from England, intending to make her home with us. Her father was the Earl of Arundel, you know."

"I remember But why is that your good fortune? As I remember it, the earl wouldn't give you a shilling."

Franklin nodded. "Yes, well, he lost his fortune before he died, which is why the new earl, Andrew Townsend, washed his hands of his niece and shipped her here to live. But his letter mentions a dowry, property rich with rents that was left for the chit from her mother's side. Kendra's uncle is unable to touch any of it, which is chafing him real good. He hinted that if I could get rid of the problem he would pay me most handsomely."

"He wants you to kill your niece?" Martin's eyes widened. He knew Franklin to sometimes cheat, more often lie, but murder? The man didn't have it in him.

"I know. Crazy fool. I've had a better idea

and it will be much more profitable than a few hundred pounds."

"And what, pray tell, is that?" Martin leaned forward, interested despite himself.

"If she dies, her uncle Andrew gets the property, but if she marries, all of that lovely money will go directly into her husband's pockets."

Martin shook his head at Franklin as if he had lost his wits. "What has that got to do with you, or me for that matter?"

Franklin gave Martin a slow smile. "She can only marry a man I approve of . . . the man I give permission to wed her . . . the man I will split the inheritance with."

Franklin's plan was suddenly clear. "Wed her? You want *me* to wed your niece? Don't even consider it." His tone was as dry as dust. "I am not a fan of the honored state of matrimony, as you well know."

Franklin smirked at him. "Ah, but you have yet to see her, my friend. She is enough to make a man's blood boil."

Martin knew of Franklin's taste in women and flicked an imaginary piece of lint from his coat sleeve, his voice thick with sarcasm, "Undoubtedly."

"Come to dinner and see for yourself."

Martin shook his head. His parents' marriage had been a brutal affair and he wanted no part of being shackled down by a woman. No fortune was worth that and besides, he enjoyed his roaming freedom and the ability to make a living off games of chance. "You will have to find someone else for your groom, Franklin. I'm content with my lot in life."

Franklin's mouth flattened and his face fell. "You may think that way now, but I'd wager a goodly sum that you'll change your mind once you meet the wench."

Martin smiled his slow smile at his friend. He always made it so easy to fleece him of what little money he had. "How goodly an amount? I believe I will take you up on that bet."

Franklin stood, eyes alight again. "One hundred pounds."

"You don't have that kind of money and you know it."

"I won't need it."

Martin laughed and held out his hand to shake. He might not get the hundred pounds but he would find something of value that he could take from Franklin when he won. "Very well. I'll meet the girl and we'll see."

They shook on it. Martin chuckled as Franklin rushed from the taproom, prob-ably in haste to tell his wife the news. Martin leaned back in his chair and downed the ale, almost feeling sorry for his friend. No woman was worth marriage, not even one with a rich dowry across the pond. It was too bad he would have to take Franklin's paltry profits from his little farming endeavor again this year. Too bad, indeed.

When Franklin arrived home he found both Kendra and his wife surrounded by gowns. He had expected Kendra to be in bed, as she always retired early, and was more than a little disgruntled that she and his wife were both up and jabbering about some nonsense.

"What is the meaning of all this?" he asked as he took off his hat.

Amelia rushed over. He looked down at her face with a start. She hadn't looked so animated in a very long while. She looked almost . . . pretty.

"We received an invitation to a ball! Mr. Colburn's birthday ball. Can you believe it? It's been so long since anyone invited us to a party. Kendra and I have pulled out all our dresses to decide what to wear. She's helping me make over one of her dresses so that I will be more fashionable. Isn't that kind?"

Franklin looked askance at his niece. She

was a slender thing with curves in all the right places and he couldn't imagine his plump wife fitting into anything Kendra could wear.

"A ball." He barked out the words. He needed to keep Kendra out of society until he had her safely betrothed to Martin. The last thing he wanted was a horde of suitors at his door. And Colburn. Wasn't that the captain fellow who had delivered her? The Colburns were wealthy and powerful. "Let me see that invitation."

His wife picked up a card from the desk and brought it over to him. "We must inspect your clothing too, dear. I do believe we can come up with something suitable from your wardrobe."

The look in her eyes made him feel a bit off center. This was the woman he'd married. This was the woman he used to love.

With a shake of his head he read the invitation. It was the captain's family. He remembered the possessive way Dorian had been with his niece, the intimacy they seemed to have. It hadn't meant anything to him at the time but now it was a threat indeed. He was her uncle and the one who would give permission for Kendra to wed. She would not be prey to the likes of Dorian Colburn.

"Yes, well it's late and time for bed. Get this mess cleaned up, Amelia. You'll have time enough to plan your wardrobe tomorrow."

Amelia's eyes turned disappointed. "I suppose so. Come along, Kendra. Let's lay them in a neat pile on the sofa here."

Kendra agreed and didn't seem to mind the order. She gave Franklin a kiss on the cheek and then hugged her aunt. "Goodnight, Uncle, Aunt. Pleasant dreams." She smiled and waved at them as she turned toward her room.

Franklin fought against the melting feeling around his heart. He'd never really desired children, but in that moment he wondered if it would have made a difference, if he and Amelia might have loved each other more and grown closer with a child as a bond between them. Shaking his head, he huffed aloud. A child would have only been another mouth to feed, and they were barely feeding themselves as it was.

With a jerk of his head, he motioned toward the door. Amelia nodded, went to get her shawl from the hook, and followed him outside.

"Well, did Martin agree?"

They were mere steps away from the house, walking toward a big oak tree.

"Hush," Franklin cautioned until they were standing beneath the tree under the moonlight. "Not exactly." Franklin frowned down at his wife. "He says he won't ever get married but I convinced him to at least meet her. Once he sees her, he'll be smitten. I doubt there's a man alive that can resist her."

Amelia squinted up at him. "Martin's a handsome devil with a smooth tongue, but I am starting to feel uneasy about this plan of yours."

"Don't tell me the chit has dug her claws into you, Amelia."

"She is my sister's daughter! My only niece."

"We need this money and the only way we can get our hands on it is to come to some agreement with Martin. Once he sees her, gets to know her, I wager he'll agree to split the dowry to have my permission to wed her. I'm sure of it."

Amelia looked down at her clasped hands. "I suppose you're right. I just hope he tries to make her happy."

"Happy? Since when do you care about such things? Stop feeling sorry for her and remember what she really means to us." He put his hand on her shoulder and turned her toward him. With one thumb Franklin touched his wife's cheek for the first time in ages. "I'm actually looking forward to seeing you all dressed up for the ball."

His wife sputtered in embarrassed protest but she took a tiny step closer. "Kendra will look beautiful. Perhaps we should wrangle an invitation for Martin. He should see how desired she is sure to be."

Franklin took another step closer and pulled his wife into his arms. He was somewhat appalled by her shape but he suppressed the revulsion. He needed her firmly on his side and one night of reminding her why she fell in love with him might just do the trick. He leaned down and kissed her. "An excellent idea. See what you can do."

The eve of the ball was a clear summer's night with the scent of lilacs drifting through the air. Kendra peeked around the corner at her waiting relatives, excitement beating in her breast. Amelia, squeezed into the makeshift gown they had managed for her, was standing beside her husband. Franklin looked grave and out of place in his best, though faded, waistcoat with its ostentatious golden trim. They looked as nervous as she felt.

Stepping around the corner, her aunt gasped as Kendra came into view. She had donned an emerald satin gown that had a tight-fitting bodice with an ivory-boned corset underneath. The skirt was made full by two petticoats, the top petticoat made of white Brussels lace. The overskirt was brocaded in silver with a small ribbon at the waist. It was raised a little at the hem in the front, showing off the lace which matched the end of the gown's sleeves, falling in a graceful tumble to mid-forearm, and also just peeping over her heart-shaped neckline. Her golden hair was caught up in a delicate coiffure with ringlets framing her face and several thick curls arranged to hang down her back. She had threaded emerald ribbon throughout her hair, but her hat! Her hat was the pièce de résistance. Black felt on the outside trimmed in black satin ribbon and emerald green silk on the inside. It was bi-cornered, with both sides turned up to reveal a great deal of the green lining. Around the crown was a wide green and cream-colored striped ribbon which tied in the front in a large bow. Just behind the bow were dyed green feathers and then mounds of wispy black feathers all around the crown. It made her look a full foot taller and was among her most prized possessions. She couldn't believe she finally had an opportunity to wear it.

Kendra smiled at the awe on her relatives' faces and took her aunt's hands into hers. "Aunt, you look very lovely indeed. Why I believe we've outdone ourselves on the remaking of that gown." Her aunt flushed and looked down at the floor. Kendra looked at her uncle, raised her brows, and then nodded her head toward her aunt. Surely the man was not so dense as to realize his wife could use an occasional compliment, and if he was, Kendra thought to remedy the situation.

Franklin looked askance at Kendra and then spurted out, "Quite the thing, my dear. You look lovely." He gave her a little peck on the top of her head, which dislodged one of her aunt's carefully positioned hairpins.

Kendra watched in dismay as one of her aunt's gray curls slid to her shoulder. Amelia elbowed her husband. "Now look what you've done, you oaf!"

Kendra tried not to roll her eyes. It was quite hopeless — trying to get these two amicable with each other. "Here, Aunt, let me fix that for you." With a quick twist and a jab with the pin, Kendra repaired the damage. Smiling at both of them, she took a long breath. "There now, are we ready?"

Franklin smiled at the two women, relief on his face as he escorted them to the borrowed carriage.

Dorian stood at the far end of the ballroom watching the door with a hum of anticipation coursing through his veins. It had been over a fortnight since he'd dropped Kendra off at her relatives and while he had tried to keep busy, tried to block her from his mind, he had not succeeded. It had taken all his self-control not to deliver the invitation to tonight's ball himself, but at least with that he had managed.

Angelene circled the area where he stood yet again. She wore another shocking gown and the men in the room were hard put not to openly stare at her display, but she was not accomplishing her obvious mission of gaining Dorian's attention. She was, instead, making him clamp down his teeth in irritation as she sailed over to him and grasped his arm in the most forward manner.

Dorian glanced down at her with a frown. She loosened her grip, her voice coy, "Are you having a pleasant time, Dorian? Faith did such a fine job decorating."

Dorian's eyes swept over her face. She really was striking but there was nothing there, not in him toward her, nor inside of her worth being interested in. He tried to disentangle her grip from his arm. "A fine time, and you?"

Angelene took his question as interest and launched into a detailed description of how she helped his mother and Faith pull off the celebration. Dash the woman. He hoped he didn't appear as bored as he felt. He was just about to make up some excuse to move to a different spot when a sudden quiet fell on the crowd.

"Lord and Lady Rutherford and Lady Kendra Townsend," the butler announced the trio from the top of the stairs.

Dorian's head jerked around, his body following as he dislodged Angelene from his side. He looked up and sucked in his breath hearing the rustling and whispers of their company as he made his way to the entry where his parents stood receiving the guests.

"Who is she?"

"Is she the passenger from England?"

"Why, I haven't seen the Rutherfords in society in years."

"Isn't that Franklin and Amelia? That must be their niece from England. What a striking creature."

Dorian walked up to Kendra, took her gloved hand in his, and bowed. His smile was slow and secretive, his voice rough, deeper than usual as he spoke into the sudden quiet of the room. "Lady Townsend.

You have rendered them speechless and have quite taken my breath away."

Kendra blushed, looking from his eyes to the staring crowd, and then back at him. Her wide, violet gaze was a mixture of mortification to be the center of attention and a pleading for his help to get them out of it. Instead, Dorian winked at her and turned them toward his parents. "Mother? I believe now would be a good time to start the music, don't you think?"

Hannah looked from Dorian to Kendra, a small smile playing across her lips. "I do believe you're right, dear." She turned toward the six-piece orchestra and motioned with her gloved hand to begin, and then looked back toward Dorian. "As we are still greeting latecomers, would the two of you be so kind as to start the dancing? Lord and Lady Rutherford and we have so much to catch up on."

Dorian choked back a laugh and extended his arm to Kendra. "Duty calls, my lady."

Kendra took his arm, laughing up at him. "I seem to forever be putting upon your good graces, Captain. Shall you rescue me again?"

"Let's try, shall we?"

■ ■ ■ ■

She couldn't possibly reject him in front of
the throng's watchful gaze but this was only
going to add fuel to the fire of speculation
that they were already generating. Why was
he singling her out? She had so hoped to
edge quietly, slowly into society. Now she
would have immediate, jealous enemies that
she would have to charm into giving her a
chance. Men didn't understand anything
about the women of polite society!

She looked over toward her aunt and
uncle, seeing her uncle's scowling face. Oh
dear, to make matters worse Uncle Franklin
didn't care for the captain. It was just as
she had suspected. Unable to think of any
other recourse, she took Dorian's arm and
allowed him to lead her to the dance floor.
The music struck up the first flowing notes
of a waltz just as they reached the center of
the room. Dorian turned her and took her
into his arms, and within moments they
were gliding over the polished floor to the
first dance of the night.

One, two, three. One, two, three. The
numbers ticked off inside her head as she
threw back her shoulders in the remembered stance of long-ago lessons. If only

there had been opportunities to practice she wouldn't be feeling quite so nervous, but there had been few dances since their financial disaster. What if she tripped and fell or trodded upon his toes and embarrassed them both?

"Relax. You're doing fine," Dorian pulled her closer and murmured the words into her ear, sending a peculiar type of excitement coursing through her body. Her gaze snapped to his and there in his dark blue eyes she saw a mix of mischief and admiration. She smiled back at him, unable to *not* smile, unable to remember that they were the focus of over a hundred sets of eyes. She floated, lost in the strong arms encircling her.

"You are an accomplished dancer, Captain." She thought to make small talk and break the tension straining between them but the comment came out rushed and out of breath.

He flashed her that wicked grin that made her knees soften. Her steps slowed so that he had to take her waist in a tight grip to keep her moving to the beat. "My vast experience, I suppose. I do so love a ball."

He was teasing her again. She didn't know whether to berate him or laugh. She decided for humor. "Ah, yes. I can just imagine you practicing the dance steps during the long, boring hours on your ship. Does the fair John partner you?" She looked up with innocence shining from her eyes and dimpled one cheek.

"John is light on his feet, but I must confess . . ." here he leaned in so close that she could feel his breath in her ear, "that I prefer Smythe."

The vision of the short, balding, overly hairy sailor came to mind and made Kendra miss a step. Suppressed mirth caused her chest to shake. "Oh heavens, I should like to experience such a thrill. Is he here this evening? I need to fill my dance card somehow."

The last strains of the music came to a halt and Dorian slowed them to a graceful stop. He bowed low over her hand and said just loud enough for her to hear, "Turn around, Lady Townsend, and you will see the line forming. I have a feeling your dance card will be full within moments."

She turned to see that, indeed, several men were positioning themselves at the edge of the crowd for an introduction. "Oh, my goodness." She looked around the room as Dorian took her arm and led her back toward where her aunt and uncle and his parents stood. "Save me another dance, won't you?" he murmured as he stopped her in front of his parents.

She looked up into his eyes and saw a smoldering look that made her heart quicken its beat.

"Of course." She tore her gaze from his face and saw Dorian's mother watching them. The love she had for her son was obvious but what would Mrs. Colburn think of her?

"Mother, may I introduce my passenger from England, Lady Kendra Townsend. Kendra, this is my mother, Hannah Colburn."

Kendra curtsied and glanced up to see a radiant face beaming at her. "So this is the woman whom my son cannot seem to say enough about."

"Oh, I —" Kendra gripped her skirt with clammy hands.

Hannah laughed. "I assure you, my dear, he only sings your praises."

He'd been talking about her? To his mother? "Thank you, Mrs. Colburn. I'm pleased to meet you." She turned to Dorian's father, a dashingly handsome man himself who took her hand and bowed over it. "My father, Clayton Colburn."

Clayton's eyes twinkled at her as if they shared a great secret. Her heart hammered a little stronger. Dorian would look just like him as he grew older. "So good to meet you, sir."

Before he could answer, a young woman with dark brown hair and blue eyes pushed her way through the crush of people around them and grasped up Kendra's hand. "Hello, Lady Townsend. I'm Faith, Dorian's sister. I have so been looking forward to meeting you. Dorian has never allowed a passenger before and we knew you must be special, indeed, for him to break his own rule."

Kendra flushed. "I'm afraid it wasn't his doing. My uncle convinced John to take me aboard. The captain was not pleased when he discovered it."

Faith laughed and his parents smiled. "Oh, but I do believe he has since changed his mind."

It was as if they'd all decided to like her and there wasn't anything she could do to change that, not that she wanted to, it was just so . . . wonderful and frightening, feeling this happy. *Joy.* How long had it been since she had said that fruit of the Spirit to herself? It had been a leap of faith — coming to America — but thanks be to God, He seemed to be making a way for her.

CHAPTER THIRTEEN

Her uncle was scowling at her when she turned from the introductions. Dorian said he would get them something to drink and strolled away. "Kendra," her uncle grasped her arm and pulled her closer, "I don't want you dancing with that man again."

Kendra frowned. "Why ever not, Uncle? Do you dislike him?"

Franklin ignored her question. "There is someone else I want you to meet." His eyes scanned the crowd. "He said he was coming. Where is he?"

Her uncle seemed to be talking to himself so Kendra didn't bother to try and answer. Was there someone her uncle wanted her to be interested in? He'd never mentioned anyone.

"He'll be here soon, Franklin. Kendra will have plenty of dance partners in the meantime. Let's dance, shall we?" Her aunt looked up at her uncle with a flushed, pleading face.

"Yes, do dance with Aunt Amelia," Kendra added. "I promise not to dance with Mr. Colburn while you're gone." Her aunt deserved some happiness and if Kendra had to avoid Dorian for her to get it, she would obey her uncle. Why he felt so strongly against the sea captain was something she would have to discover.

"Oh, very well," Franklin gave in, sounding none too pleased. "Do not move from this spot, Kendra."

Kendra's eyes widened. Was she not going to be allowed to dance with anyone? But seeing the look of excitement on her aunt's face she only nodded her head. "Yes, Uncle."

As they walked off she heard her name being called and turned to see John coming toward her. There was a tall woman on his arm with hair the color of honey and warm amber eyes to match, who must be Victoria.

"Lady Townsend, how do you fair?" John winked at her and kissed the back of her hand with exaggerated flourish.

"I am wonderful. Thank you, kind sir. And this must be your fiancée, Victoria?" Kendra shared a smile with the woman.

Victoria bobbed a small curtsy. "It is such a pleasure to meet you, Lady Townsend.

John has told me so much about you."

"Please, call me Kendra." It would seem she had been the topic of conversation on many lips these last weeks. "How is your house coming along? I heard a wedding date is in the making as soon as it is finished."

Victoria nodded. "You must come and see it. They are nearly finished and I would love some decorating advice. The styles must be advanced in England."

"As if you haven't had every female in the county out there giving advice," John groused. "She changes her mind almost daily and I despair of ever knowing what color we will paint the drawing room."

"I can't say as I'm very accomplished in such matters." Kendra grimaced, thinking of all the lovely things they had sold and the shabby way her father and she had lived that year before his death. "But I would love to see it sometime."

Victoria took her hand and squeezed it, making Kendra feel she'd found a true friend. "You shall. I will have John pick you up and bring you by later this week."

As the three of them chatted, Kendra spied Dorian on the dance floor. A few seconds later, her heart dropped as she realized the stunning woman in his arms was none other than Angelene Monteiro. Something, shock maybe, must have shown on her face as Victoria and John turned toward the dance floor to see what she was staring at.

"Oh, her." Victoria sighed and then quickly turned back to Kendra. "She's no doubt tricked him into dancing with her. Do not let it worry you, Kendra."

"Worry? I have no claims on the captain."

"That's not what I have heard," Victoria said in a soft voice. She looked up at John with a *why don't you do something* expression.

John cleared his throat. "Ah, yes." He turned toward Kendra. "Women have been throwing themselves at Dorian since he was fifteen, I'm afraid. But none have captured his attention like a certain Englishwoman." He gave Kendra a kind smile.

Kendra's cheeks grew hot. Was she so obvious in her attraction to the man? She would not be one of those women who threw herself at him as Angelene was doing. Just watching the way the woman held tight to his shoulder and gazed up into Dorian's face was enough to make her nauseous. Turning away she said, "It's so warm in here, don't you think? I believe I will get some air out on the terrace. Will you excuse me, please?"

Victoria nodded, her face concerned. "Would you like us to accompany you?"

"No, I will be fine. You two should dance," Kendra assured her. "It was so very nice to meet you, Victoria. John, wonderful to see you again." She nodded good-bye and pushed through the crowd to the wide-open doors at the back of the house, forgetting her promise to her uncle to stay in one spot.

Leaving the ballroom she wandered out onto the terrace and stood, alone, as the cool breeze soothed her cheeks. She inhaled the delicate floral bouquets that wafted through the air from the many pots of overflowing flowers but she couldn't stand still.

So women threw themselves at him, did they? How very convenient. Why that knowledge upset her as much as it did was something she didn't want to probe too deep for answers. *Lord, he is so wrong for me and I fear he'll just break my heart. Besides, Uncle Franklin despises him; there must be a reason for that. Help me guard my heart!*

"I've caught you at your prayers, I see," a deep voice chuckled from behind her.

Kendra's eyes fluttered open as she spun around. Her breath caught. The man standing behind her, between the house and herself, looked like the very devil. He watched her the way a cat would crouch down in the tall grass and watch a mouse. Her heart thudded with fear. He was very tall, dressed entirely in black, with black hair, a mustache, and a little patch of hair beneath his lower lip. His eyes narrowed as one corner of his mouth quirked up in a disdainful smile. He looked her up and down, a stare that made her feel instantly stripped and sullied.

He took a few steps toward her. Kendra stepped back, casting a glace about the area. She sank inside as she noted that they were alone in the dark corner of the garden. How had she wandered so far from the house?

He laughed with a low chuckle and a seductive curve of his lips, seeming to enjoy her obvious fright. "Forgive me, I've forgotten my manners. My name is Martin Saunderson. And you are Lady Townsend, no?"

"Yes." Her gaze darted toward the yellow glow shining from the back of the house in the distance. "How do you know my name?"

"Your uncle is an acquaintance of mine. He has spoken of you" — he flashed a feral grin at her — "although it would seem that for once he was right." Again his dark eyes flicked up and down her form, making her wish for a heavy cloak to hide in.

"I must be going back inside, sir." Her

voice squeaked, making her sound more like a startled hen than the firm assertion she wished for. Her heart hammered inside her chest as she turned to leave.

"Not quite yet, my sweet." His arm snaked out and caught her wrist.

Now would be the time to scream. She opened her mouth to do just that, when he yanked her into his chest. His lips closed over her open mouth. With a survival reflex she didn't know she possessed, she pounded her fist against his chest with all her strength and bit down on his lip.

He pulled back, enraged. "You vicious wench!" He held one hand to his bleeding mouth and lifted the other one to strike her.

"Don't even think about it."

Kendra whirled around to find Dorian standing behind them. She took advantage of the surprised slack in the horrid man's arms and jerked free, backing up until she was close to Dorian's side and breathing as if she'd run a race.

"I don't remember inviting you, Saunderson. I must request that you leave, immediately."

"I'm not so sure the lady wants me to leave. She was quite amorous in my arms before you interrupted us." Martin sneered, blood smeared across his chin.

Kendra sucked in a breath at such a bold-faced lie, unable to respond.

He mocked her with a low bow. "Until another time then, my sweet, when we have more privacy."

Kendra collapsed against Dorian's side as Martin strode toward the terrace. "Who was he?"

"Martin Saunderson, a cheating thief of a gambler who resides in Yorktown at times." His words had a bite to them as his arms circled around her.

"He said he knows my uncle."

Dorian set his chin on the top of Kendra's head for a brief moment. "Yes, well I've learned some things about your aunt and uncle since our return." He placed his thumb underneath her chin and tilted her face up. His voice was more serious than she'd ever heard him. "Your uncle has had dealings with Saunderson in the past. They are not honest men, Kendra."

Kendra nodded. She had wondered how her aunt and uncle made a living, knowing their farming efforts were sad indeed. "I don't believe my relatives would harm me."

"Maybe not, but I don't like it. Be careful of Saunderson. Considering the kind of women he keeps company with, it is doubtful he believes you to be uninterested."

Kendra gasped. "Are you saying he forces kisses on women and they like it?"

Dorian shot her a speculative glance and appeared to be smoothing down a smile. "Some women like a direct approach."

The conversation about his vast experience with the fair sex rushed back to Kendra. She took a step back and then another. "I suppose you know all about that. Mayhap I should guard myself from you too."

Dorian took a step closer, just as Martin had, but this time jolts of excitement raced through her instead of fear. "That would be wise indeed, Kendra." His voice was like warm silk gliding over her heated skin.

She reminded herself that she would not be like those other women, throwing themselves at him. And she would most certainly not be like Angelene. She would continue to pray and await God's will for her life with patience and . . . long-suffering . . . and . . . the image of Ruth lying at Boaz's feet flashed through her mind, causing her to frown. The Bible did have some peculiar stories in it. She would have to study that one again in light of this new knowledge of men. Nevertheless, she would uphold her high morals just as her father would wish. She lifted a hand to stop Dorian. "Don't prove yourself no better than that horrid man."

Dorian's mouth quirked up in a crooked smile as his eyes flashed mischief at her. "You dare compare me to him?" He grasped her upper arms in a tender, tight hold. "Next, you'll be calling me names again, black-hearted pirate names."

Kendra shivered under the force of his hands and not because of the chill in the air. He did look like a pirate, a reformed gentleman pirate with his long, dark hair and dark blue waistcoat with a stark white cravat and shirt glowing under the light of the moon.

He leaned in and pulled her toward him. His hands rose to rest on her shoulders, his thumbs a butterfly touch against her flushed cheeks as his breath moved in and out above her hair. She stood still in his trap — unable to move, unable to think, unable to breathe.

An aching hungriness grew in her chest. She was no better than the rest of them — poor, besotted women indeed. She would give anything if he would only kiss her.

She let her head fall back and closed her eyes, letting the moonlight reveal his victory. She waited for what seemed an eternity and then let out a held breath as his warm lips brushed against each closed eyelid. The kisses trailed to her ear, sending waves of bliss through her body. She took a shuddering breath as his lips made a trail of heat down her throat. Her senses swirled together, her mind spun down a dizzying path to where she did not know or care.

He was a pirate after all.

Oh, not the kind that took loot from another ship, reveling in the spoils of jewels and golden coins. No, he was the pirate of her heart, taking what she was terrified to give and heaven only knew what he would do with it now that he held it in his hands.

Dorian groaned as he finally took her willing lips. He heard both their ragged breath and knew he would have to stop, pull back, and protect her innocence. But something was happening, something strange and not welcome. His independence, his life as a sea captain and the freedom he'd reveled in, all swept away with the intensity of her response. If he didn't stop, and soon, he would have to make her his wife.

The choice hung between them like the strongest silken thread, connected by their lips. With all the strength he possessed he pulled away and gazed at the flushed splendor of her face. He groaned deep in his throat as the violet-hued eyes opened to reveal a smoldering she couldn't know was there, couldn't realize the effect she was having on him, could she? Her lips were swollen from his kiss, her hair fallen down in wild disarray. She was the picture of seduction and it took all of his strength to step back.

"Why did you stop?" she whispered in a husky voice.

Was she really so innocent? "I think you had better go inside. Quickly."

Kendra took a step back and with a deep breath, a shocked breath, as if she were just coming back into the land of the living, she lifted her hands to her cheeks. "Oh! What are we doing?"

With a feminine squeak of a sound, she turned and rushed toward the light and safety.

CHAPTER FOURTEEN

The low fire was the only light in his bed-chamber as Dorian walked in and shut the door behind him with a small click. He walked over to a chair beside the fire, rubbing the back of his neck. A trickle of sweat ran down the side of his face. He squeezed his eyes closed, trying not to think, and then removed his coat and tossed it over the back of another chair. Sitting down, elbows braced on his knees, he blew out a long breath and buried his face into his hands.

What was he doing? Playing with her like that?

Images of people and places he hadn't thought of in years paraded across his memory. Captaining his own ship had turned out even more satisfying than he'd dreamed. He enjoyed every aspect of his life — making deals for goods that other men couldn't seem to get their hands on; courting contacts and business associates with a natural charm that made easy friends of everyone; the surge of his heart pumping when life on the high seas turned dangerous, when it demanded nerves of steel, decisive leadership, and the thrill of overcoming odds time after time after time.

She'd called him a pirate and in a way, it was true. He looted pockets using calculated charm instead of sabers, plundered relationships to achieve his goals, and even turned off the internal voice which whispered he'd gone too far when he accepted a midnight offer from a beautiful woman with greed on her mind. He'd been living a charmed life and he hadn't dreamed that anything or anyone would ever change that.

Kendra's face flashed behind his closed eyes as he pressed his fingers against his face. What had she done to him? Like a cannonball being fired at his middle she'd exploded into his perfectly happy life and blown it to bits. It didn't make sense. It was as if he stood on the edge of a steep cliff unable to stand against the cyclone coming right at him. There didn't seem to be any stopping this fast-fall obsession.

A pair of violet-hued eyes had quite simply ruined him.

With a short, hard exhale of breath he stood and removed all but his drawers. The fire barely made enough light to see the bed but he was too exhausted to light a candle. He edged around to the side, turned back the edge of the coverlet, and slid into bed. His elbow slammed into something solid, something soft. He sprang back. Something was in his bed! No, not something . . . someone!

It moved toward him as he leapt from the bed and grasped his pistol from the bedside table. As soon as he had it pointed at the bed he heard a low chuckle. Prickles of unease ran up and down his back and then outrage burst through him as Angelene's dark head poked out from the covers.

"You."

"Hello, Dorian." A bare shoulder showed above the top of the coverlet.

"Angelene, what do you think you are do-ing here?" He knew the answer — it was hammering at his head in a tap, tap, tap-ping way but the shock had yet to wear off. Trap! This was a trap — his body and brain screamed at him to run.

"I would think that would be obvious," she purred. She started to sit up, covers clutched fetchingly to her chest. "Tell me you don't want me here."

Dorian swallowed hard and looked away. "Angelene, please, get dressed and get out."

225

She chuckled with throaty certainty. "Come now. I always get what I want and I want you. I will make you very, very happy, Dorian."

Dorian looked back at her, incredulous. "I have tried to be polite. I have tried to spare your feelings, but I see that my efforts have been wasted. If you do not leave, immediately, I will. I would save your reputation if possible. Angelene, think what you are doing."

"Oh, I have thought of nothing else." Her gaze was like a searing iron with her brand on it across his chest. With a big inhale, Angelene threw back her head and let out a bloodcurdling scream. Dorian dove for his pants and yanked them on. A moment later the door burst open as Angelene's father and two other guests who were staying in rooms down the hall, rushed into the room. Her father's face turned ashen as he took in the sight that met his eyes.

"What in blazes!" His gaze swung to Angelene as she clutched the coverlet to her throat. "Daddy," she screeched, "he seduced me!" She began to cry, real tears streaming down her face.

Dorian stood motionless in the trap that was tightening around his throat. He was finding it hard to breathe. "Mr. Monteiro, I assure you that I was not seducing your daughter. I'm sorry to say it, but I found her in my room waiting for me." He wasn't sure how to go on. As much as he disliked her, he despaired of seeing her chances of ever making an honorable marriage disappear like a puff of smoke.

Angelene burst into a fresh round of tears at his words. "Forgive me, Daddy," she cried. "You saw how he danced with me earlier and then, and then, he kissed me in the garden. Before I knew what was happening, I was coaxed in here." She peeked up at her father, tears still bright in her wide, blinking eyes.

Monteiro started to rush Dorian but one of the other houseguests held him back while the other, a young gentleman who couldn't keep his gaze off Angelene, closed the door and made shushing sounds to them all.

"He'll pay for this, my dear. I promise you that," Monteiro hissed with an outraged glare toward Dorian. "We will leave and you will get dressed. Be quick about it. I am taking you home." Turning to Dorian, he shook off the restraining hands and stood as tall as his frame would allow. Shaking with anger he stated. "I will discuss this matter with your father, sir. You shall be called to account for your despicable actions."

Dorian said nothing to that. He was a grown man and his father would never interfere in his life unless asked to. Dorian watched as they all quit the room. He gave Angelene one last look, a look of pity, before following them out.

Angelene looked as she always did when about to win the desires of her heart.

Angelene looked smug.

Kendra closed her eyes, a dreamy smile on her lips, and leaned out the open window of her bedchamber, breathing in the cool night air. Had there ever been a more perfect evening?

Dear God, he's the one, isn't he?

Her smile grew into a soft laugh as happiness expanded inside her chest, filling her with an almost painful joy. She wanted to remember his kiss, but she was saving that. First she had to remember every smile, every touch, being in his arms while they danced, even that ghastly man had turned out part of her fairytale. All fairytales needed a villain and the way Dorian had rushed to her rescue, so brave and so strong! She inhaled and then let out a big sigh.

American pirate captains were very nice indeed.

A sudden rustling sound from across the yard jerked her attention to the outdoors. She poked her head further out the window looking from side to side and then, as two large figures came around the side of the house, she pulled back inside the darkness. She straightened, skirting around to the side of the window, and pressed her back against the wall. Leaning ever so slightly toward the open window she was just able to make out a voice.

"So, where's my money, my friend?"

It was Uncle Franklin's voice. Who was he talking to out in the middle of the yard at a time like this? Kendra leaned a little more toward the window, her ear coming around the frame, but still kept her back pressed to the wall so that she couldn't be seen.

A low chuckle, one that sounded strangely familiar, answered her uncle. Wait. Was that the sound of coins jingling? "You've won at last, Franklin. Your description of her was, ah, not exaggerated. You've truly foiled me. Well done."

Uncle Franklin laughed with a hearty sound Kendra had never heard from him before. He must have realized how loud it was as he cut the bark off and took to whispering. "She is something, isn't she? But that's not even the half of it. She's so . . . pleasant. Yes, yes, that's the word. She's brought sunshine into this house and I should hate to see her go and the gloom reappear I assure you, but then it must be so if we are to have what we want, eh? Why, she made me a rhubarb pie yesterday, slaved over the thing for hours I'm told to get it just right, just because she heard it was my favorite. I shall miss her!" He sounded louder and magnanimous. "She'll make a fine wife, that she will. Make a man happy, I say."

Oh dear. *She* had made a rhubarb pie yesterday. They were talking about *her!*

"Yes, well, I fear I've misstepped on making a good first impression."

"Heh." Her uncle's voice growled. "You were just over eager. Understandable. Quite understandable. Let's have you out to dinner. You'll make a better impression here at home with us than standing in a crowded ballroom vying with all the other men for her attention. She was belle of the ball. I couldn't keep track of how many she danced with."

"One in particular is worrisome."

"Yes, that Dorian Colburn. Something will have to be done about him."

The voices paused.

Kendra's mind reeled with everything she

had heard, but the greatest, strongest thought was the knowledge that they might harm Dorian. Peeking around the window frame, she saw the face of the man speaking to her uncle. Her heart sped up as the moonlight cast a shadowy pall on his sharp, angled face. It was him. The man who had forced a kiss on her. She shuddered.

Why was Uncle Franklin talking to him like they were some sort of partners? And why was Uncle Franklin acting like he was plotting something? What was this bet they had? It didn't make sense. Her relatives had been kind to her of late and she had thought, hoped, and prayed that she was being accepted into their family. She bit her lower lip while hot pinpricks of tears scalded behind her eyes. Her nose swelled and she sniffed — a loud interruption in the dark quiet. Oh, no! They'd heard her! Her hand rose to her mouth as she shrank back from the window.

Lord have mercy, what if they saw her?

With legs that trembled and a painful throbbing against her temples she rushed to her bed, eased under the covers, and turned on her side toward the wall. *Don't let them come to the window. Please, God, keep me safe, keep me safe, keep me safe.*

Her heart was roaring in her ears so that

she wondered if she could hear anything should they come to her window to investigate. Taking short breaths, she squeezed her eyes shut and concentrated on calming down. Uncle Franklin wouldn't hurt her, she was sure of that, wasn't she? But it sounded like he wanted that horrid man to court her. Oh, stop thinking like that. Trust in the Lord, remember? He had promised to be her Father now that she was an orphan and she was going to hold Him to that promise!

Finally, after several minutes of silence, she started to breathe evenly again. A few more minutes and she mustered up the courage to turn her head and look toward the window. Nothing was there but a wide breadth of moonlight spilling through the half-open curtains. Big, deep breath. *Thank You, Lord.*

More moments of silence went by and then she took a deep breath and by slow degrees turned over and slid out of bed.

She would not be sleeping with the window open this night.

Dorian was fully clothed and pacing the length of his room when he received his father's summons. As he walked into the library, he saw the other occupant in the room, his stern face accusing him. Clayton stood up and motioned for Dorian to take the seat opposite Don Monteiro. "Mr. Monteiro has told me what he walked in on tonight, son." Clayton sighed. "Dorian, I'm sure there is some kind of . . . explanation —" He stopped and leaned against his braced hands splayed on either side of the desk.

"Father," Dorian asked in a voice that was deadly soft, "do you think I'm such a fool that I would invite a woman into my bedroom? And in your house? I may have been foolish in the past, reckless even, and I will admit to the folly of naming my ship after her and no doubt giving her false hopes, but I did not invite her into my room. I am not that big a fool."

Clayton nodded, his features relaxed. He turned to Monteiro. "You know your daughter, sir. In all honesty, what do you think happened?"

Monteiro's face turned a telling shade of red as he sputtered, "My daughter is ruined, that's what I think. And foolish or not, your son is going to marry Angelene posthaste."

Dorian shook his head and stared at Angelene's father with pity in his eyes. "I'm sorry, sir. Sorry if I, in any way, encouraged her. Sorry she lost her mother at a young age and hasn't had a mother's guidance in such matters. I'm sorry you've given her everything she ever wanted and that she has become this . . . this spoiled woman. Because, truth be known, she is beautiful on the outside and miserable on the inside. Truth be known, she has been hurtling toward this moment for a very long time and you know it. You've been dreading it, haven't you?"

In the deathly silence of his words, Dorian walked over and poured Don Monteiro a drink. He took it to him, his steps steady and sure. The look in his eyes matched his steps, a mix of compassion and truth. It was like an inborn weapon, this ability to show truth and direct it in such a way that people recoiled and capitulated. He felt sorry to wield it, especially to a father who had probably done the best he could, but his back was in the proverbial corner and he fought with the instincts of the trapped. Dorian thrust the drink out to the man — a talented man, a man who was revered in his place as a shipbuilder, a man that had never known how to be a father. Dorian held the glinting crystal out with a steady hand and in a firm voice encouraged, "No one will know what she's done, I promise. Just take her home and let this quietly subside."

Monteiro's hand shook as he took the glass. He took a large gulp and nodded his head. "Yes, yes that's probably best."

Dorian gave him a grim smile and shrugged. "She needs a husband and brood of children to keep her occupied. I suggest you find someone and be quick about it, before she gets herself into further trouble."

The three men looked at each other a bit sheepishly and then they all broke into quiet chuckles. Picturing Angelene with a brood of children clutching her skirts was quite the mental image.

After Monteiro went back to his bedchamber, promising an early departure for Angelene and himself, Clayton's face grew serious. "Son, you handled that well, as you do in all your dealings, but I have a bad feeling that this ordeal is not going to go away that easily."

Dorian nodded. "Angelene is a worthy opponent, I agree. What do you suggest I do?"

Clayton steepled his hands under his chin, his eyes narrowed in thought. "I think you should take a trip, get away for a little while and let things simmer down a bit."

Dorian paused and then nodded. "I know just where to go. John and I have been meaning to inspect a new shipment of horses up north in Stafford County. We could leave first thing in the morning."

"Good. I'll deflect any questions and work on controlling the rumors." His father winked at him. "Your mother has her heart set on another female for you. I don't believe she will find it difficult to convince the guests that walked in on Angelene's little scene to remain quiet."

Dorian chuckled. "Mother can be quite ruthless and convincing when she desires."

"Yes." His father looked up and smiled with closed lips, his eyes alight with something that Dorian hadn't seen in awhile. It was a look of pride as he thought about his wife, a look of love mingled with pride. "I would dare to say your mother is more competent than President Washington when she sets her mind to something." His father's eyes twinkled.

"Are you threatening me, sir?" Dorian quirked a brow at his father, playing along.

"Not me! I know better than that." He stood and took Dorian's shoulders in a hug. With a mock sigh he shook his head and stared Dorian in the eyes. "Sorry son, but I do believe your bachelor days are numbered."

Dorian let out a soft word.

His father threw back his head and

laughed.

"Good-night, son."

Dorian scowled. "Thanks for the pleasant dreams."

CHAPTER FIFTEEN

Dorian jogged up the wide steps of John's plantation home. It was almost finished and his best friend would be a married man soon, but not yet. He could still show up on his doorstep and demand a favor.

John listened with restrained mirth as Dorian related the night's happenings to him. "You've got yourself in a pickle this time, Dorian, loving two women at the same party. Tisk. Tisk."

Dorian gave him a black look. "I'm not in love with anyone and well you know it."

"I know nothing of the sort!" John snorted. "A particular Englishwoman strikes me as someone who has occupied a great deal of your thought and attention."

Dorian swished his riding crop hard through the air with a hissing sound. "Nonsense."

But they both heard the paltry, shallow sound to the word.

John threw back his head and laughed. "Oh, very well. How may I be of assistance, Captain?"

"Pack your bags, my friend. We're off to Stafford County to inspect some newly arrived horseflesh."

John's eyes brightened. "It's true then? Cameron has Spanish stock? Just arrived?"

"That's what we're going to find out." Dorian looked heavenward for patience. "Hurry up, man. I've got marriage-minded females dogging my heels. We haven't got all day!"

Dorian chuckled, thinking how very glad he was to have such a good friend, as John turned tail and ran into the house for his baggage.

Pastor Higgins, Don Monteiro, and Angelene wheeled into the Colburn drive in a dust cloud of what looked to be impatience. Clayton had been half-watching for them the last two days from his study window. He frowned as he saw Angelene step out of the carriage in an elaborate pale blue gown and veil — wedding finery.

"This won't be that easy, Angelene," Clayton muttered to the glass. He settled himself behind his desk and awaited the knock on his door.

"Come in." His voice was low and harsh, too harsh. *Get control. They have no power over your son.*

The threesome sailed into the room, with Angelene making a grand entrance with swoops and swishes of her skirts. Her voice could be heard complaining that someone was stepping on her train but Clayton blocked it out the best he could. Instead, he stood up and assumed an astonished mien. "Mr. Monteiro, I wasn't expecting you today."

Don Monteiro cast a sheepish glance at his daughter. "We felt it was best to clear up this matter as quickly as possible, Mr. Colburn."

Clayton raised an eyebrow. "I thought our conversation that night had concluded the matter. Dorian is not at home. I'm afraid this will have to be addressed some other time."

Don Monteiro cleared his throat, eyes darting about the room. "Angelene said" — he stared at a speck on the floor — "she, ah, said that your son agreed to wed her. Insisted it, you know."

Clayton felt a stab of sorrow for the man. His own children had found their mates and married in every appearance of happiness. He stared at the young woman determined to have his son. She was a dark beauty, to be sure. Wide, slanted cat's eyes, full crimson lips, high cheekbones, and thick black hair that coiled like shining ropes around her shoulders. Lord have mercy upon them all. How did his son get himself into such a predicament?

Just as he was about to despair how to answer, Hannah flew through the door as if on dove's wings. Clayton's heart settled back down, his breathing returned to normal. He smiled. His wife would know how to take care of this.

"Mr. Monteiro, so good of you to come!" Hannah tilted her elegant blonde head and smiled at the man, catching him off guard with her gaiety. He started to reach for her hand but Hannah turned her bright smile to Angelene. "Child," she muttered, her chin tilting down, her eyes turning soft and kind. "My dear child."

Clayton held his breath. What was she about?

Hannah reached out and took Angelene's stiff arm, squeezing her hand and coming up closer. "What a beauty you are. Just look at you!"

Angelene eyed Hannah in wide-eyed distrust. But she allowed herself to be drawn closer to Hannah's side. "We need to have a chat, you and I. Don't we, dear?"

Hannah reached up and patted Angelene's shoulder.

"Come now. I have a story to tell you. A story that I think you are going to like, very, very much." Hannah took a firm grasp on Angelene's gloved elbow and led her toward the door. She turned back to the men and smiled.

"Clayton, you entertain Mr. Monteiro and Pastor Higgins. Enjoy a ride or something? Angelene and I have so much to talk about."

"Now see here. What kind of story are you telling my daughter?" Monteiro's cheeks puffed out as he put his hands on his hips.

"Why, Mr. Monteiro, I'm only going to tell her of the first love story. How God made Eve as the perfect mate for Adam and how Angelene has an Adam out there somewhere."

Monteiro dropped his arms and nodded. "Oh. Well, that's alright then." He turned toward his daughter. "You listen to what Mrs. Colburn has to say."

Hannah tugged on her arm before she had time to react. "Would you like some tea, dear? I do believe Cook has those little pastries you're so fond of. Let's go and see, shall we?"

Hannah's coaxing voice faded down the

hall. Clayton looked at Monteiro and grinned. "How about a little hunting? I heard geese overhead not an hour ago."

Don Monteiro shrugged a shoulder. "Sounds better than a wedding."

The three men chuckled as they quit the room.

Kendra set the bowl of boiled potatoes and turnips on the table and closed her eyes, dread filling her chest. Her aunt and uncle had cheerfully announced that they were to have a dinner guest this evening. The identity of the person was a surprise they said, but Kendra was certain who it would be. After the conversation she'd overheard, she had been expecting just such a guest.

She turned back toward the kitchen to fetch the roasted duck. She and her aunt had spent the last two hours in the kitchen preparing the meal. The garden had begun to produce fresh vegetables and Uncle Franklin had even bestirred himself enough to go hunting. They'd been so pleased to see him return with two plump ducks, but the dread of seeing Martin Saunderson again had dampened any joy Kendra would have felt on this festive occasion.

"Do take off that apron and go and freshen up, Kendra," Aunt Amelia said, shooing Kendra out of the kitchen. "Our guest will arrive any moment." Her eyes were shining with excitement as she hefted the meat platter into her arms.

"But don't you need my help?" Kendra reached for the tray that looked ready to topple to the floor.

"No, no. You'll want to look your best. Now, go!"

"Very well." Kendra sighed as she untied her apron and folded it into a neat square. She started to turn toward her bedchamber but stopped. There was a small, sharp knife sitting on the worktable. It glistened in the sunlight, beckoning to her. She reached out her hand, thinking to hide it on her person just in case Martin attempted to get too close. The thought of actually using it though . . . she shuddered and backed away. She would trust God to save her if she needed saving. Stabbing someone wouldn't do much good even if she could gather the courage to use it. Best to continue to pray as she'd been doing all day. *Lord, if only You would intervene and cause this to be called off.* She stopped and listened for her miracle. A small earthquake? A sudden thunderstorm? A dreaded eclipse of the sun? Nothing. Only her aunt's voice nagging her to go and make herself look pretty.

She hurried to her room and stood in front of the hooks on the wall, deliberating on changing her dress or just remaining in the faded, striped cambric she was currently wearing. She'd scared off one marriage-minded man, why couldn't she scare off another? Even as she thought it, she shivered. Martin Saunderson was nothing like Lord Barrymore. There was something ruthless in his eyes and a wiry strength about his body that made her truly afraid. She could not be alone with him.

She pulled a pale pink gown from the back and stared at it. Still pretty and fashionable but modest too. It would have to do. After donning the dress she moved to the small mirror hanging on the wall and pinned her hair into a simple chignon. A sound from the front of the house gave her a start, causing her heart to race. She rushed to the door and opened it a crack. Martin's voice was like a deep velvety trap coming from the parlor.

Her knees shook beneath the gown as she made her way down the short hall. *Stop it, silly. Nothing is going to happen to you. Faith!* She lifted her chin and turned the corner, standing in the doorway where Uncle Franklin was conversing with Martin.

"Ah, Kendra. Come here, my dear. My,

but don't you look like a vision." Her uncle beckoned her with an outstretched arm and warm smile. Kendra took a small breath, giving him a slight smile. She managed to cross the room without looking directly at Martin. Her uncle took her elbow and turned her toward his cohort. "Kendra, this is Martin Saunderson, a very dear friend of mine. Martin, this is my niece, Lady Kendra Townsend."

Kendra looked up for the first time and locked gazes with a set of dark gray eyes. He smiled, a sensuous stretching of his lips, and then had the audacity to wink at her. "Lady Townsend," he reached for her hand and bowed over it.

Kendra snatched her hand away. "We've met before, if you recall."

Martin nodded his head, his mouth pulling down at the corners. "You must forgive me, my lady. I fear I had a little too much champagne that night and was not quite myself. If you could be so kind, as your uncle insists you are, I beg you forgive me and give me another chance at a first impression." He raised black brows at her with a hint of pleading in his eyes. But there was a glimmer of humor behind that look, making sport of her, she was sure of it. Taking a haughty mien she turned away and pressed her lips together. "You were unconscionable, sir. If my uncle only knew the . . . the liberties you tried to take. It will take more than a pretty apology to regain any degree of trust from me."

Kendra ground her teeth as her uncle took steps toward her and dove into the fray to rescue his friend. "But Kendra, a man makes mistakes. I've made so many and you've forgiven me. You have been the very picture of grace and forgiveness. Won't you extend that same consideration toward my very good friend?"

Her aunt chose that moment to enter the room. She was red faced and perspiring. Her eyes flashed back and forth between the three of them. "Dinner is served." She pulled Kendra toward her and whispered in her ear, "I'll keep an eye on Martin. Don't you worry about a thing."

Kendra looked down into her aunt's determined eyes and relaxed a little. Who would have thought her aunt would become her ally?

"Come now" — Amelia motioned them toward the dining room — "before it grows cold."

Kendra ignored Martin's proffered arm, which gained her a frown, and walked into the room unescorted. They sat across from one another at the small, rectangular table. There was a chipped blue pitcher in the middle filled with wild flowers that Kendra had picked the day before and around it four plates, bowls, and platters of food.

Dear Father, thank You for this food, please bless it for the nourishment of our bodies and help me get through this!

"Lady Townsend, how do you find America?" Martin asked.

Kendra swallowed a bite of roasted duck and answered, "I find it different than I thought. It's as if polite society decided to set up camp in a wilderness. Some of it is quite civilized, but all around those insulated areas is a sense of wildness."

Her uncle barked out a laugh. "Do you think us wild, my dear?"

"Not at all." Though her relatives' life had shocked her at first. Working the land, no servants to cook and clean for them, eking out a living. It wasn't that she abhorred what they did; on the contrary, she admired it. But they weren't content in it and so many Americans — like John and Victoria, the Colburns, and some others she had met — loved the freedom and independence that was available to them as Americans. She didn't want to explain it out loud to the people at this table but she had seen a satisfaction, a faith and hope in those people that her relatives did not seem to have. A knot formed in her throat but she pushed it down. Amelia and Franklin were bitter with their lot in life but she was determined not to be. "I find America to be stirring . . ." she hesitated, not wanting to share her heart with this stranger she didn't trust. "I find it fascinating," she finished with a shrug.

Martin had paused as she spoke. He was watching her face very closely, too close for comfort. Kendra looked away, down at her plate. Some inner strength gathered inside her, in her stomach. She met his eyes and challenged, "What do you think of America, Mr. Saunderson? I've heard you make your living in the gambling establishments. Do you enjoy fleecing your fellow countrymen for a living?"

Everyone gasped except for Martin. He turned that sly smile upon her and narrowed his eyes. "I assure you, my lady, that there are moments I enjoy very . . . very much. Mayhap I can introduce you to some of them."

It was Kendra's turn to gasp, but she stifled the impulse, narrowing her eyes back at him instead. "I have a pastime that I enjoy, sir. Would like to know what it is?" She smiled a small smile and looked up at him through her eyelashes.

His eyes turned heated.

Kendra tried not to laugh. She shot a glance at her aunt and uncle and let out a tinkling laugh. "I would like to share it with all of you!" She took a bite of bread and laughed around it, suddenly happy, confident that indeed, her God could save.

"I'd like to take you all to church with me!"

All three faces fell. Kendra just nodded and chewed.

Two hours later and after quoting Scripture verses whenever possible and once even bursting out in a hymn, Kendra was able to escape the evening.

"Time for my bedtime prayers!" She sighed with overbright eyes and a big smile, then stood and waved good-bye to the three of them. It was hard not to feel a little smug as she closed her bedchamber door with a sigh of relief. The evening hadn't been so very different from the evening with Lord Barrymore after all. To repel a man, one only had to find out what a man disdained and make it one's main passion. She squashed a giggle as she unbuttoned her gown, hung it back on the hook, then slipped into her nightgown. *Not that I don't truly love You like I said I did, Lord. I just exag-*

gerated the demonstration of it a bit.

She slipped into bed, pulled the covers up to her chin, and let out a contented sigh. Sleep came easy. Sleep came sweet. The sleep of the victorious.

Or so she thought.

CHAPTER SIXTEEN

Kendra twisted her gloved hands in her lap as the carriage swayed and jerked over the rutted road toward Yorktown. Would he be there? She had good reason to believe that he might from the inquiries she had made of Faith Colburn the night of the ball. Grace Church. The church the entire Colburn family attended every Sunday and the church she had finally convinced her aunt and uncle to take her to.

She leaned out the open window of the ancient coach and yelled up to her uncle, "Do hurry, Uncle. We don't want to be late on our first visit."

Franklin scowled down at her. "This horse doesn't go any other speed. We shall arrive when we arrive."

Kendra pulled her head back in and chewed on her bottom lip. Her aunt reached over and patted her restless hands. "No good will come from all this fretting. A body would think you were on your deathbed and needing last rites, the way you're carrying on."

Her cheeks turned pink and she looked away, out the window at the rolling countryside. It was unseemly, the way she thought of him, well, constantly. She drew a deep breath and commanded herself to relax. She was going to church, after all, to hear about God. Not to moon like a daft cow over a sea captain. *Lord, forgive me. I am foolish at times! It's no wonder You compare us to sheep. My brain feels full of wool!*

Sooner than expected they ambled to a stop at one of the many hitching posts lining the street in front of the church. It was crowded but the big clock tower in the center of town had only reached five minutes until nine so they weren't late. Kendra didn't wait for her uncle to climb down and open the door, but sprang out on her own, causing a grumbling noise from her aunt. The people from the town and the surrounding countryside were decked out in their Sunday best and heading toward the front doors. Kendra smiled. It was good to be back at a church.

Her uncle came around the side of the carriage with Aunt Amelia's arm linked in his and looked around the churchyard. "Ah, this way then, ladies." Kendra followed in their wake as they merged with the crowd entering the large, one-roomed building.

Kendra tried to keep her eyes on her uncle's back or at her feet, trying not to gawk and make a fool of herself. Uncle Franklin led them to a long bench and she followed them down it to almost the middle point and then sat down. From the corner of her eye she thought she saw Faith and another of Dorian's sisters. Her heart sped up a little but she kept her eyes downcast, determined to be good. A pair of men's elegant shoes came into her line of vision. She pressed down a smile. The shoes turned in the direction of facing the front and then she saw him settle in, quite close, beside her. Surprised pleasure filled her. She looked aside and up, allowing the happiness she felt to sparkle in her eyes.

Martin Saunderson grinned back at her. "So good to see you, Lady Townsend. As you can see, I've taken your advice and decided to become a reformed citizen. Your words, nay, your passion for the church has convicted my black soul to the very depths of my being. I owe you eternal thanks."

Kendra clamped her gaping mouth shut and doubted it to the *depths* of her being. But she couldn't say so. She only turned her head toward the front where the service was beginning. "I'm so glad, sir. I pray your many sins be forgiven and you remain . . . reformed."

Martin leaned close and chuckled into her ear. His warm breath made her recoil. "Ah, but I fear that will require a constant dose of your goodness, my lady. Perhaps even . . . a daily dose."

Kendra sucked in a breath. Would he declare himself right here as the service was beginning? She turned toward him, eyes flashing with warning. "You are mistaken if you think me a paragon of virtue, sir. It is our Savior, Jesus Christ, who makes a way for all sinners, me included."

She turned forward and pressed her lips tight together, determined not to speak to him any longer.

The dark chuckle reached through her meager shield and sent a chill of fear through her spine. He murmured words, a low hiss of sound, as the preacher instructed them to open a hymnal. "I daresay I should like to see the sinner's side of you. I should like that very much."

Outrage burst like flames through her as she stood and opened to the appointed page. The blackguard! What man would accost a woman in church? The man had no scruples whatsoever. She took a step away, crowding her aunt and gaining a frown and dig from her aunt's elbow as she began to sing. The words barely registered as the skin on one side of her body crawled where Martin stood.

As soon as the song was over she looked up and saw a slight wave from someone on the other side of the room. Faith was smiling and waving and then as Hannah leaned over and said something, she quickly lowered her hand and turned toward the front. Kendra smiled as the pretty young woman glanced back at Kendra and winked. The look and the wink reminded her so much of Dorian that the familiar longing rose up and she took a moment to scan the room for his dark head. Nothing. Her heart sank a little. He wasn't there.

As soon as the service was over Kendra ignored Martin's attempt at further conversation by brushing past him and rushing over toward Faith. Faith's eyes brightened as she hurried to meet her, grasping her hands in a tight squeeze. "I'm so glad you've come! You must meet the rest of the family."

Kendra nodded happy agreement. "I should love to. Is, ah . . ."

Faith giggled and leaned in, saying in a

low voice, "No, Dorian's not here. Some mission to look over horseflesh in Fredericksburg. But you must meet Louisa, Charity, and Marjorie. They've been dying to meet you."

Kendra allowed herself to be dragged over to a tall woman who looked very much like Clayton Colburn. She carried a little girl on one hip and two boys only slightly older than the next clung to her skirts. One of them was sucking on a thumb. Kendra paused, taking in the scene of the harried mother. A knot formed in her throat and she didn't know why — couldn't fathom why it was suddenly hard to swallow — except that they were the most beautiful children she had ever seen.

"Lizzie, this is Lady Kendra Townsend," Faith gushed as if she were presenting the queen of England. "Lady Kendra, this is my eldest sister, Louisa Fairchild."

Louisa grinned with a broadness that took up most of her face. "You must forgive me, Lady Townsend." She twisted around until she had a grip on one of the boys. "Thomas, you're going to suck that thumb right off if you don't give it up, my dear," she admonished in a tone that said she was crazy in love with him. "As you can see these children are like living shackles. I can't even offer you my hand."

"Please, there is no need." Kendra smiled down at the wide, brown-eyed boy with his curly mop of white blonde hair who had ignored the parental advice and was doggedly working on his thumb. "Your children are so . . . beautiful."

Lizzie laughed and then shared a look with Faith. "You'll not think they are so angelic after an hour or so, I promise. But thank you. I can see that you mean that."

Faith took her arm and squeezed, looking at her sister as she said in an excited whisper, "I told you, didn't I?"

Lizzie nodded, her eyes happy and thoughtful as she stared at Kendra. "I didn't think it would ever happen to him. I shall have to revise my opinion on miracles. They do occur in modern days after all."

Faith giggled and admonished at the same time. "Shush. We are standing in church after all!"

"As if the good Lord doesn't know my every thought anyway." Lizzie shrugged, her eyes sparkling with mirth.

Faith gave Kendra's arm another excited squeeze. Kendra didn't understand what they were talking about but she was almost certain, by the way they were both stealing such pleased glances at her, that they were talking about her.

With a wave of her hand Faith rounded up the other sisters, Charity and Marjorie. Charity was blonde, short, and plump like her mother while Marjorie had the darker looks of Clayton and Dorian. They both eyed her, up and down, Charity bubbling with laughter as one of her nephews plowed into her demanding candy, and Marjorie looking shy and stealing glances at Kendra. Kendra smiled encouragingly at her and wondered if these two sisters were married with children also.

Before she had time to ask, she heard a shriek and turned to see Angelene staring at her, her eyes wide and face gone white. "Lady Townsend."

Kendra raised her brows. "Miss Monteiro. I didn't know you attended services here."

"For quite some time." Her red lip curled. "I didn't know you were interested in *church*."

"Oh yes, back home in Arundel I attended every Sunday. I've missed it since coming here and was so glad Faith invited me to come here to Grace Church."

Angelene's gaze flickered down to Faith's arm entwined with Kendra's. She looked up at Faith, but not quick enough to extinguish the slash of betrayal. "I see that the two of you have gotten quite chummy. Faith is such a dear soul to anyone in need."

"You sound as if you don't approve, Angelene." Lizzie jumped into the fray. "I assume you agree that anyone can attend church?"

Kendra pressed her lips together as a wave of compassion swept through her. It must appear to Angelene that she was taking her place in the Colburn family.

Angelene looked away from them and shrugged. "Of course. I was just curious as to why she chose this church. There are several closer to that *farm* where her ladyship lives. It is so . . . out of the way."

"I doubt it's a further distance than from my home!" Lizzie seemed to grow another inch and her chin jutted out. It wouldn't be wise to be on the other side of that ire, Kendra realized as she eased away from Faith. Even though Angelene had been nothing but a thorn in her side, Kendra couldn't bear to feel that the three of them were ganging up on her.

Turning toward the dark beauty she held out a hand. "Miss Monteiro, let us begin again." Kendra smiled with genuine warmth. "It is so good to see you. I've only a few minutes before my relatives drag me back to that *farm*." She laughed, making fun of it too. "Would you show me around the church?"

Faith let out a little gasp but Lizzie just raised her eyebrows and inclined her head toward Kendra in a brief move that seemed to say, *touché.*

Before Angelene could react, Kendra took her arm and led her away, chatting about the service and the choir and inquiring if Angelene liked to sing. She would look so wonderful on stage, she must love to sing.

As they eased through the crowd Kendra heard Faith's excited voice, "Our brother will be the veriest fool if he lets her get away."

"Mayhap he'll need a little help," Louisa's voice answered. "Sometimes God lets us participate in His miracles."

Feminine laughter followed Kendra and Angelene out the door.

Once outside in the open sunshine, Angelene cast a glance toward Kendra, her chin cocked to one side, her eyes narrowed. "Have you seen Dorian since the ball, Lady Townsend?"

"No, I haven't. Why?"

Angelene looked down, her cheeks filling with a becoming rose color. "I didn't know if you'd heard the news."

"News? I was just visiting with his sisters,

as you know, and they didn't mention any news."

Angelene glanced aside as if embarrassed. "Well, it was something of a scandal really. I'm sure they don't wish it common knowledge."

Always these games with this woman. How was she to handle her? *Patience, kindness, goodness, self-control.* La! She would need all of the fruit of the Spirit to keep her head above these choppy waters. Kendra tried not to grind her teeth. "Why don't you just tell me? You seem to want to."

Angelene shrugged a slim shoulder. "It's just that I know you imagine yourself having particular feelings for him and I wouldn't want you to get hurt. But after what happened that night, after you left the ball . . ."

"What, exactly, happened?"

"We danced and he strolled with me in the garden. I —" She clasped her gloved hands in front of her skirt and looked up at Kendra with big innocent eyes. "I let my emotions get away with me and allowed him kiss me. And then —"

Kendra's stomach plummeted with each word. It was the same as what Dorian had done with her. "And then?" She couldn't help but ask.

"Oh dear. It's very bad of me, I'm afraid. I was just so swept away. I don't even know how it happened but I ended up in his room. We were caught. My father caught us. He's demanding a wedding."

She had the audacity to stare at Kendra with a broad smile and glowing eyes. "I've already bought the dress. I'm just waiting for him to return from that trip north to see some horses." She waved a hand in the air. "You know men, he just had to go, and what could I say? I do plan to be a very accommodating wife."

Kendra couldn't speak. Her breath caught in her throat. Was it true? If so, why hadn't Faith told her? Would Angelene really make up such a monstrous lie? Would anyone?

Before she had a chance to regain any semblance of composure, Aunt Amelia spotted her and hurried over to Kendra's side. "There you are, Kendra. Come along. Your uncle is past ready to go."

Kendra nodded good-bye to the smirking Angelene, unable to get a word through her stiff lips, and turned to follow her aunt to their carriage. Her heart thudded dull and heavy, her legs seemed unable to take the next step. She glimpsed Faith and her parents coming out the church door. Her gaze locked with Faith's, the silent question in her eyes. Faith bit her lower lip and turned away.

So, it was true. The Colburn girls must have been talking about Angelene, not her. What a fool she'd been. She bit her lower lip trying to keep the tears back as she climbed into the carriage and stared out the open window, praying the pain slicing through her stomach would go away.

CHAPTER SEVENTEEN

"Come in." Andrew Townsend accepted the morning post from his butler and then waved him from the room. He flipped through the letters wondering if today might be the day he would hear from the Rutherfords as to how *the plan* was proceeding. After his pirates had failed to dispatch his niece, a fact he'd only learned about a few weeks ago, he'd been forced to rely on that letter to the Rutherfords. How hard could it be to arrange an accident for a naïve Englishwoman in the wilds of America? It was taking far too long.

He paused over a grimy looking envelope. At last! It was from Virginia. He closed his eyes and clutched the missive to his chest. It was so close — just within reach. Finally he would own all of the Arundel fortune, every plot of land, every tenant, every investment . . . every last shilling, even Kendra's paltry dowry. She had no right to it. It was all meant to be his — every last dirt clod. His plan was about to be complete. He broke the seal with shaking fingers and scanned the message.

Dear Lord Townsend,

My name is Martin Saunderson and I have some news concerning your niece that I believe you will find quite valuable. You see, I am a friend of Franklin Rutherford, a close confidant, you might say. He explained that you were intent on getting rid of a certain young woman for her dowry and hoped Franklin would see to it with a generous reward, of course, at the end. Alas, our dear Franklin has had other ideas. He offered me half the dowry if I would marry Lady Kendra, saying that only he had the right to give her away as a bride to the man of his choice. At first I declined, having never thought to marry. But after meeting her, well, I'm sure you can understand my change of heart.

Of course the more I considered the idea, the more I realized that as her husband I should have every legal right to the full inheritance. Why share any of it with either of you?

Andrew put down the letter and threw his head back with a savage curse. He should have known better than to trust a couple of grasping colonists! Picking up the letter, his hand shook with rage as he continued:

On the other hand, it would be so much easier to have your cooperation as the chit has not as yet come up to scratch. There is a sea captain she has her heart set on, a Dorian Colburn. I believe you know him? My instincts say you'd rather not have him in the family fold, as the Colburn family can be a force to be reckoned with. I would like to suggest myself as an alternative. I can be very accommodating and believe we can come to some sort of compromise that will suit us both.

Andrew threw down the letter and pushed away from the desk, the vein in his forehead throbbing with rage. He was being black-mailed by an American! It was unconceivable! He stood, walked over to the crystal decanter on the sideboard, and poured himself a brandy. It burned down his throat but brought no relief. He reared back and flung the glass as hard as he could into the empty grate of the fireplace. He balled up his fist and slammed it onto the sideboard, causing the other glasses to rattle and move across the table, then braced his arms on either edge and leaned over it, his fair hair flopping in his face. "Alright. Get a hold of yourself. There must be a way to salvage this."

He took a deep breath, turned, and walked back over to the desk. Picking up the paper, his chin held high, his eyes narrowed, he read the remainder of the letter:

Land in England means little here across the pond, but money — gold — that is a very different matter. It's quite simple, really. You keep the land and pay me what it is worth in gold. You'll have your estate intact and I will be able to support your exquisite niece in the manner in which she is accustomed. It's all very agreeable, no? If you are wondering what I will do about the Rutherfords, make no mistake, they will be taken care of and bother us no more. I will take Kendra west, far away from anyone she knows, and start a new life with her so buried in the American wilderness that you may forget she was ever born.

In the essence of the time it takes to receive a reply from you, know that I will be pursuing my courtship of her. I hope you find my suggestions an acceptable alternative.

Yours,
Martin Saunderson

Andrew pulled out a fresh piece of paper and wrote a stiffly formal reply. He set the wax with the Earl of Townsend's seal and rang for his servant. "Find the quickest messenger to get this on board the first ship sailing to America. Spare no expense."

"Yes, my lord."

"Kendra, an invitation has come for you" her aunt called from the back door.

Kendra stood up, a ripe tomato in hand, her lower back aching from working in the garden these past two hours. My goodness, but was it hot. Her cheeks radiated heat and sweat trickled down her back in what felt like enough to fill a bucket. Upon hearing her aunt's call, she turned, ducked under the low archway of dangling ivy, and hefted the basket of beans and tomatoes higher on her arm. Her apron flapped in the hot summer wind and her big, floppy garden hat flapped against her cheeks. Had it ever been this hot in England? She didn't think so.

A letter. The thought brought only anxiety

to her already quickened breathing. Whoever could it be? And what could they want? It seemed everyone wanted something of her and there was so little left to give. She could feel it leaking out, as if someone had cut her and the lifeblood was trickling out, little by little, until all that was left was a limp version of what used to be herself. After Dorian's betrayal she'd realized how much strength she had been gaining from the hope that someday they would be together. Now. *Oh, Lord. Now.*

She didn't want to cry any more tears and she didn't know what else to pray, except for strength. *Please, Lord. Give me what I need for these people, this place, the here and now. This day.*

She quickened her steps, trying to put some courage into her backbone. Ouch! Her thin slipper trod upon a large stone, making her jerk her foot back and stumble. Tears sprang to her eyes as her foot began to throb. She sank down onto the dirt path and brought round the injured foot. Her slippers were in tatters. What had she been thinking to come here with no more than dancing shoes in her trunk? And she couldn't ask her relatives for new, sturdier footwear. They were barely able to keep body and soul together as it was. She took off the delicate satin and looked at the quick forming bruise on her sole. She touched it and cried out, and then looked around to see if anyone had heard. It wouldn't do to bring more hardship upon her poor aunt. She would just have to manage through the pain.

The thought of her aunt, a younger, happier version, came to her mind in a sudden way. Kendra closed her eyes and saw her as a young woman with Eileen, Kendra's mother. She imagined the sisters dressed in frilly muslin with bows and ribbons and lace. She imagined them laughing together and smiling at each other, her mother tall and willowy and her aunt plump and grinning from ear to ear. She saw them at a dance, twirling with dark-coated, elegant gentlemen, bright-colored slippers flying. She saw them flying and happy.

And then she imagined her dear father. He was so tall, so reserved, but he couldn't take his eyes off her mother. She had heard the story from him many times. He'd gathered up his courage and asked her mother to dance.

Kendra smiled, thinking of it. Her shy father and her stately mother. He'd been brave indeed to ask the beauty of the country, the most sought after woman in a decade, to dance. And she'd loved him. She must have. Who could not?

The tears finally came, racing down her cheeks one after the other so fast that she knew she'd been bottling them up for some time now.

"Oh, Mother. Father said you wanted me to choose. That you said I would know. But I was so wrong. I thought I found him, but I didn't."

"Kendra, what are you doing there in the dirt, girl?" Her aunt broke in on her imaginary world. "Didn't you hear me? You've got a letter! It's from the Colburn house. Now come open it, I'm dying to know what's inside it."

Kendra wiped away the tears and saw her aunt's excited face peeking around the back door. It was just the face she'd imagined on the dance floor. Full of mischief and fun. In a flash she saw that she'd brought her aunt that. She had brought life back to her. The feeling overwhelmed her — that one person — one person in a household could uplift and give hope and laughter and joy back. Even when making a poor living from the dirt.

"Coming!" She rose, dusted off her skirts, and determined that whatever that letter said, she would make the most of it.

God help her, she would rise to this occasion.

Kendra tore open the plain wax seal and read the invitation. The Colburns were having a weekend house party and she was invited. There was to be a tour of the plantation, quail hunting, musicales in the evening with cards and games, and a picnic on the last day, complete with a horse race. Dorian and John were going to be riding their new Spanish stallions in a race against some other local fellows and their breeds. Buggy races for any ladies brave enough to try. It was to be a grand affair. And she was to bring a chaperone of her choosing, should she like.

"Oh, my!" Amelia clasped her round cheeks, her eyes alight. "That sounds like such fun, doesn't it, Kendra? I can't imagine such fun."

Kendra looked down at her aunt, and even though the last place she would like to be was at the Colburn Plantation, she could not let her aunt down. "Of course you should accompany me. I couldn't go alone."

"Do you mean it?" Her aunt exclaimed and then seemed to remember her place. "Well, of course you couldn't go alone." She turned her head this way and that. "We have so much to do! Why, the clothing alone will take us all week to wash and press. Come. Hurry along and help me with dinner so we can plan our wardrobes. A whole weekend! I hope Franklin won't baulk, but don't you fret. I can manage him."

Her aunt's voice faded down the hall toward the kitchen.

Kendra looked down at the signature. Faith Colburn. What would Dorian think to see her there? Did he know she'd been invited? And Angelene? She would most certainly be there. The thought of that brought true despair sinking through her.

She sighed and looked at the ceiling of their meager home. "You had me pray that before seeing this letter, didn't You?"

She didn't know whether to laugh or cry, but what she did know for certain is that the Lord wanted her to serve her aunt. "As long as You're there with me. I can do all things with You there with me."

She hoped she believed it.

CHAPTER EIGHTEEN

The crowd around the stable yard clung to the fence and clapped, their quiet murmurs of excitement reaching him across the yellow-bathed expanse of green pasture. Dorian led the Andalusian into the middle of the field and let loose her head. He backed away, a gentle but firm pressure on her lead line. Her eyes were fearful and uncertain, but turned toward him and his voice.

"Good. Good girl."

He tugged a little on the rope and she turned, four feet skidding across the grass and kicking up a cloud of dust as she looked at him. Dorian held tight, firm but without too much pressure, as she lifted her elegant, arched neck and whinnied at him. "There now. Come on. Come on."

Dorian held the lead rope in one hand, a braided leather whip in the other. He flicked his wrist. The whip snapped beside the horse, turning it to the other direction. She took off in a gallop, making Dorian grin. Such a thing of beauty. He laughed, watching her hoofs and black-socked feet pound the earth, dark mane and tail flying, waiting for the next signal from him. *You've outdone Yourself with this one, haven't You, Lord?*

They had been at this particular exercise for over an hour now, all the stable hands, John and his father and Faith hanging on the fences, watching. It had been a long time since he'd broken a horse to saddle but it had come flooding back to him. Not so different than training a new recruit on one of his ships. He chuckled at that thought. Green sailors were often more wild than tame, and not too keen on taking orders from a stranger. But this animal, God bless her, she was amazing — spirited, intelligent, and yet quick to trust him. He could sense the push and pull inside her. She clung to her independence, but her eyes rolled toward him in a liquid way when he chirruped at her, telling him she wanted to please him. It wouldn't be much longer now and he could start with the blanket.

"Don't think to make it look too easy," John shouted over at him. "We've the stallion to break yet!" The crowd of onlookers laughed and nodded at him.

Dorian cracked a grin but kept his eyes on the high-stepping, Spanish mare. Fredericksburg had turned out to be more surprising and rewarding than he'd imagined. His friend Dirk Donovan had done the impossible — got his hands on some famed Spanish breed, the Andalusians, horses of kings. Dorian had managed to outbid many others for two of the prized mares, thrilling enough. But then Dirk led out a real beauty, a rare Palomino thoroughbred stallion. Tall, at least sixteen hands, and as majestic as any animal he'd ever seen. He loped around the stable yard, a fine cream-colored coat with white mane and tail fluttering. *Dangerous.* That's what everyone called him. Bucking and wild-eyed, no one had been able to get him on a lead line. Dirk gave Dorian that look of challenge with a hint of laughter, then slapped him on the shoulder and demanded an outrageous price. Dorian looked across the field at the grace of his lines, the elegant savage toss of his head, and paid it. And it had taken all he and John's combined strength to get the blindfolded animal on board the barge home.

A sudden commotion from the front of the house startled the mare, causing her to rear back and turn before he'd given her the signal. Dorian glanced over to see an ancient black carriage rumble up the drive toward the stables. His sister squealed and turned toward the visitors, but Dorian kept his focus on the mare. She had already noticed his divided attention and wasn't turning as quickly as she had been to the whip's snap beside her.

The commotion grew louder and he heard his sister's high-pitched laugh. His gaze slid back. It had to be guests for the house party. *Please God, don't let it be Angelene!* Faith had promised not to invite her but Dorian wouldn't put it past her to come anyway. Why did Faith have to have a party now of all times? Just what he needed, an even larger crowd watching and distracting the horses. Faith needed a husband to keep her occupied.

A flash of blonde hair caught his attention. Kendra. He'd been trying not to think of her since the ball. He enjoyed his single life too much to be brought down by a female and his brush with Angelene had cemented that thought. Just this past week had been another example of his freedom. John had only come back with one mare due to the cost of building the house for Victoria. He would have never been able to spend the kind of money he'd just spent if he was married with a family. That life meant sacrifice and he just wasn't ready for it. He flicked the whip and glanced back toward Kendra. Her smile from across the green shocked through him as if a lightning bolt had struck. Her startling eyes shone like jewels in her pale face, her smile lighting up her eyes and bringing a squeezing to his heart. Even the curled brimmed hat covered in pink flowers and trailing ribbons around her shoulders seemed endearing rather than outlandish. He forgot to breathe and nearly dropped the whip. Clearing his throat, he looked at the mare. She'd stopped, sucking air with loud puffing sounds coming in and out of her nostrils. His own breath was loud too. He flushed and turned away from the women heading toward them. With gritted teeth, the sweat coating his shirt to his chest, he threw himself back into training the mare.

I shouldn't have come. This is too hard, Lord.
Kendra studied a large painting in the foyer of the Colburn mansion and chewed on her lower lip as Faith prattled on about their rooms and the planned activities for the weekend while leading her aunt up the grand curving staircase. Kendra motioned toward Faith to go on without her, a silent plea for a moment alone with upraised

brows and pleading eyes. The dear girl understood in an instantaneous way. She always seemed to know things like that which made Kendra sigh. This was what it would have been like to have a sister — someone who knew what she wanted without needing to say it aloud. That was Faith, since the moment she'd met her, there had been that kinship connection that Kendra hadn't known she was missing.

She smiled up at her with closed lips as Faith grinned knowingly back and took her aunt Amelia's arm, leading her further away, her aunt bubbling with enthusiasm and chatter about the weekend to come.

Kendra took a long breath and stared up at the dark colors of the painting that must be some battle of a war. There was a man, stout chested with a white wig, aboard a boat with several other men. Their faces were so serious, so determined, the water and sky around them so dark and foreboding. She brought her hand up to her mouth and covered it, feeling the moment with them, the salt spray against their faces, their coats, their bravery as they plunged their oars toward a battle that they couldn't have known the outcome of. *Lord, what do You have planned for this place? And what is my place here? I want to be a part of it, like these brave men.*

A sudden noise broke into her thoughts. She turned around with a swish of silk and swaying hat ribbons. Dorian burst through the front door. He was hatless and even more handsome if possible — tan and rugged — wearing only a full-sleeved white shirt and tan breeches with black top boots. He turned his head toward her and his black hair waved back upon his shoulders, having come loose from his queue. Kendra swallowed around the knot in her throat. When he saw her, he stopped, just as his beautiful new horse had done with the whip each time he commanded her. Had he seen her watching him break the mare? She had hardly been able to tear her eyes from the sight but he had been completely focused on his task and had not once looked in her direction.

Dorian stood for several seconds, seeming not to know what to do. He stared at her as if she were a ghost or the swishing snap of the whip.

She turned toward him, finding her mettle. "You needn't be so skittish," she remarked, glancing toward his face. "I've heard the news."

"The news?" His black brows went up in question and then down over his eyes, eyes that resembled the gray clouds of a coming thunderstorm on the horizon. He stepped toward her, his boots ringing against the floor, making her breath quicken. He took her by the elbow. "Please, come with me." He pulled her toward him.

Kendra allowed the pressure of his hand to pull her forward. Side by side he guided her into the drawing room. The door shut behind them with a soft click. He reached toward her but she backed away. "Congratulations, Captain."

His eyes narrowed. "Captain, is it?"

Kendra turned aside toward the window and looked out at the rolling countryside. Her voice was softer, resigned. What good was it to bait him? Angelene had won. Not that she wanted an American sea captain for husband anyway. Let her have him. They were perfect for each other.

But she didn't believe it. He was perfect for her, only her. *Oh, Lord! What went wrong? Did I do something wrong?*

"Please. Don't play the fool. Angelene told me that you are to be married."

Silence lengthened like the late afternoon shadows across the wall. Kendra turned her face slightly toward him. "I wish you every happiness." She said it to the wall, an empty sound of breath and voice that meant nothing the words said. Despair filled her when he didn't answer until she could stand it no more. She turned toward the door and rushed toward it, sudden tears blinding her.

Halfway there he stopped her, spun her toward him, held her entrapped within the cage of his strong arms. "Kendra." He said her name like someone would say a rasped-out prayer. She looked up into his dark blue eyes not knowing what to hope for, what to expect.

"It's not true. I don't know what she told you, but it isn't true."

She bit her lower lip and looked deep into his eyes. "I've heard . . . she was found in your room. That same night we danced. You danced with her like that, I saw you. Then after I left, she was found in your room, in your . . . *bed*. Do you deny it?"

Dorian turned his head away and exhaled with a sharp sound. "She tricked me. She was trying to trap me into marriage. I did not invite her there."

Kendra reached up and turned his head back toward her. She stared up at him. "I'm sorry, Captain, but from all accounts you have encouraged her from the beginning." She shrugged and gave him a sad smile. "You named your ship the *Angelina* after all. It's no business of mine. As I said, I wish you every . . . happiness."

She turned to go. He reached for her arm but she sidestepped his grasp. "Good-night, Dorian." It was hard. She closed her eyes as she reached for the doorknob and turned it. She bit down on her lip, wanting to turn around and hear his side of the story but not trusting him, not knowing what game he was about. He had never proclaimed any love for her, only danced and flirted and continually tried to kiss her. A rogue. An American rogue. A pirate — taking what wasn't his and then throwing it aside when it turned out to be less than what he expected. That was not the sort of man she needed. She turned the knob and walked out, shutting the door behind her, and made her way up the stairs toward whatever room was assigned to her for what would be an interminable weekend. She only hoped there was a quiet place where she could be alone . . . and cry . . . unnoticed.

There was no denying that the Colburn home was lovely, she thought as she made her way down the long hall, looking for her aunt. The second floor had two wings, one on either side of the winding staircase. There were four bedrooms in the east wing but no one in them. In the west wing there were two bedrooms, a small library at the end, and what looked to have been the schoolroom across the hall. Familiar smells of chalk and old books drifted to Kendra as she stepped inside the schoolroom. She couldn't help but smile, her own schooling rushing back over her. She wandered over to a small bookcase and picked up a primer that might have been one of Dorian's or his many siblings. She flipped to the letter E and saw a picture of an elephant. An instantaneous and bright memory assailed her. Pain shot through her chest as she remembered her father as her teacher.

"What is an elephant, Father? I've seen its picture in the book, but what is it?"

He'd risen up on all fours and used his arms as a great swaying trunk, pounding about her schoolroom as if he weighed thousands of pounds, and then as he neared her, made flapping motions with his hands, huge ears that flapped into her face and made her giggle with delight. The highlight was when he threw back his head and made a loud trumpeting noise that had both startled her and sent shivers of excited fear through her. "You've seen one, haven't you? A real live one! Tell me! Tell me!" She'd climbed up on his knee and grasped his whiskered face in her small hands, tilting him toward her, so demanding, so in love with him, so sure he had all the answers and would always be there to take care of her.

He'd told her all of his stories, his adventures in India and Africa and England, before her mother, before her, before having to become the Earl of Arundel.

Oh, God, I miss him so . . .

She sunk down into a small wooden chair and let the tears silently fall. She laid her head on her upraised knees and felt small and alone and very far from home.

After a few moments Kendra rose and wiped her wet cheeks on the back of her hand. Straightening, she decided to try to cheer herself up by finishing her tour of the house. Making her way down to the first floor, Kendra realized how empty the house felt. Come to think of it, she hadn't seen any sign of Dorian's large family since arriving, only Faith and Dorian. Shrugging her shoulders, she decided that they must be out, and she would most likely see them at the evening meal. Dorian's parents had been so kind to her the night of the ball and she was looking forward to seeing them. Kendra brightened and made her way down the hall of the first floor, looking for Faith or her aunt.

Most of the doors were open to reveal

drawing rooms, a larger library that must be Clayton Colburn's, and kitchens in the back. The other wing held a large bed-chamber and then, at the end of the hall was a door, slightly ajar, giving Kendra a small view of the room. She hazarded a knock, growing anxious in the feeling that she was alone in the house. "Hello, is anyone there?" No one answered so she pushed the door open and stepped inside. It was Dorian's room, it had to be. There was a large model of a ship sitting on top of a chest of drawers. It looked so familiar that she walked over to it and ran her fingertips over the beautiful wood. The *Angelina.* How he must have dreamed and worked to create a ship so beautiful. Her sleek lines were almost delicate, but Kendra knew the power behind her. She was certainly a prize. Turning, Kendra surveyed the rest of the room. It was decorated in gray-blue — almost the color of his eyes — with clean, masculine lines. The four-poster bed was large but not massive, covered with a heavy counterpane of blue and cream. There was a colorful rug beneath her feet that was thick and oriental in design. The tables were heavy oak, intri-cately carved and spoke of their English origin. It was the room of a traveler. A vase from China, delicate French candlesticks, and Italian statues were on the mantle above the fireplace, and hanging above it was a painting of a ship being tossed in a stormy sea.

Moving to the adjoining room, Kendra saw maps strewn about on a large, round table. Two comfortable chairs were on either side and a tall wardrobe in one corner. Without thinking what she was doing, nor why, she walked to the wardrobe as if it held some magnetic power over her. Kendra opened the door and picked up the sleeve of a white shirt. She brought it to her face, inhaled his scent, and closed her eyes. It was almost as if he was right there beside her.

"Do I need to have my clothes laundered, my lady?"

Kendra jumped at the sound of Dorian's voice. Whirling around she stared at him, her face flooding with heat. "I-I was just looking for my aunt. I couldn't find anyone. The house seemed so empty." She backed away from his advancing stride.

Dorian laughed and caught her, taking hold of her upper arm. "I don't suppose your aunt is hiding in my closet?" His deep voice sent shivers of excitement down her spine. "I've been looking for you. Why did you run away?"

Kendra titled her head back to reply but she couldn't seem to think of anything. She couldn't seem to think at all. His arms tightened around her, bringing her closer. She shook her head no as his lips closed over hers. Her knees went weak and she sagged against his wide chest. She was melting into his embrace. All the reasons why she shouldn't be floated away into nothing.

He broke away with a heavy breath. "Now do you believe me when I say there is nothing between Angelene and me?"

Angelene. That was one reason. She pushed away, her hands against his chest. He grasped her shoulders and held her to him in a gentle hold.

His voice was low, angry. "Do you really believe I could kiss you like that while in love with another woman? Engaged to be married? You don't know me very well if you can even think it."

Kendra wrenched her arms free and turned away from him. She lifted the back of her hand to her mouth and took a deep breath. "What does it mean then?" If he was to declare his feelings for her, then she would like to hear it.

A long silence stretched out. So. He couldn't say it. He would not declare himself for Angelene or her. She looked over her shoulder at him, brows raised in challenge. He stared back like a man choking on the words, his lips pressed together, his eyes uncertain. She'd been right. He was only interested in dalliance and flirtation. Hard-headed American scoundrel. Well, she wasn't going to let him take any more liberties, that was for certain. She took a fortifying breath, turned to leave, and stormed out of the room, slamming the door behind her.

Gentleness be darned.

CHAPTER NINETEEN

Kendra was just putting the finishing touches on the ribbon's wide, lime-colored bow that sat cocked to one side amongst her blonde curls when she heard a knock. She had been toying with the idea of adding a little black bird as an accent to the bow but had run out of time. "Come in."

Faith peeked her head around the door. "If you and your aunt are ready, Kendra, I'll take you down to dinner."

"Coming." Kendra took one final glance in the mirror above the dressing table. How was she to get through this evening, never mind the rest of the weekend? She would just have to avoid Dorian Colburn and his smoldering gray eyes at all costs. She stood up and studied the black-and-white striped skirt with white bodice she had donned. The dress had a rounded neckline edged in black lace which fell slightly off the shoulders to reveal her neck, but little else. Quite modest compared to what many of the women wore, Kendra decided with a nod of acceptance.

Her aunt hurried to her side in a peach gown that was very fetching, her face rosy with excitement. "Shall we?"

Faith, lovely in a lavender dress that set off her dark hair and eyes, motioned with a sweep of her arm toward the staircase. The three of them hurried toward the gold drawing room where the sound of happy chatter confirmed that the party had gathered.

As soon as Kendra entered the room she saw Dorian. He seemed to fill the room with his hooded hawk's eyes, dark and confident, lounging against the ornate molding of the fireplace. His black hair had been neatly combed back into silky waves and his evening dress was a simplistic, impeccable suit of dark blue with a white shirt and stock. He straightened at the sight of her, his gaze narrowing, penetrating her calm. Kendra took a shuddering breath, tore her gaze away, and walked to a group on the other side of the room.

The bell rang for dinner to be served and Kendra smiled at a young, sandy-haired gentleman who looked to be gathering his courage to ask to escort her into the dining room. He took the hint, stepping up and offering his arm with a wide grin. She must have grasped his arm a bit too hard, as he gave her a surprised smile and then pulled her in close to his side in a manner that was entirely too intimate. Fortunately, his name card turned out to be at the other end of the table and she was mostly able to ignore his longing glances thrown in her direction. Unfortunately, she was seated at Hannah's right — directly across from Dorian.

The dinner dragged by as she picked at the food on her plate. Any other time she would have been happy with such fine company and delicious food, but now she only wanted to go home. The ache in her heart moved to her throat when she heard Dorian's deep voice from across the table, causing the food to stick and her water glass to empty much too often. She gritted her teeth and took another bite, but moments later the deep rumble of his laugh made her look up.

That was a mistake.

Her breath caught at the sight of his head bent in the direction of the pretty auburn-haired lady seated next to him. She was enjoying the captain's company very much, despite the fact that Kendra was sure she was married. She must be entertaining indeed if Dorian's mouth, quivering in mirth on one side, dark eyes alight with humor, were any indication. *Long-suffering.* Kendra clinched her hands together under the table and focused on the spiritual fruit.

"Lady Townsend, won't you tell us about life in England? I've always wanted to go but Roland says he'll not let me leave him until the children are grown." Lizzie winked at Kendra as everyone around their end of the table laughed.

Her cheeks grew warm as she wondered what to say. Should she tell of life after her uncle had come back and cost them everything? She had loved that year with her father all the more because it felt like the two of them against the world, working together with wit and will to pull the estate back into working order. Oh, the pride she'd felt when he had pulled her next to him at his desk and showed her their first profit. The fields yielding crops again, the livestock increasing as they studied, head to head, on quiet winter nights the most advanced methods of agriculture, husbandry, and accounting. She'd been glad at times, secretly glad, that their lot had changed and made them dependent on each other.

Or should she tell them what they must want to hear — the grandeur of Arundel Castle, the haute ton social circles, the gowns and jewels, the earl's sleek carriage and matching four — life in London. The theatre, musicales, and shopping trips. She blinked hard, thinking of how her father had taken her once a year for a few weeks to London and shown her about town as if she were princess, the only princess on earth. She'd been so young then. So very young.

The quiet of the table and the attention of every eye finally dawned on her. She turned hot and then cold, her eyes flooding with tears. With a sudden move she pushed back from the table. "I'm . . . so sorry. Please excuse me."

She turned and fled from the room, running down the back corridor and out into the rich smells of the rear garden. She turned in a slow circle in the moonlight and sniffed, not knowing where to go or what to do. She pressed her hands to her cheeks, making them wet as tears that wouldn't stop raced, stubborn, one after the other, down her face and neck and — *oh, God. I miss him so. Why is this week so hard? Why do I keep thinking of him wherever I turn?*

"Kendra? Are you alright?"

She whirled around at the deep, familiar voice, shaking her head, not alright, not knowing how to answer. She wanted nothing more than to rush into his arms. It was all she could do not to rush into his arms.

"Kendra, come here." He took several steps toward her and held out an arm in invitation. She allowed him to gather her close, curled up within the strong places of his chest, and gave way to shuddering breaths. "I'm so silly. So stupid. I don't know what came over me."

Dorian leaned his chin onto the top of her head and she could hear the vibrations of his chuckle more from her ear buried in his chest than from his throat. "You've dealt Lizzie a blow I'll not soon forget. I've not seen her without words . . . ever!"

"Oh, I feel just horrible. It was a perfectly ordinary question. I'm just . . . I don't know what's come over me, but I keep seeing my father. It's this house, I think. I keep being reminded of him here. Maybe it's your family. They are so close and everything is so, so loving here." She looked up into his shadowed eyes and blinked away the last of the tears. "He seems nearer here. And I miss him so much."

Dorian pulled her close again and kissed the top of her head. "Here now, let's go for a little stroll through the garden and see if that makes you feel better, shall we?"

Kendra nodded and backed out of his embrace. "I could use a bit of fresh air."

Dorian tucked her hand in his arm and started off at a slow pace down the garden path, his voice soothing, rich like velvet, as he pointed out flowers, guessed at their name, and plucked some for a haphazard bouquet. She was feeling better, smiling at his humorous bumbling with the stems of the bouquet, when he led her to a curved stone bench and beckoned with a hand that she sit down. He presented his posy to her, which she accepted with all the seriousness, the suppressed mirth that she could manage, and sat down next to her.

As soon as he had seated himself, taking her hand into his and squeezing it, a sudden rustling sound came from the bushes behind them. Kendra turned in time to see a large, dark form rise from the greenery. She screamed as shadowy arms rose, a large object in the hands. Dorian turned, tried to stand, but it was too late. The object crashed down upon his head. Before she could move, Kendra saw him crumple to the ground beside her. A gash in his head welled, quick and strong, with dark blood where he had been hit over his head with a long object. Kendra stood and gathered her skirts to run, taking a breath to scream again, but strong arms pulled her backward into the bushes. A wad of musty-smelling cloth was stuffed into her mouth, making her gag. She kicked out, thrashing her arms back toward her assailant while thorns pricked through her gloves and caught on her skirts. The man took a tight hold around her waist, trapping her arms and dragging her backward. He clamped his legs around hers, making her immobile, and secured her arms together with a length of rope. She was hoisted up and over his shoulder where she was bounced so hard she felt she might be sick. Must not be sick. Not with a gag in her mouth. She could choke to death. Terror made her break into a sweat. *God help me!* She kicked out with her legs but that only made him clamp down on her back, driving his shoulder further into her stomach. Her breath whooshed in and out her nose. Dizzy. Black and dizzy. *Oh God, don't let me faint!*

Abruptly, he stopped. She heard a door open and was dumped inside a carriage. Her shoulder rammed into the seat, sending a fresh shock of pain through her body. The door slammed shut behind her and, with a jerk, they were off. Kendra pushed herself up into a sitting position, trying to balance herself against the swaying of the fast-moving carriage. Leaning to one side, she managed to get her feet underneath her enough to push up onto one of the seats. She peered through the darkness of the interior of the carriage, praying that she was alone. She could barely keep her seated position as the vehicle flew over the rutted, dirt road.

Pushing back into the far corner of the seat, the panic she had managed to keep at bay surfaced into her throat. Who was her captor? What did he want?

And then there was Dorian. Was he hurt? Alive? The thought that the blow might have killed him made her sick with fear. He had to be alive. She willed herself to focus on that thought.

She closed her eyes and prayed.

Some time later the horses slowed to a walking pace and then stopped. She held her breath, panic lancing through her chest as she waited for whatever was to happen next. The door swung open and strong hands grasped her around the waist. She kicked out and heard a satisfying grunt of pain from the man.

"You will regret it if you fight me," a low voice snarled into her ear.

She was slung over his shoulder, the air whooshing from her lungs, and hurried up some steps. Once inside, he carried her up a further flight of stairs, through another door, and deposited her on a bed. She struggled to rise to a sitting position as male laughter filled the darkness of the room.

"You may sit up now but you'll be on your back soon enough, *Lady* Kendra."

The voice was familiar — fearless, ruthless, assured of his goal, but it was too dark to see his face. That surety sent shivers of fear up and down her spine.

The door opened and closed again, leaving her alone in the darkness. Rising to her feet, Kendra crept forward, determined to find the door, or something to cut through the ties around her wrists. After bumping into the wall, she turned her back to it so her tied hands could feel along the wall. The room had little furnishings in it, making it easy to find the door frame. There it was. Now for the knob. It turned, but the door wouldn't budge. She pounded on the door with all the anger and fear churning inside her. "Help me!" She tried to yell around the gag.

Nothing. If only she could cut through the rope. Kendra inched forward hoping to find a sharp object, something to release her hands. A few shuffled steps later she bumped into a table. Turning around, she felt along the top with grasping fingers. Nothing, the table was bare. She circled the room several more times but still came up empty-handed. With a leaden heart, she sank down on the bed. Deep, even breaths. She thought of the rescues she'd read about in the Bible — Joseph, Daniel, Isaac, Jonah, for goodness sake. She almost smiled imagining her room the belly of a fish. Well, it wasn't as bad as that. At least it didn't smell. *Lord, I am losing my mind for certain this time! Will You rescue me? Of course You will. How will You rescue me?*

Kendra fell back on the bed and curled up on her side. She tried to stay awake knowing that she needed to be alert for any opportunities of escape, but the softness of the bed crept over her tired, aching body. Just a few minutes of rest couldn't hurt. After all, the Lord must have angels watching over her. With that thought she drifted off to sleep.

Pale streaks of dawn crept into the small room, rousing Kendra from her slumber. At first a strange disorientation swamped her mind. Her gaze darted about the room, taking in the bedside table and colorful quilt that she slept on as the details of the night came flooding back to her. The capture, the rope around her wrists that was making her shoulders stiff and sore. She struggled up into a sitting position and scooted to the side of the bed. Her arms ached from being tied together. She arched her back in an attempt to stretch from head to toe and closed her eyes as her muscles spasmed.

Her eyes shot wide as the door burst open. "Did you sleep well, my lady?"

Kendra turned toward the voice and saw the man she suspected had taken her — Martin Saunderson. He walked toward her. She reared back from his grasping hands. "Hold still," he demanded as he fumbled with the knot at the back of her head. She gasped in relief as the gag fell into her lap. "You. What do you want with me?"

Martin's red lips stretched over his perfect teeth. His gaze raked over her from head to toe, dark brows lifted. Grasping Kendra's upper arms, he pulled her to stand in front of him. "The first thing I want is to keep you from making the biggest mistake of your life by cavorting with Dorian Colburn. His intentions are not honorable, my lady."

"And yours are?" Kendra demanded, twisting from his tight hold.

"Actually, I believe they are. We will be married immediately. I have it all planned." He sounded genuine in his excitement about the prospect. "After tonight you will be all mine."

Kendra gasped as his meaning sunk in.

"You are deranged if you think I would ever marry you." She struggled against the hold on her arm. "Let me go."

"I'm afraid you will have little choice in the matter. We are to be married by the magistrate, a, er, friend of mine, and then off to a pleasant inn for the consummation."

"I will never agree to wed you. You can't force me to say vows and no magistrate would condone to marry us without my co-operation."

Martin chuckled. "This one will, I'm afraid. Let us just say that he has a penchant for gambling and now owes me a great sum of money. He gladly agreed to perform the ceremony without your willing participation in exchange for the removal of his debts."

Kendra shook her head in a desperate attempt not to believe it. "Why do this? I'll not make you a good wife. I don't love you. I loathe you."

He leaned into her face so that his breath wafted over her. "I have every confidence that you will learn to desire me. You're such a . . . bright girl."

Kendra pressed into the cruel pressure of his arm around her back. "You will regret this, let me assure you. Unhand me!"

Martin released her in a sudden move that caused her to stumble and fall back on the bed. She saw him raise his hand in the air but it was too fast to stop. She remained frozen, unable to move as he slapped her across the cheek. "Don't fight me, my lady. I will break you to my harness if need be, but I must confess I had hoped you would come willingly. It will be so much more enjoyable for both of us if you do." He bowed, suddenly polite, and tipped his hat toward her. "Think about it." Kendra watched in stunned silence as he walked from the room, shut the door, and slammed the bolt into place with a loud click.

Kendra crumpled into a little ball, trying to hold back the tears. Her cheek throbbed, the inside raw against her teeth. Oh no! Would a magistrate really marry her without her consent? How could that be legally binding?

She had to escape. There must be a way, but how?

The scraping of the door being opened sounded a few moments later. Kendra sat up as a serving girl made her way into the room. Shutting the door behind her, she turned and gave Kendra a broad, gaping smile. "I'm Maybelle," she began. When she saw Kendra's face she clucked her tongue. "Ya must 'ave done somethin' purty bad for Martin to hit ya like that, miss. I ain't never seen him hit a woman before."

Kendra stared at the woman, shocked further by her speech. Would she help her if she knew what Martin was planning? "Please, I only refused to marry him." Kendra scooted to the side of the bed and stood up. "He's holding me captive here. Please, help me escape!"

Maybelle chuckled. "Martin said ya was given to theatrics and that ya can't help yourself. Now don't be givin' Maybelle any trouble, ya hear. Martin wants ya cleaned up and dressed in this here weddin' gown for your upcoming nuptials." She opened the bag she was carrying and pulled out a garish-looking gown.

Kendra took one look at the dress and wailed. This couldn't be happening. Why would he bother to buy her a dress when this wedding was such a farce? Kendra shook her head. "I won't wear it. Take it back down to him and throw it in his face or I swear I will tear it into a million pieces."

A look of momentary shock passed over Maybelle's face and then her eyebrows drew together in a stubborn, angry way. "Ya listen here, miss high and mighty. Any girl would be lucky to have Martin as a husband. Girls four counties over and more have been tryin' to get their hands on him for years. Ya needs to stop these hoity-toity acts of yers and be thankful."

Kendra curled toward her middle in frustration. "Maybelle, listen to me. Whatever he told you was a lie. He has abducted me and is planning to force me to marry him. I'm . . . I'm in love with someone else. Please, I beg you, you have to help me escape."

Maybelle took in her pleading eyes and shook her head again. "Enough of this, miss. Let's get you ready for the magistrate. He'll be here within the hour and you'll be wantin' to look yer best for yer own weddin'."

Kendra gave up on Maybelle's assistance. "I don't care what you believe. Just take the dress back to him and tell him I won't wear it because I'm not going to marry him. Tell him that. Now go!" Kendra advanced as she spoke, her voice getting louder and louder.

Maybelle's eyes grew wide as she backed away, clutching the dress to her ample bosom.

Kendra watched with some satisfaction as the servant rushed from the room. Unfortunately, she didn't forget to latch the door.

Not more than five minutes later Martin stormed into the room. His face was red with rage, his hands balled into fists. Kendra backed away but he caught her and pushed her back on the bed. Placing both hands on either side of her, he leaned into her face and ground out the words. "If you don't put that dress on right now, I will strip you down and put it on myself."

"Please, leave me be." Tears filled her eyes.

"I had thought to give you Maybelle's assistance getting dressed but if you prefer mine, I will be happy to oblige."

His head descended toward hers with the look of a hungry tiger and she knew she had no choice. Jerking to the side before his mouth touched her lips she rasped out, "Alright, I'll wear it, but only if you cut these ropes from around my wrists."

Martin leaned back and considered her. "Making demands already, are we? Very well, *Lady* Kendra. As a testament to my good nature I will accommodate you. If you will stand up, I'll unbind you."

Kendra held out her arms. The touch of his hands on her wrists made her shudder. As soon as her hands were free she walked across the room, as far from him as possible, and shook her arms in an effort to restore proper circulation.

"I'll be back in a few minutes with the magistrate. You had better be ready."

CHAPTER TWENTY

Dorian came to with a jerk and a groan. He sat up, dizzy, disoriented, but with a sense of panic connecting the images and thoughts flashing through his mind. The garden, someone had hit him. Kendra! Where was she?

He reached up and probed into his hair at the place of most pain. A giant, throbbing lump and a gash as long as his finger. His hand came away sticky with blood. Rising from the ground he searched the garden, calling out for Kendra. When his search proved futile he came to the conclusion that whoever had bludgeoned him over the head had abducted her. But who would have taken her? And why? Whoever it was, they had known Kendra was at the Colburn house.

Dorian took off his neck cloth, wadded it into a ball, and pressed it against the bleeding gash on his head. He hurried back to the house, yelling orders to the servants as he passed them. "Locate John and have our horses saddled! Lanterns, food, and water. Millicent" — he nodded to the wide-eyed maid — "if you would be so good as to hurry!"

She jumped to obey. "But yer head is bleedin' like a sieve, sir. Shouldn't I fetch your mother?"

With a sigh, he nodded. He did feel a bit dizzy. "Yes, yes and some bandages and a bowl of warm water." She turned to go. "And a needle and thread," he shouted after her. His mother was an old hand at stitching up wounds. Everyone for miles around called on her for doctoring and she would no doubt demand to stitch him up before he began the search.

It didn't take long for the news to travel throughout the house party. Amelia collapsed into a chair and burst into tears when she heard that her niece had been taken. Dorian's sisters rushed to comfort her with patting hands, soothing words, and a ready bottle of hartshorn. Dorian gritted his teeth and sat under his mother's ministrations.

John looked on, wincing every time the needle pierced Dorian's flesh.

"You say you were sitting on the bench and heard a rustling from the bushes behind you?" Clayton asked.

"Yes. Before I had time to turn around I was hit. I must have blacked out. I don't remember anything after that, just waking up with this headache."

"I've questioned the other guests. No one has seen anyone suspicious and everyone is accounted for," John said. "We must make haste before the trail grows cold."

Dorian shot him a dark look. As if he didn't know that they were wasting precious time. But there was no use going off ill prepared and leaving a trail of blood in their wake.

"It's going to be difficult to track her in the dark," John asserted with a frown.

"We'll have to spread out. I've gathered every able-bodied man in the stable yard. We'll find her."

His mother tied off the thread and Dorian stood. The world started to whirl around him and darkness crept into the corners of his vision. "Blast this dizziness," he murmured, leaning down to regain his equilibrium. John was at his side in a moment. "Easy, old man. It won't do to pass out on us again." He tried to take his arm but Dorian brushed him off.

"I'm fine."

"Well, your face is as white as a ghost's."

"I'm fine, I say. Let us be gone."

"Wait!" Amelia stood up, her face splotchy with tears. "I–I think I know who took her."

Dorian crossed the room to stand in front of her, his brows together in a scowl. "Does Franklin have something to do with this?"

She nodded, her eyes full of fear and shame. "He and Martin Saunderson. They've been planning this for weeks. I overheard them talking before we came. I didn't know they meant to take her here. I thought Martin would show up and keep her attention away from you, but I didn't know they meant to actually kidnap her!"

"Where, Amelia? Think back to the conversation. Did they mention a place?"

She nodded. "Hanover. Martin said he knew of an inn there. I think he means to force her into marriage." Her bottom lip began to quiver.

"You've done the right thing, Amelia. Thank you. We won't let them get away with this."

Dorian and John headed out to their horses. It was decided that the other men would fan out as planned, just in case Amelia was wrong.

They followed a set of carriage tracks on the road north toward Hanover, riding fast and hard. By morning they'd reached the

311

little village.

Please God let her be here. He didn't know why or how, but he felt like God was helping them and as grateful as he was, it made him uncomfortable too. It made God alive and *personal.* It made Him care . . . and Dorian just wasn't sure he really believed that. God hadn't cared enough to stop Molly. Why care now? Why with Kendra?

The town was small — a mercantile, a boarding house, a couple of taverns, a livery, a blacksmith, a constable's office, a church, and a few other small, scattered establishments. They headed toward the livery to feed and water their horses. A tall youth ran out to assist them.

"Sir, what a fine horse! Might I brush him down?"

Dorian clapped the lad on the shoulder and nodded. He had ridden Trista, one of the Andalusian mares, and had begun to regret it. The beautiful gray attracted too much attention as evident by this starry-eyed youth. Dorian dug some coins from his pocket and passed them to the young man. "Take good care of them both and keep them out of sight, will you?"

He looked up wide-eyed. "Yes, sir."

"What's your name, boy?"

"Stephen Fowler."

"Your father own this place?"

"Yes, sir. My ma is fixin' to have a baby and he stayed with her this morning. I'm watching over the livery."

"You know horses? Been doing this awhile?"

"Oh yes, sir. Been around horses since I could walk. I've a natural way with 'em, I'm told. You can trust me to take good care of these fine animals."

"Glad to hear it."

John passed over the reins of his mare. "Where's the inn around here?"

Stephen pointed toward a weathered plank building. "Aunt Judy's Boarding House. She serves breakfast if you're lookin' for a meal. She usually has plenty."

As they walked toward the boarding house Dorian made their plan. "As much as I would like to bust in, guns blazing, let's sit down for breakfast, ask questions, and have a look around the place."

John patted his stomach. "Exactly what I was thinking."

Minutes later they were seated near a window with a good view of the street, drinking strong coffee and waiting for their promised apple tansy, fried eggs, and pork.

"How's the head feeling?" John tipped back his chair and looked at Dorian over the rim of his coffee cup.

"Feeling like someone bludgeoned me with a hammer." Dorian's tone was dry. He looked out the window at the townsfolk passing by and clenched his teeth together. "John, what if she's not here? What if we can't find her? Amelia isn't exactly an excellent source. We have so little to go on. I . . ."

"You love her, don't you?" John asked in a quiet voice.

Dorian jerked his head up to look at his friend. "What?"

"You've been like a man possessed since you clapped eyes on her on England's shore. Admit it to me, at least."

Dorian stared at John for a long moment, anger and frustration rising to heat his face. "I don't want to love her."

John chuckled. "Not what you thought it would feel like, is it? You'd think falling in love would feel good, but most of the time it feels like your guts are all tied up in knots. It's downright painful at times."

The arrival of their breakfast stopped the conversation. The serving girl set their plates in front of each of them and gave them a broad smile. "You'll be wantin' some more coffee, I suspect. Goodness gracious, but this town is full of folks lately. What with the doc in town for Mrs. Fowler's baby and that new couple, they're so elegant and mysterious! And now two handsome gents like you. I ain't ever seen Aunt Judy's so busy."

Dorian's head snapped up to look at the girl. "An elegant couple, you say? We're looking for someone. A young woman with blonde hair. She was wearing a blue gown. She has an English accent and goes by Lady Kendra Townsend?"

The girl nodded, wide-eyed. "Oh, yes sir. I didn't see her come in, but I heard Maybelle, the other serving girl here, talking about her. Maybelle took a tray to her room this morning. She came in with a man who is near famous in these parts."

"What's his name?"

"He's a gambler and so handsome." She patted her chest. "Martin Saunderson. You heard of him?"

"Yes, I have." So Amelia had been right. Thank God.

"Would you like me to go and fetch him for you?"

Dorian leaned in and murmured in a low voice. "No thank you, miss. What's your name?"

"Marie, sir."

"Marie, Martin Saunderson is very dangerous. Can you show us to the room where

315

the lady is staying? I need to see that she is safe."

Marie edged closer, eyes wide as saucers. "You think she's in some sort of trouble with him?"

"Yes, I do. Will you help us?"

"Oh, sir! You're making me afraid, but I reckon I could sneak the two of you up the back stairs. Go on outside, to the back of the building. I'll let you in that door."

John took a giant bite of his apple tansy as he stood, gazing down at his food with a look of longing. "Can you wrap this up for later?"

Dorian frowned at him and tossed down the appropriate coins, handing an extra one to Marie.

"Come on, John. I believe the good Lord is rolling out the carpet with His help and I aim to take Him up on it. There will be time for breakfast later."

Kendra stood, knees locked and shoulders back, chin up and jaw clenched, wearing the awful dress and waiting for the sound of the bolt on the door to slide open. She shook with fear and anger but determined not to show it. Martin must find her strong and determined. When he entered with the magistrate they must both find her steadfast and resolute against them. No tears. Resolute. It was all she had left.

She waited for long moments, breathing so shallow that she felt faint. Finally, the door scraped open. A tall man with slumped shoulders and wearing all black walked in ahead of Martin. He was perhaps thirty, brown nondescript hair, a long face and somber eyes. His pinched face appeared afraid and sad and . . . guilty. His gaze darted from her eyes to the floor as Martin pushed him further into the room. He bowed, a short action of head and shoulders, his gaze lingering on her bruised cheek. Martin must have noticed it as he stepped up to he and grasped her elbow with a tight squeeze, pulling her arm against his chest, and smiled down at her. He brushed his hand against the throbbing cheek. "So clumsy, that fall." He looked at the magistrate. "She had a small accident, but will be fine in a day or two. Isn't that right, my dear?" Martin raised his eyebrows and dared Kendra to defy him.

The memory of him striking her was like another blow. She exhaled, lips trembling as she looked from Martin to the magistrate, mute, knowing that anything she said would be turned against her.

"Shy, are we?" Martin propelled her

toward the magistrate in the center of the room. "A bride's nerves, you know. Let us get on with it."

The magistrate nodded his head with a bewildered expression and opened the leather-bound book in his hands.

Martin secured Kendra to his side with a strong arm and rasped into her ear, "It doesn't matter if you speak or not, we will be wed."

Kendra pretended not to hear as she stared at an ugly brown stain on the wall in front of her.

The magistrate paged through his book with shaking fingers and then launched into a lengthy speech about marriage. He did not once look at Kendra.

Martin grew impatient, fidgeting beside her. "Yes, yes, get to the vows, man. We haven't got all day."

The magistrate cleared his throat and swallowed, his Adam's apple bobbing up and down. "Do you, Martin Saunderson, take this woman, um, y-you d-didn't say what her n-name was," he stuttered.

Martin looked down at Kendra with a devilish grin. "Lady Kendra Townsend."

The magistrate started to nod and then looked up, startled at the title.

"Just go on!"

Kendra jumped at the shout.

The magistrate cleared his throat again and looked at Martin. "Wilt thou have this woman to be thy wedded wife, to live together after God's ordinance in the holy estate of matrimony? Wilt thou love her, comfort her, honor, and keep her in sickness and in health; and, forsaking all others, keep thee only unto her, so long as ye both shall live?"

"I will." His voice held a note of mock gravity as he stared down into Kendra's eyes. Anger, like she'd never felt before, filled her. She looked away, breathing hard and trying not to burst into tears.

The magistrate nodded and then turned toward Kendra. "Wilt thou have this man to be thy wedded husband, to live together after God's ordinance in the holy estate of matrimony? Wilt thou obey him, and serve him, love, honor, and keep him in sickness and in health; and, forsaking all others, keep thee only unto him, so long as ye both shall live?"

Kendra turned her gaze to Martin's, held it, stared into his brown eyes. She shook her head and stated, "No, I do not. I will not. Never."

The magistrate paled and looked to Martin, who motioned with his hand for him to continue with the ceremony.

"Do you have a ring?"

Martin dug into his pocket, took Kendra's hand, and shoved a plain, gold band on her finger.

"Repeat after me," the magistrate instructed Martin. "With this ring I thee wed, with my body I thee worship, and with all my worldly goods I thee endow —"

"Yes, yes. Just do the ending."

Kendra shook her head as the man's eyes skipped down the page. "In as much as Martin Saunderson and Kendra Townsend have consented —"

"Consented!" Kendra yelled. "How will you sleep at night, knowing you've done this thing? God is our witness, sir."

"Continue and your debts will be paid in full," Martin reminded him with raised brows.

The man hesitated, his mouth working in silent indecision.

"You have exactly three seconds," Martin challenged. "Three, two —"

The magistrate cleared his throat and looked back down at his prayer book. ". . . together in holy wedlock, and have witnessed the same before God and this company, and thereto have given and pledged their troth either to the other, and have declared the same by giving and receiving of a ring, and by joining of hands; I pronounce that they be —"

Kendra fell forward but Martin caught her and forced her to stand upright. "Noooo! I beg you!"

Dorian turned from following John out the front door. "Wait. Forget the back way. It's Kendra." He knew that voice. He would always know that voice.

He turned and dashed up the stairs, John on his heels. A loud scuffling noise from behind one of the doors gave him his direction. He ran to the door and threw it open.

The occupants of the room turned and gaped as Dorian and John rushed into the room, pistols aimed at the two men.

Martin cursed while trying to grab the fleeing Kendra. Catching her, he pushed her behind his back, breathing hard. Dorian lost all conscious thought at the sight of her, eyes wide with fright. He took the steps toward Martin and punched him in the jaw. Before Martin had time to react, Dorian followed that punch with another to his stomach. Martin bent over with a harsh sound and tried to swing at Dorian but it lacked the strength that Dorian knew flowed through him from his fear for Kendra.

"Get back," Dorian ordered Kendra. While his attention strayed to her for a brief moment, Martin knocked his arm, the one holding the gun, and sent it sliding across the floor. They both dove for it, but Martin was closer. Dorian watched in dread as he grasped it and turned it on him, standing up with a slow grin. Dorian didn't pause, didn't give Martin time to even raise his arm and point the gun. He swung with all his might, punching Martin in the side of the head. Martin's eyes rolled back into his head and the gun clattered to the floor as he went down, the table falling over with a crash.

Looking around, Dorian saw that John held the man with the prayer book. He was pale and panting, not even trying to get away. Dorian tossed some rope to John. "Let's tie them up and then fetch any law we can find around here."

Dorian turned toward Kendra. "Are you alright? What was going on in here?"

"If you'd been a second later, I might be a married woman right now. Martin was bribing the magistrate to wed us without my consent."

Dorian glared at Martin who had come to and sat tied to a chair, his mouth bleeding on one side. "He lied to you, Kendra. The courts would never support a marriage that you didn't consent to."

Martin's upper lip curled in a disdainful smirk. "We would have been long gone from here and the marriage consummated before she figured that out."

"Come. Let's get you away from here." Dorian took her elbow and led her from the room, saying back over his shoulder, "John, hold the pistol on them while I fetch the constable."

"Gladly, Captain."

Dorian led Kendra into the hall, shut the door, and pulled her close. "Kendra," he whispered her name into her hair. "I thought I'd lost you. I thought . . ."

"Yes?" Kendra leaned back and looked into his eyes.

He held her for a long moment while they both just breathed.

"I believe I've made a discovery," he finally said.

She looked up, dark lashes wet with tears. Her ivory throat contracted with a hard swallow.

"There is only one way to keep you safe."

Her brows raised in question. Her voice was threadbare, a breath. "And what is that?"

"Make you mine."

"Yours?"

"Yes. For always."

A shiver went through her spine and he felt it in his arm clasped around her. "What are you saying, Captain?"

He grinned, allowing the freedom of the thought, the capitulation, to overtake him. Yes. This was what he wanted. More than the sea. More than a bachelor life that he'd put on a pedestal. More than the fear of another bad marriage. This. Kendra. This was what he had been searching for. His mooring place. The solace, the grounding place, the roots . . . that was here . . . now . . . in his arms. And he'd almost lost it.

"Will you be my wife, Kendra?"

Her mouth quivered and a little cry burst from her throat as she buried her face in his shoulder. She nodded her head.

"Yes?"

She looked up, touched his face, and leaned toward him. "Yes."

He took a long breath and laughed. Then he pulled her closer still, pulled her up off her toes and into his arms. His lips crushed down in gentle assault. He plunged them into whirling sensation until he felt dizzy and reckless like on the deck of a ship tossed by wind and sea. A voice resounded within him like a song, like a sea chant overcoming the storm.

Abandon the fear, turn away from independence. Embrace love. Embrace this woman . . . her glorious being that lights your heart on fire. Love her. Love her. Love her . . . forever.

I will.

CHAPTER TWENTY-ONE

It was evening by the time Dorian helped Kendra down from the hired carriage in front of the Rutherfords cabin. "Are you sure you don't want me to come with you to tell them the news? I don't trust your uncle."

Kendra placed a hand on his arm. "I can handle them, trust me. And anyway, John is eager to get home, I can tell." She smiled up at him. "You may call on me tomorrow."

She could see the silver flecks in his eyes reflected in the dusk sunlight. He caressed her cheek with the back of one gloved finger. "I don't know that I can let you out of my sight for that long. Who knows what trouble you will find yourself in." He was teasing, of course, but there was a note of seriousness in his voice that warmed Kendra's heart.

"Trust me. I will have a better chance of winning them to our side without you standing beside me like a fire-breathing dragon."

Dorian leaned down and whispered in her ear, "A dragon, eh? First I'm a pirate and now a dragon. And here I thought I was your knight in shining armor, rescuing you and all. Your opinion wounds me, my lady."

Kendra cocked her head toward him and grinned. "I'm sure you will think of something to remedy it."

"Lord knows I'll have time enough, being shackled to you for the rest of my days." She could feel his smile against her cheek as he moved even closer to her lips.

"Having regrets already?" Kendra turned her face ever so much.

His lips hovered over hers. "Oh yes. Deep regrets. But I am sure you will think of something to console me? Reassure me?" His kiss deepened and cut off her laugh.

For a few breathless minutes she forgot her very real dread of the conversation to come with her relatives, forgot John waiting in the carriage, forgot everything but the man who would soon be her husband. Her mind went blessedly blank as sensation ruled — his exploring lips and the firm muscles of his shoulders as she clung to him, the —

A throat cleared. Loudly. "I told you we

should have demanded the magistrate's services before the constable hauled him away." John's voice was like a bucket of icy water thrown over them.

Kendra jumped back, choking back a laugh. She pressed her hands to her hot cheeks. "Sorry, John."

"Oh, never mind. As Dorian said, his mother would have never forgiven us had you wed without the family present. Let's just hope you can pull together a ceremony soon." He chuckled. Dorian glared at him. John cleared his throat again and looked away.

Kendra turned toward the house. "I will see you tomorrow then?"

Dorian gave her a brief bow. "Tomorrow, my love."

Her heart sang at his words as she turned toward the door and opened it. She waved good-bye and then, with a deep breath, entered the sitting room.

"Aunt Amelia? Uncle Franklin? Anyone home?" There was a single candle burning on a low table, but no sign of her aunt or uncle. She moved through the dark house, checking the few rooms. Could her aunt still be at the Colburns'? Dorian had assured her that the party had broken up and he'd sent word that they had found her. She stepped into the kitchen and saw a shadowy form out the back window. Walking to the back door, she opened it and peered out at the vegetable garden. Before she could say anything she heard her Uncle Franklin's voice.

"He will have married her by now. Might even be consummating the marriage right now." He chuckled.

"Franklin. I beg you. You have to stop this nonsense," her aunt's voice rebuked.

"What's gotten into you?" Franklin growled. "You know this is the only way to get our hands on that fortune."

"I can't be a part of it anymore. I won't help you. As a matter of fact . . ." — Amelia's voice quivered but there was a note of steel underneath it — "I told them that it was Martin who took her, and I told Dorian Colburn that I had heard you and Martin mention the town of Hanover. If anything is going on right now, it is probably Kendra's rescue."

There was a rustling sound and then Kendra heard her aunt make a terrible rasping sound. Without thinking, she rushed out the door, closing it with a loud bang, and ran toward them. "Stop it!" she yelled, seeing now that her uncle had his hands wrapped around Amelia's throat. She ran at Franklin

329

and started beating his back and arms with her fists. "Don't hurt her! Stop it right now!"

Franklin took one hand off his wife, reached around, and shoved Kendra to the ground. He spun around with Amelia still in his grasp, eyes alight with rage.

"Uncle Franklin, please. This isn't you. Don't do this." Kendra sat up and wiped the dirt from her cheek, breathing heavy.

He stopped at her words, his face drooping, eyes registering shock. He dropped Amelia's arm, turned, and walked away from them into the darkness of the fields.

Amelia gasped. "Hurry, before he changes his mind and comes up with another plan to get your dowry. We don't have much time. We have to get away from here."

"My dowry? Is that what he and Martin were planning?"

"Yes." Her aunt pulled her back to the house as she explained. "The letter you brought from Lord Townsend told of your dowry, and Franklin came up with a plan to get his hands on it. If you married his good friend, Martin, they were going to split it."

Kendra stopped inside the house. "And you were helping them?" It had all been a lie. Their care and concern. All this time they had been plotting against her to get to her dowry. Memories of time spent with her aunt crashed over her in stark clarity — all their talks, working side-by-side, her aunt smiling more, laughing more often . . . Tears filled Kendra's eyes until she could hardly see where she was going. These people didn't love her. They just wanted something from her, some paltry dowry she hadn't even known about.

"At first I did, but as I got to know you . . . and love you . . . I told Dorian where to find you. Franklin will never forgive me for that, but I had to do what was right. Now hurry up. I know him and his mind is plotting on what to do next. He could be back at any moment."

They hurried through the dark house toward her room. What might her uncle do when he found out she planned to marry Dorian within the week? Could he stop her from marrying him? Did he have that kind of power over her? She had to get out before he locked her in her room.

Once in her room, they pulled a trunk from under her bed and began to stuff her most prized belongings in it. She had a little money in the toe of one stocking left over from the trip from England, some clothes, some jewelry and pretty hairpins, the precious dragonfly brooch . . . but what she really needed when traveling alone at night was a gun. Uncle Franklin had a gun. "Aunt, go and fetch Uncle Franklin's gun. We may need it and we certainly don't want him coming after us with it. And pack a quick bag for yourself."

"Good idea." Amelia hurried from the room.

A little while later a noise from the back of the yard made her stop and turn, prickles of fear racing down her spine. *Oh God, help us get out of here!* She eased down the lid and sidled over toward the door, standing behind it. Her aunt came back with the gun and thrust it into Kendra's hands.

"He's coming!"

With a burst of strength, she lifted the trunk, motioned to her aunt to follow her, and bolted from the room. When they reached the door, Amelia stopped. Kendra turned as she ran out the door and yelled in a whisper, "What are you doing? Come on!"

"I'm not going. I will be okay, I'm sure of it. I'll stay here and try to talk some sense into him. It will buy you some time. Now hurry! Go!"

There wasn't time to argue with the plan. Kendra turned and fled, amazed at her aunt's courage.

■ ■ ■ ■

Kendra jumped and stifled a shriek as an owl hooted nearby. Taking a deep breath, she kept on, putting one foot in front of the other as fast as she could and dragging the heavy trunk behind her on the dirt road. Worry for Amelia kept her going. Would Franklin fly into another rage? What would he do when he found her gone?

She looked up at the moon and judged that it must be well beyond midnight. She had come four or five miles by now but still hadn't found the Y in the road that she remembered Dorian saying to take to get to his home. Her feet ached in protest of each step, begging her to stop. She looked down at the dainty slippers that matched the light sash of her gown and frowned. What she needed was a decent pair of boots, but there had not been money for that.

A howling sound pierced the air and made her throat close in fear. She took up the gun, swung it around, and aimed it in the direction of the noise. Little good a gun without powder would do. She hadn't considered wild animals when she'd thought to bluff about her skills in weaponry. Another howl, closer this time.

Oh . . . oh. What is that, Lord?

Another sound, off to the right. Was there more than one? Kendra's gaze darted around the shadowy trees on either side of the road. It seemed unwise to leave the cleared path where the bright light of the moon gave her some feeling of safety, but they sounded like they were coming right for her. A tree. Could she climb a tree in these skirts? She hadn't climbed a tree since she was a girl but if she could find one with low enough branches . . .

Wolves can't climb trees, can they? I'm about to marry the man of my dreams and I can't be eaten by wolves right now!

With the empty gun still pointed toward the sound she backed toward some low trees. The dancing shadows made by the moon and wind caused her breath to rush in and out of her chest. Just as she was about to throw down the weapon and leap for the lowest branch, she heard the pounding sound of a horse's hooves. She pressed back into the rough bark of the tree as a tall, pale horse came galloping into view, its white mane like a silvery flag whipping in the wind. She couldn't speak as the magnificent creature raced by, throwing up clods of earth from his hooves.

Everything was quiet once the dust from

the rider settled. She took a few steps after him and then stopped. Despair filled her as she realized she was alone again. Cocking her head, she listened for the wolves, but there was no sound except the breeze blowing through tree branches. Her hand curled tight around the rifle as she took deep, calming breaths. She would just have to keep walking. At least the streak of horseflesh had scared away the wolves. She only hoped they would stay away and not follow her.

An hour later she stumbled over a large rock and fell to the road. Tears of exhaustion and pain streamed down her dirty cheeks as she sat in the middle of the road and cradled her bruised toe. She rocked back and forth, looking up at the near-full moon, and allowed the crying to reach her chest. What was she to do? She would never make it all the way to the Colburn Plantation injured and without water. Her throat ached with dryness and quivered with emotion. Why hadn't she thought to bring water instead of clothes? She could have gone back for the clothes after she was safely married. Stupid. Stupid. Stupid Englishwoman. What was she doing in this savage country anyway?

The image of her uncle Andrew brought

on a fresh wave of tears. Why didn't he love her? Why hadn't he wanted to care for her, care about her well being, after her father's death? How could he have changed so thoroughly? And her only other relatives? Oh! It wasn't fair! *God, it's not fair to lose both parents and have no one care. They all hate me so!* She wiped her running nose on the back of her sleeve and let her head fall forward on another broken sob. "I can't go on and I won't. I can't stand it anymore. I'm . . . so . . . tired . . ."

"If you're quite done feeling sorry for yourself, I've come to rescue you."

The voice, dry with sarcasm, made her turn around with a squeal. She scrambled to her feet and tried to dust off her skirts. Peering through the dark, she saw a pale coat flash as it walked toward her. The horse. The white horse with silvery tail and mane. She took a step toward it. "Sir?"

"You don't recognize my voice? I'm crushed, my lady."

She took a quivering inhale and then laughed and cried out "Dorian!"

She limped toward him, his face coming into the light as he dismounted. His raven hair and teasing eyes, his knowing smile. She propelled herself into his arms.

"I can't believe you found me. How did

you know?"

He grasped her close and pulled her face next to his, breathing in her hair as he held her for a long moment. "When I arrived home, I heard that Franklin had come and fetched your aunt Amelia. Father said they were both acting stranger than normal, even for them. It didn't set well with me and I couldn't sleep, thinking of you alone with them, so I decided I had better come and check on you. Imagine my alarm when I arrived to find you gone. Your uncle was in a high temper about it, saying you'd run off and good riddance, but your aunt pulled me aside and told me you'd taken this road back toward my house. It was a dangerous decision, Kendra. Wild animals being just the beginning of it."

"I didn't really have a choice. Uncle Franklin tried to choke my aunt when she told him that she told you about their plan. He was the one who came up with the scheme for Martin to marry me. They were after a dowry that I didn't even know existed."

Dorian considered that for a moment. "That would explain it, I guess. Your uncle Andrew must be holding a dowry for you until you marry. Franklin hoped to marry you to Martin to get their hands on it."

Kendra shook her head. "It can't be much. I told you how Uncle Andrew ruined us. We had nothing left but the shell of a castle and a little land."

"There must be something to it. They wouldn't go to all this trouble for nothing."

Kendra took a deep breath. "I suppose we will find out when we are married." She looked up at him and raised her brows. "You're not marrying me for my paltry fortune, are you?"

Dorian laughed and leaned down to give her dusty lips a brush of a kiss. "Would that I had such an excuse. I'm afraid my motives are far more dire."

"Dire? Surely not?" Her eyes widened in mock dismay.

"I fear I want to do more of this," he kissed her again, a mere touch of his lips against hers, a breath over her face, "And this," he pulled her to him and cupped her cheek with one hand while wrapping her tight with the other at her waist.

Kendra held him back but excitement rushed through her. "First things first, Captain." She ticked off her needs on one hand. "The most immediate need is some water, then an introduction to this magnificent beast you are riding. Next, a bed for the night, a special license? Is that how things are done in America?" She didn't wait for a response. "A wedding," she added softly, "soon. And then you might pick up where your pirating, rebel, American lips have left off."

Dorian looked to be considering her demands. "Or I could just leave you here in the road."

Kendra pushed against his hard chest with a huff. "Don't even consider it."

Dorian reached back, pulled his flask from his saddlebag, and passed it over to her, chuckling. "I do relish your particular brand of endearments. Can't say that I want to live without those."

Kendra took a long swallow, the water feeling cool and wonderful as it slid down her throat. When she finished she wiped her mouth on her sleeve and stared into his eyes, eyes that were glowing like molten silver under the moon's light. "Take me home then, you backwoods, thieving, scoundrel." She giggled.

"Thieving? Why, I've never stolen a thing in my life." He lifted her into his arms.

She looked up at him, a slow smile curving her lips. "You stole my heart, didn't you? I will never forgive you for it."

"No?"

"Well, maybe . . . you can start with letting me ride this magnificent horse and then we'll see. But what shall I do with my trunk?"

Dorian looked askance at the heavy object.

"Let's hide it in these bushes. We'll come back for it tomorrow."

They each took an end and covered it with branches. Dorian took her hand and led her back to the horse. "Up you go then." Dorian turned and lifted her high in the air, like thrusting up a bag of potatoes, he propelled her onto the saddle. Kendra screeched, almost falling to the ground on the other side of the horse. At the last moment she turned, a neat twist of her upper body, and swung one leg over the horse's back. The horse sidled in response and blew a huff of air from his nostrils. Kendra let out an astonished breath as the power of the animal moved beneath her. "Dorian?"

"Right here," he said in a calm voice as he climbed up behind her and steadied the horse with gentle words.

"I'm right here." He leaned toward her and pressed his cheek to hers.

With a soft clicking sound they were off. Flying on moonbeams and wind song — safe again — with his arm wrapped tight around her middle.

CHAPTER TWENTY-TWO

"I'm sure they don't deserve to be invited, but consider it, dear. What can they do with all of us here to support you?" Hannah asked the next morning as they sat in the parlor and discussed a quick wedding.

"No." Dorian pushed away from his place at the fireplace, dark brows drawing together in a frown. "I've sent a servant to check on Amelia and make sure she is unharmed with a note of warning to Franklin. But I don't trust them. I wouldn't put it past them to put together some sort of mutton-headed scheme. I won't let them upset Kendra again."

"But she will have no one from her side" — Hannah worried her hands in her lap — "and I just can't believe it of Amelia. I think she gets pulled into these awful ideas by her husband."

"You're right, Mrs. Colburn, my aunt has changed. She told Dorian where to find me and then helped me escape. I even heard her praying as I left. We can invite them but I really don't think that my uncle would attend or allow her to attend. And anyway, I'll have Faith, who already feels like a sister to me, and you and" — she nodded with a shy look at her soon-to-be father-in-law — "Mr. Colburn. It's enough."

"You know," Clayton said "I have been thinking about your aunt and uncle, Kendra. Farming is just not their strong suit, but Franklin has a knack for numbers, doesn't he?"

Dorian tried not to snort. "If you consider gambling —"

"Yes, but gamblers often make good men of business."

"What do you have in mind?" Dorian raised one brow at his father.

"I heard of an opening at the Custom House in Yorktown. I was thinking to help him get the job, sell that farm they hate, and get a little house in town. Franklin might do better in that sort of job and if we can get the two of them more stable . . . you won't have to worry about them so much."

"Oh, Mr. Colburn" — Kendra clasped her hands together in her lap — "what a wonderful idea! I know my aunt would love to live in town and Uncle Franklin, too. It would be a fresh start for them. How can I ever thank you?"

Clayton beamed. "I'll ride over after the wedding, then. And none of that formality, my dear. Please call us by our given names, or if you like, as all our children call us, Momma and Father." Clayton took a sudden sip of tea and looked hastily away.

Kendra gave him a gentle smile, thinking how blessed she was to have these new parents who were so kind and good to her. "Thank you, sir."

"Thank you, Father. It is most generous of you. Now," Dorian continued with the planning, "I will leave for Yorktown to procure the marriage license and the reverend. Father, if you could round up the family and send messages to any neighbors we want to invite."

"You're putting me in charge of invitations?" Clayton frowned, reminding Kendra of his son, and opened his mouth to complain more when Faith rushed into the room, eyes wide and bright. "Millicent says we're to have a wedding!" She looked from Dorian to Kendra and back again. "Thank God they found you! Are you alright? Is it true?"

Dorian grinned at her with brotherly affection. "It's true, poppet. And we are going to need your help."

"I'm so happy for you both." Faith hurried to Kendra's side and took up her hand. "Who abducted you?" She turned to Dorian. "How did you rescue her? Tell me everything."

Dorian motioned for her to sit down in a chair beside Kendra. He gave her a quick accounting of finding her about to be married to Martin.

Faith turned round eyes toward Kendra. "You must have been terrified. I was praying so hard!"

"Thank you, Faith. I can't imagine where I would be right now if they hadn't come. Martin was going to spirit me away to another town right after the ceremony."

Faith paled. "He would have forced himself on you."

Hannah cleared her throat. "Don't think of it, my dear. We have much to be thankful for."

Faith turned her face toward her brother with a dreamy sigh. "So you brought her back and proposed. When is the wedding?"

"Tomorrow, if possible. I should be able to bring back Reverend Worthington and the marriage license by then. Can the three of you come up with everything else?"

Hannah laughed. Kendra blushed and looked down into her lap. "I don't want to cause any trouble. Please, it should be a simple affair."

"Nonsense" — Faith reached over and squeezed her hand — "Momma is a miracle worker with situations like these. Aren't you, Momma? We will call the troops home to help — Lizzie and Charity and Marjorie. And I will make the bride's cake!"

Hannah set her teacup down and stood up. "An excellent plan, Faith. Send notes to your sisters right away. Kendra, we must find you a proper gown. Come and show me what you have and we shall see if we can't make something into a wedding dress. I dare say we have enough fripperies lying about in Faith's armoire alone to make something festive."

Dorian frowned at his sister. "Now don't overwhelm her. I don't want to find her frightened away when I return." He walked over to Kendra and pulled her to stand in front of him. In a low voice he said, "I'll be back by nightfall, God willing."

"I will miss you." She bit down on her lower lip. "Do be careful." Her voice was low but everyone in the room had become suddenly busy looking elsewhere.

"Always." He bowed and kissed the back

of her hand but not before Kendra saw a look of uncertainty pass through his eyes, a shuttered look that lasted only a moment, but still, it was there. Oh, dear. Did he really want this marriage? Or was he only doing this to "keep her safe" as he'd said. She thought back to his proposal and realized, belatedly, that there had been no mention of love in it. She started to say something, to ask, but he had turned away, nodding farewell to his sister and parents, and then strode from the room.

"Girls, do come along." Hannah's eyes brightened with excitement. "We've so much to do."

Clayton came over and gave Kendra a kiss on the cheek. "Welcome to the family." His voice was so warm and kind, so sincere, that she determined to forget her worries about Dorian. This is what she wanted — a family that loved her and that she could love in return. Dorian just hadn't said it yet, that was all. It was up to her to make sure he knew what a wonderful wife she would be and how she would pour her whole heart into making him happy. He would say it soon. Maybe on their wedding day.

Hannah's arm wrapped around her waist as she led Kendra out the door toward her bedchamber. Kendra squashed her doubts, only too glad to be carried away on their wave of excited happiness.

They'd done it.

Not that he had doubted his mother and sisters' ability to pull off a wedding and celebration party afterward, but still, it was impressive, all that they'd managed.

He stood with the Reverend Worthington at the end of a grassy aisle under an old walnut tree that he used to climb as a boy and tamped down the raw fear that gnawed at his stomach. The smell of hot honeysuckle from nearby bushes floated on the breeze toward him, making it impossible not to remember the other time he had stood up to be married.

Tricked. Made a fool. The worst mistake of his life.

And now, here he was doing it again. Was he making the same mistake?

He took a deep breath and reminded himself for the hundredth time that Kendra was not Molly Simpson, not even close. Molly's face flashed through his mind. Shame filled him when he thought of her, which was rare. It filled him now as he stood and waited for his bride. He knew what he should be feeling — joy, anticipation, *love* — the fact that those emotions didn't come easily made him grit his teeth and look down before someone saw the anger in his eyes.

Music lifted on the fragrant breeze. He looked up from studying the tips of his shoes in the long grass and saw her come to stand at the end of the long line of chairs set up for the guests.

His breath caught in his throat.

She was wearing a pale blue dress, almost silver. It floated as she came to a stop, settling around her in a cloud like some magical creature of light and beauty. He swallowed hard. She looked up and caught his gaze, held it. There was questioning in her eyes, as if she, too, feared this thing they were doing. And why wouldn't she? Dorian realized. Her parents had loved and lost. She had her wounds too.

God, help me be brave enough to love her. His eyes glossed over and he stretched out his hand. *Come to me. Marry me. We'll figure it out . . . together.*

She couldn't have heard him, but it seemed she did. Her lips curved in a slow smile, a smile that said she was willing to step off the cliff with him into the unknown. She started walking, a little faster, and then her hand gripped his, her eyes shining with unshed tears too.

He wanted to lean in and kiss her but something told him to wait, it wasn't time yet. He turned toward the preacher, hoping he would hurry with the ceremony. Kendra hoped no one could hear the loud pounding of her heart. He'd had that look again, like a trapped animal, wary and unsure. It had only lasted a moment but it brought back all her doubts. They were doing the right thing, weren't they? *Lord, You know I love him. I will make him a good wife. I won't give him any reason to regret this day whatever his reasons for marrying me.*

She said her vows with determination, staring into his eyes with all the conviction she could muster.

His voice was determined too, as if he'd made an inner decision.

Her hand shook as Dorian slid a delicate ring with a small stone the color of deep amethyst onto her finger. "I'll get you a prettier one later," he leaned in to whisper.

Kendra shook her head. "I love it."

Reverend Worthington said the final words of the blessing and pronounced them husband and wife.

Dorian leaned down and kissed her before he'd finished the last words. The crowd behind them chuckled. She grasped Dorian's arm with a laugh — *joy* — a shaft of light bursting through her, and then they walked toward the aisle and the congratulations of these kind people who were now her family, her friends.

She had finally found *home.*

On the other side of the long yard, standing hidden amongst a stand of trees, stood Angelene, gnashing her teeth, a lone tear running down her cheek, and promising herself revenge.

CHAPTER TWENTY-THREE

"Good morning, love," Dorian murmured as he leaned over his wife who was obviously pretending to be asleep. She smiled, eyes still closed, and snuggled closer to him. "Having trouble waking up?" Dorian wrapped his arms around her before rolling them both over and over, and then completely out of the bed. They landed on the floor with a thud and a squeal from Kendra.

"You sir, are a cad. You did that on purpose!" She sat up, straddling his stomach. "Married a mere two months and you're already trying to kill me. What's next, poison? From now on you have to taste everything I eat before I eat it."

Laughing, Dorian rolled her over so that she was pinned beneath him. "Oh gladly, my lady, and I'll start by tasting this." He slowly lowered his head toward her.

Kendra pushed him back with a laugh.

"Don't you have to leave soon? John's showing you his finished stables today, isn't he?"

"Aye. But I'm sure he won't mind waiting."

Kendra wriggled out from beneath him. Backing away with her hand out, she shook her head. "Victoria will mind, and I'll not have it my fault that you're late."

Dorian rose up off the floor in a sudden move and reached for her.

She shrieked, laughing harder, and jumped out of his reach. "Stop it, knave. We have no time for pillage and plunder and you know it."

One of Dorian's brows rose in a wicked-looking question. "I'm a pirate now, am I? That is one of your favorites."

Kendra squeaked as he dove for her, catching her nightgown in one hand. He hauled her backwards until her back hit his chest. She had the good grace to know she wouldn't convince him and with a sudden movement, turned in his arms and wrapped her arms around his neck.

"I suppose pirates always get their way," she murmured near his lips.

"Oh, yes, my prize. Always."

When she finally got Dorian out of the house she looked at the clock in a panic. A quarter past nine and there was so much to do to prepare for his twenty-sixth birthday party that she was throwing for him that evening. She had been planning a surprise dinner party with their closest friends all week. Now they only had a few hours to decorate the house, go over the menu, and help Cook with all the different dishes. She shouldn't fret though. Faith was a testament to her name and would assure her that all things were possible and pitch in wherever needed. She and Hannah were as excited about Dorian's birthday as Kendra was. Well, that was close to true. Kendra had a surprise for all of them.

A thrilling hum filled her and tears stung her eyes as she put her hand over her stomach. A baby. What a perfect birthday gift to give her husband. Walking over to her chest at the foot of the bed, she knelt down and opened it. Closing her eyes, she inhaled the familiar lavender and cedar that greeted her from the contents. She lifted out the miniature portraits of her father and mother, wishing they could have met Dorian and what would have been their first grandchild. They would have been so happy for her. Laying them aside, she lifted out her other treasures she had brought from England — a few slim books, her mother's dragonfly brooch, fine linens for when they had a home of their own, and her first sampler. She smiled at the crooked stitches and could still feel the prick of the needle as she rubbed her finger against her thumb before setting it aside. Near the bottom she withdrew a small bundle wrapped in paper. Her fingers were clumsy with excitement as she untied the ribbon. Folding back the paper, she lifted out a tiny garment. A white christening gown with white satin embroidery and a lace-trimmed bonnet. It had been her christening gown and now it would be her baby's. It was still in perfect condition and snowy white, being wrapped and always stored in the chest. Yes, this was perfect. She would give it to Dorian as a gift and watch his eyes light up when he understood the meaning. She held it to her, closed her eyes, and imagined his happy, surprised face. *A baby. Thank You, God!*

Kendra stood hidden beside a tall Longcase clock in the front drawing room with family and all their close friends, who were hiding behind various pieces of furniture, waiting for Dorian to walk through the door. It had been John's duty to keep him occupied until six o'clock when they were to have dinner with John and Victoria. No one had mentioned it being Dorian's birthday, and Kendra didn't know if he had guessed at the reason behind the dinner or not. Either way, he would not know it was going to be a much larger affair.

A clatter of hoofs sent all the guest diving for cover with muffled giggles and exclamations. Kendra put her hand to her mouth to still the laughter bubbling up inside her and peered around the clock.

The front door opened with a blast of sunshine and fresh air. "Surprise! Happy birthday!" Friends and relatives sprang from their hiding places. Kendra bit down on her lower lip as she watched Dorian's eyes grow round with shock. He saw her then, gave her a sideways look that was half-accusing, half-laughter, then strode over to her and caught her up to him, giving her a tight squeeze. His smile was brilliant, the one that always melted her heart. "What have you done? I didn't think you knew it was my birthday."

"Your mother told me. Are you happy?"

"I've never been happier in my life." His eyes were intent and voice thick with emotion as he said it.

Kendra couldn't respond, only basked in the perfect moment.

The dinner was a huge success. There was

more food than they could eat in three days — veal chops and lamb, duck and monkfish. There were all sorts of colorful garden vegetables — peas, carrots, turnips, and potatoes. Giant bowls of roasted corn on the cob dripping with butter, and platters of corn bread soaked in maple syrup. Gingerbread, apple dumplings, and then, in the center, on a raised dais made from a linen-covered box and crystal vase, sat Dorian's favorite dessert that Kendra had made herself — spice cake with almond-flavored icing. A meal to rival Christmastime!

After supper the party gathered in the drawing room where Charity played cheerful tunes on the pianoforte, with various guests volunteering to sing. After a time, the men pulled back the furniture to the walls and couples began to twirl and dance about the room. Kendra felt her heart might burst with the happiness of it all.

"May I have this dance, my lady?"

Kendra curtsied and took her husband's offered hand. He led her to the center of the room and then pulled her in close for a waltz. Her eyes glowed with happiness as Dorian swept her into his arms, circling and turning, his hold so secure she felt she was floating.

"I still can't believe you've done this."

Dorian grinned down at her.

"Oh, there is even more to come. You haven't even opened your presents yet."

"Presents too? You'll spoil me."

Kendra raised her brows and cocked her head to one side. "I am determined to make you a good wife."

A small frown creased his forehead but his smile remained intact. "Why would you say that? You have nothing you must prove."

Kendra looked away, realizing she'd expressed too much of her fears out loud. He seemed so happy — they were so happy — and yet, he had never said those three words, that he loved her. The music came to a halt and everyone swung to a stop around them, breathing deeply, laughing and talking. Kendra took the opportunity to slip away. "I have something to do now. Go and dance with someone else, one of your sisters perhaps?"

Dorian nodded, watching her go, his smile a little stiff.

He was so astute to her every mood. She must be more careful and keep her silly doubts to herself. She hurried over to her mother-in-law. "Hannah, I need to run upstairs and fetch my present for Dorian. Could you round everyone up and direct them into the back sitting room? The children are getting tired and we should have him open his presents soon, don't you think?"

Hannah laughed, the crinkles around her eyes endearing. "The adults are getting tired, too." She waved her toward the stairs. "You've done a wonderful job, Kendra. He's never had such a day just for him."

Kendra leaned over and gave Hannah a quick kiss on the cheek. "Thank you. I will be right back."

When she came back down she spotted Dorian in a secluded corner, his head bent, seeming in a deep conversation with John. Probably talking about all the improvements he meant to have in the home he was building for them. He would be lost in that conversation for half an hour if she let him. This was a party. She would have to pull him out to join the guests.

She jostled her way through the crowd, stopping beside a high-backed chair where she watched her husband unobserved. He looked so handsome in a waistcoat of dark silver, black breeches, and shining top boots. His jet-black hair lay combed against his tanned neck. She lost her train of thought as she watched him, smiling to herself, but then she became aware of what he was saying.

"I should have never married her, John. She knows too. I can tell she knows. I will have to tell her."

"You had no choice, man. Just be glad it's all behind you, or at least it will be, as soon as you tell Kendra."

Everything inside her stopped at the words. It made no sense . . . and then it made perfect sense. Before she even thought what she was doing, Kendra turned and fled through the crowd. She ran up the stairs and into her bedchamber. Closing the door to their room behind her, she leaned back against it.

He didn't want her.

He didn't want to be married to her anymore. He never had.

Despair swept over her in great waves, rolling over her and taking her under. Nothing in her life, not even her beloved father's death, had prepared her for such complete pain. It was an agony that robbed her breath.

"I can't breathe. I can't breathe," she rasped out to the room, stumbling toward the bed. "God help me, I can't breathe." The words kept ringing in her ears over and over until she thought her mind would explode with it. Lies, the last few blissful weeks had all been lies. Why? Why would he marry someone he didn't love?

He'd never said the words. He never said *I love you.*

He'd only said he'd marry her to keep her safe.

Face it, Kendra. She felt like shaking herself. He married her to protect her and she had let him, encouraged and led him to that moment. She was as bad as Angelene in her attempt to win him, just more subtle. Oh God, I've been manipulating him and now he is stuck in a marriage he doesn't want and regretting it. This is all my fault.

She fell to her knees and bent her head. "Forgive me. I'll make it right. I won't let him sacrifice himself for my selfish mistake." *Love.* It was time for her to exercise sacrificial love.

CHAPTER TWENTY-FOUR

The early morning air was cold on Kendra's face as she led the gray-dappled mare through the wooded path and then down a quiet street to Angelene's house in Yorktown. If Dorian knew she was out riding alone he would be furious, but then it really didn't matter anymore, did it? She couldn't fathom what he would feel when he found out she had left. Would he be relieved? Now he wouldn't have to find a way to get rid of her.

He wouldn't even know she was gone for several days. Luck had been on her side when she made her plans. Dorian had received an inquiry from a man interested in captaining the *Angelina* and was headed to Williamsburg to speak with him. Kendra hadn't known he had decided to no longer captain the ship himself and found it puzzling, but her heart was too heavy to really ponder the point. All she knew was that he would be gone for four or five days, giving her the opportunity she'd been waiting for.

She told the Colburn family that she would like to spend some time with Victoria while Dorian was away and she would be staying with her for awhile. Hannah had given her such a frown when she told her that Kendra almost believed she had read her mind, or at the very least knew something was wrong. She hated to deceive her, but there was no other choice. She couldn't bear to wait until Dorian left her. Just the thought of it brought back the waves of despair and the feeling that she couldn't catch her breath. No. She couldn't wait for him to do that to her. She would go home and put her life back together. And Angelene would be glad to help her find the first ship sailing back to England.

Ducking beneath a low branch, she adjusted her seating and kept a steady pace. She rounded a bend in the road and saw the house. There. Last chance to change her mind. She stopped and pulled a letter from her pocket. It was the letter that Dorian had received, the one that told of her inheritance.

Uncle Andrew wasn't happy about their marriage, that much was clear, but he had included a deed to a cottage and some land in Arundel. Kendra couldn't remember ever having been there. The letter said it was from her maternal grandmother and had passed down through the eldest daughters for centuries. Andrew assured Dorian that it wasn't worth much. There were some bank notes for a few hundred pounds tucked inside the letter that was said to be the extent of the dowry. Andrew apologized that it wasn't more, in his snide way. Kendra had taken the notes and the deed, they were hers after all, packed up the bare essentials and now, here she was, at Angelene's house looking for help. A sad, choking sound escaped her throat as she spurred the horse further down the drive.

Taking a deep breath, Kendra dismounted and secured her horse to the hitching post. Picking up her skirt, she walked up the steps to the wide porch and knocked. A manservant answered and smiled at her in a kindly way. That was unexpected. She imagined Angelene's servants to wear armor beneath their livery in order to survive her barbs.

She handed over her card. "Is Miss Monteiro at home? I would like to pay her a call."

"Miss Monteiro? Gracious ma'am, she isn't up this early."

"Oh, dear." Kendra twisted the glove she'd taken off in her hands. "It's a matter

363

of great importance. I don't know what I shall do without her help." Kendra felt the quivering of her bottom lip increase.

"Well now, that's a different matter, isn't it? There aren't many ever needs Angelene's help, but there's always that first time, now isn't there?" He looked alarmed with wide eyes and his lips pressed down into a frown. "Come in the drawing room here and I'll go and see if I can rouse her."

"Thank you." Kendra walked into a charming room of mint green and cream decor. Sinking onto a small sofa facing the door, she waited while trying not to chew on her bottom lip. A few minutes later, she looked down at her clenched fists in her lap and noted how her knuckles were white. *Stop being nervous!* Angelene would be glad to be rid of her, there was nothing to be afraid of on that score. The thought of the woman throwing herself at Dorian after she left made her throat ache. *Help me be strong, full of patience and long-suffering, Lord.* She knew this was only the first of many hard things she would have to do in the coming months.

It was a full half an hour later that Kendra heard a rustle of skirts approaching. She looked up to see Angelene, her face flushed and hair in disarray, enter the room.

"I can't believe it's true. What are you doing here?"

She paused, and her disdain dimmed as she saw Kendra's eyes fill. "Kendra, what's wrong? Has something happened to Dorian?"

"Yes, I'm afraid something has," Kendra said quietly. Standing, she walked to a window and looked out, feeling blank inside, as if she didn't know anything anymore. "I know we haven't been very good friends, but I need your help."

"Tell me what's happened." Angelene walked to her side and took hold of Kendra's upper arm in none too gentle a hold.

"I'm going to have to ask a favor of you, and I can't tell you why. Please" — she looked out into the yard again, fighting back the tears — "I need to find passage back to England, as soon as possible."

"What do you mean, back to England? Are you visiting someone?"

"No, I'm . . . I'm leaving him. Please, don't ask why, can't tell you. It was just never meant to be."

Kendra looked at Angelene's smug face. "I was right, wasn't I? He doesn't love you."

Kendra turned away from her hard, glittering eyes. This was harder than she expected. With a little sniff, she pulled herself upright. Turning back to Angelene, she nodded. "I have to go home. And I need passage back to England before Dorian returns from Williamsburg. Your father knows everything about ships. Please, I need your help leaving America as soon as possible."

Angelene just stood there for a long moment, looking into her eyes. Kendra couldn't tell by her stoic face if she felt happy or sad for her, but it didn't matter. She just needed the woman's cooperation. Then her lips curved up into a cold, calculating smile. "Of course I'll help. I'll do anything I can. My father is even now at the docks. We will walk down together and see him."

"Perfect. When can we leave?"

"Let me fetch my parasol and gloves. I never let the sun touch my delicate skin, you know."

Kendra nodded, feeling leaden inside.

"Just leave the details to me, Kendra. I'll get you home and it will be soon, very soon. I promise you that."

Dorian pushed his steed harder as they entered the yard. He had been gone five days, and he was eager to see his wife. It was the first time since their marriage that he'd been away so long. He hadn't realized how attached he'd become, how lonely life felt without her. Dorian hurried through the front door, met by his worried mother. "Thank God you're home, son," she said as she helped him off with his sodden coat.

"What's wrong? Is something wrong with Kendra?"

Hannah led her son into the front parlor and poured him a cup of hot tea before answering. "I'm not sure, dear, but I am worried. She rode out of here minutes after you left. She seemed to be in such a hurry to leave and she hasn't been the same . . . since your birthday party. She said she was going to stay with Victoria for a few days and visit while you were away, but I haven't heard a word from her since. I sent one of the stable hands over this morning to tell her that I expected you home today and to see how she was doing but he hasn't returned yet. I don't want to worry you unnecessarily, but I have a bad feeling that something has happened. I would suggest you ride over there yourself and bring her home."

Dorian downed the rest of his drink and shrugged back into his coat. "I'll go now. I knew I shouldn't have taken this trip. Something was wrong before I left but she wouldn't tell me what it was." With a grim set to his mouth, he gave his mother a quick kiss on the cheek and hurried back out the door.

The ride to Victoria's house seemed to take forever. He had a fresh mount and it was a good thing, because he nearly drove the poor beast into the ground in his haste. When he finally saw the house come into view, he breathed a sigh of relief. He would force her to tell him what was wrong. Whatever it was, they would find a solution. There was nothing between them they couldn't resolve. Reining in his steed, he threw the lines to the waiting stable boy and raced up the stairs to bang on the door. Victoria answered it. "Dorian, this is a surprise. I'm afraid John isn't here."

Alarm rang through Dorian's mind. "I'm here to see my wife. Where is Kendra?"

"Kendra?" Victoria motioned for him to come in. "Please come in where we can talk."

Dorian allowed her to lead him to the drawing room. He ignored her motion for him to sit. Remaining standing, Dorian said as pleasantly as he could manage, "Victoria, please go and get my wife."

Victoria paled. "Dorian, I haven't seen Kendra since your birthday party. Has something happened? Is she missing?"

Dorian fell back into the chair across from

her and leaned his head into his hands. "I don't know. She told my mother she was coming here to stay while I was in Williamsburg." He looked up at her, his hair swinging in his eyes. His heart was pounding. Hard. Too hard. If Kendra had been abducted again he didn't know how he would handle it. But that made no sense. She had left on her own, telling lies about where she was going.

"Oh, dear." Victoria sat down across from him. "I haven't seen or heard from her. I don't know . . ."

Dorian was stunned. Never in all his wildest imaginations did he think that Kendra would leave him. Why? What had happened? What had he done?

"We'll find her," Victoria said in a low, calming voice. "She must have left some clues. Have you searched your rooms?"

Dorian shook his head. "I came straight here."

"We must go back. She may have left a note or something."

"Yes." Dorian stood up. "Go back." He gave a little bow murmuring, "Thank you, Victoria," and rushed from the room.

"Wait. I'll come with you!"

But it was too late. Before she had time to get to the door she heard horse hooves pounding away.

Victoria had been right.

Back in his room, Dorian found a note on the dressing table. He tore it open with shaking hands.

Dear Dorian,

I know you are probably shocked to be reading this letter. I'm sure by now Victoria has told you that I did not come to visit her. I have decided that it is time for me to go home to England. I would like to thank you for the security you gave me by giving me your name. After I was taken by Martin, I was terrified for my life. When you offered marriage to protect me, I grasped at the chance because I love you. I realize now what a great sacrifice that was for you and I thank you, but now it's time for me to make a life for myself. I'm ready to begin again and am returning to my true home to do just that. Please, if it is in your mind to follow me — don't. You won't change my mind and if you think about it, I'm sure you really wouldn't want to anyway. Please know that I will always cherish our brief time that we spent together, but I am doing the only thing I can, the right thing to do. I am setting you free. You will always hold a special place in my heart.

Forever in your debt,
Kendra

Dorian blinked several times and reread it. And then read it again, more confused than ever. "In your debt?" What did she mean? She didn't want to be his wife? What could she possibly be thinking by "setting him free"? The only freedom he had ever felt had been when he held her in his arms. He turned to pace but couldn't seem to move. Another thought occurred to him. She had only married him for the protection of his name. *God, had it all been a lie? Like the time before? Had it happened again?*

With sudden energy he searched the room and her belongings. She had taken most of her things and clothing and something else, something that made the puzzle snap into place.

The letter from Andrew Townsend.

The deed. The banknotes. Her inheritance.

Was that what she'd wanted all along?

CHAPTER TWENTY-FIVE

Standing on the deck of the ship *Liberty,* Kendra looked out toward the London harbor in the distance. Low-lying fog shrouded the city against gray, water-laden clouds. The wind chilled her to her core, causing her nose to ache and shoulders quiver. It was a sharp contrast to the day she'd left, so bright and sunny. Now, it was January, winter had come and, with it, the London drear.

The voyage had been depressing as well with bad weather dogging them, rough waves and storms, so much rain. Then she'd experienced the occurrence of morning sickness which lasted well into each day. She had hardly left her cabin for the entire ten weeks at sea. Thank heavens that was fading. She was feeling better now, physically at least. The rest of her felt strangely numb, as if she couldn't muster the strength to care about anything. Kendra placed her hand on her slightly rounded stomach. *Please God, let everything be alright.* She'd never felt so alone. Aboard another cargo ship, she didn't even have fellow passengers to talk to. But she was almost home.

Home. Seeing the English shoreline brought bittersweet tears to her eyes. It was good to be home, but at the same time the aching hole in her heart throbbed with longing for her husband. *I'll never find another man like Dorian, will I? Why couldn't it have been for real?*

I only have You, Lord. I'm sorry for even thinking that You are not enough. But I miss him. Another person to miss.

Interrupting her thoughts, the captain walked over and stood beside her at the rail. He was a wiry, red-headed man with freckles covering every exposed inch of his weathered face, who spoke with an Irish accent. He'd been too busy to do more than send an occasional sailor down to check on her and another to bring her meals each day, meals she had mostly not been able to eat. But now his blue eyes twinkled at her, seeming glad to be at their journey's end. "We'll be docking in a few hours, Mrs. Colburn. If you've not already packed, you might wish to do so."

"Thank you, Captain. I will."

With a polite tip of his hat, he was gone.

Kendra watched his retreating back. The numbness she fought settled back around her like the fog around the city. She turned and stared at the water, at the waves, and wondered what life would bring next.

And if she could survive it.

Dorian tore across the open field on his Palomino stallion, feeling the controlled muscle of the animal explode with power at the slightest signal of pressed thigh or a tug of the reins. Over the last two weeks since Kendra had left him, he spent every evening working the horse until they were both lathered with sweat. The results were showing. They were learning each other, an instinctive collaboration as to what the other wanted and was capable of. And they pushed, both of them, to the limits of flesh and bone — spirits soaring, bodies straining, souls listening.

The sun faded into a molten red glow at the edge of the horizon but Dorian didn't heed its warning. The relief these rides provided from the constant ache was too great to stop. It was almost like being aboard the *Angelina* when the wind whipped the sails flat and they clipped along at amazing speeds. It was like flying. Like running headlong into the elements and becoming one with them. It made him feel alive.

His breath whooshed out as they turned in a tight circle at the edge of the clearing and raced back toward the barn. Kahn whinnied, lengthening his neck and stride. They were both breathing in even, ragged gasps. Up and over the swells of the field and then plunging down into gentle valleys, they soared together. The landscape blurred past, a frenzy of movement, a jolting of joy flowed from animal to man. The pounding sound of Kahn's hooves matched Dorian's beating heart.

Kendra . . . Kendra . . . Kendra . . .

Noooo! He turned the echoing name aside and clenched his eyes shut. Focusing on Kahn he reclaimed his calm and urged him on even faster. Faster than they'd ever gone. Reckless. Not caring if it killed them. Ravished. Torn apart except in this moment of total concentration.

It was the only thing that worked. *Dear God, it's the only thing that works!* His throat tightened with the thought, with the truth.

A sudden dip in the ground made the proud beast stumble. It happened so fast Dorian couldn't react. But Kahn did. With an almost supernatural grace he sidestepped with his powerful back legs, haunches gathered up and exploding with power. He reared up. Dorian clung to him with all the muscle he could muster. Kahn leapt forward, avoiding the hidden hole and springing back into a run. Dorian slowed him by degrees until they smoothed into a canter across the field. He didn't seem injured but he wasn't taking any chances. He felt a fool, heat stinging his cheeks when he thought of how hard he had pushed Kahn. And yet, the horse seemed to enjoy it as much as he.

Thank God he wasn't injured in my foolishness.

They cantered at a gentle pace back to the barn where Dorian gave instructions to have Kahn brushed down, watered, and fed an extra measure of oats. He turned toward the house then. He dreaded going to his room, but it was growing dark and he would have to face it sooner or later.

Walking through the entry he heard a noise coming from his father's study. "Dorian? Is that you?"

He ignored the question and hurried up the stairs. He'd avoided his parents and, especially Faith, since Kendra had left. Their questioning, sympathetic faces were more than he could bear. He needed to get away again. Like he had with Molly, only he needed escape much, much worse this time.

Entering his suite of rooms, he headed toward the decanter and poured a drink. He slammed it back then took off his dust-smeared coat and slung it across a velvet chair. He was filthy. He should ring for a bath but he didn't care. Let the room stink right along with him. He poured another drink and took a sip, sinking down on the Persian rug beside his bed. With one knee up, he braced his forearm and stared into the growing darkness, sipping the burning talons of fire from the glass until full dark had settled around the room. His body relaxed against the bedframe behind him.

His mind slowed until even blinking made him tired. He was so tired. Tired of running. Tired of feeling the pain despite everything in his power he'd done not to feel it. Tired of not knowing . . . anything.

He slung the empty glass away with a weak flick of his wrist and heard it roll, clunking across the polished wood floor. *Why did she leave me? I don't understand. I thought she wanted to be my wife. If she really loved me, she wouldn't have left.*

The silence in the room grew thick, like the dark. Dorian took a sudden breath, afraid. He glanced around, wishing he had thought to light the lantern but couldn't seem to move, just waited.

Go ahead. Give it to me. I deserve it.

He didn't know if he was still talking to God or the devil maybe. But something in him was rising up and he needed to finish this.

I miss you, son.

The thought came in an instant way that overwhelmed him. He began to shake — like those stories in the Bible when someone saw an angel and fell flat on their face. He began to feel like that in the thickness of the room. Something, Someone, was here with him.

Lord God, is that You?

Nothing. He thought through the words he'd heard so deep that it took his mind a second to sort out the meaning. Could God really miss him?

His past flashed across his mind. As a boy he'd always been glad to go to church, stand up and sing, read his Bible, and ponder the stories of the people of God. So innocent. So believing and soft-hearted, yielding to any understanding that might come along and help him grow. He saw Molly's face, a pretty girl with brown ringlets and a fierce desire to escape the poverty of her life. He'd been the ticket out. Her manipulation had turned that naïve boy into a hardened man. He hadn't had much respect for any woman outside his family after that. Didn't trust them. Woman after woman until Angelene. They'd all been the same. Grasping, greedy, wanting to take anything from him that they could. Why were they like that? Why had he always attracted that sort of woman?

He thought back on the recent conversation he'd had with Angelene. He'd gone to see her after hearing from a stable hand that Kendra's horse was returned from Angelene's house. It was the last place she'd visited before boarding the ship to England. Angelene had tried to play her games with him again.

"Dorian, you know she was never right for you, don't you? An English aristocrat and all. You know I could make you happy. Not her. Never her."

Dorian had snapped, grasped her by the neck, and looked down into her dark brown eyes, waiting, hoping to finally see some fear there. "I will never be with you, Angelene. Do you understand? I will never love you. Never."

She nodded, fear and tears making her eyes glassy, but it was a look that said she finally understood. And he'd not heard from her since. He would never entertain that kind of woman again.

They had made his heart hard. He'd

turned from God's voice, God's presence, and thrown himself into escape. He saw his ship, arms above his head and throat raw with exalted shouts as they reveled in yet another storm. He saw himself on Kahn this afternoon, riding hellbent toward numbness. It was what he did. What he did without God.

Dorian curled over his upraised knee and allowed the anguish to encompass him. His shoulders shook with silent spasms as the full truth came into his mind and seeped through his soul. He'd replaced God with adventure. He'd replaced trust with control. And he'd let the only woman he would ever truly love leave him. *Forgive me, Father. Forgive me. I want her back. I want You back. I lay my life before You. Whatever You want. Whatever is Your will. Forgive me. Oh, God forgive me and take me back. I don't want You to miss me anymore!*

He breathed hard, rasping into the quiet room. His breathing lengthened and slowly, by degrees, evened out. Finally, a deep peace settled into his very bones. He felt he could lie down and sleep for days. He breathed long and deep, lifting his head. *Thank You, God. I praise You. Thank You for salvation and healing and revelation and truth. Thank You, Father.* A joy he hadn't felt in a very long time filled him. Peace and joy. His gaze roved the dark room and then there, peeking out from under the bed, something glowed white like a flag lit up by the moon. He stood and walked toward it. Bent down and picked it up.

It was a paper-wrapped package tied in ribbon. He turned it over and over in his hands, able to feel it more than see it. Taking up a candle, he lit it and set it on the bedside table. He sat down on the bed and folded back the paper. A folded note fluttered to the floor. Bending, he picked it up and read the familiar scroll of Kendra's handwriting. *"Happy Birthday, darling! All my love, Kendra."* His heart began to pound as he laid the note on the bed. "All my love." She'd said it, but had she meant it? Dorian turned back to the paper and reached for the white fabric. It unfolded as he lifted it out. A baby's christening gown. He swallowed hard as the garment's meaning slammed into him.

A baby. Oh Lord, a baby.

Kendra was going to have his baby. His heart raced as the realization took hold. *If she was going to have a baby why did she leave? Couldn't she have stayed for the child's sake, if for no other reason?* He had to go after her. He had to find the answers to his questions. And whatever else happened, he was going to be a father. They were a family and it was time to get them back.

Kendra looked out the window at the passing countryside. They had just crested Bury Hill and could see Arun Valley with its rolling farmland and dotted with cottages and sheep. It was cultivated, Kendra thought, pressing her chin into her hand. It seemed so civilized even though they were in the middle of the countryside. Why, you couldn't have gotten a carriage through the American countryside, it was so wild and untamed and beautiful — like its people — like Dorian.

It was night when they reached the outer gardens of Arundel Castle. She sat up straighter as they clattered over the cobblestones through the huge stone gate and then over the bridge where decades ago there used to be a moat. Her heart began hammering as the hired carriage swung around the drive and stopped at the entrance to the castle. What would Uncle Andrew do? Would he let her stay? She brushed the questions aside with determination. She'd come this far, she would just have to find out. Kendra took a deep breath and she stepped out onto the drive. She looked at the castle, up and up the massive walls to the coat of arms carved into the stone above the door. Their lion and unicorn stood ready to guard the castle from harm. The impact of the scale of the place hit her like never before. It couldn't be more different than Aunt Amelia's simple log home.

And everything appeared so fine and well cared for, much better than when she left. She had expected to see more disrepair, but the windows sparkled in the evening twilight, every one of them glowing with warm light. The ivy covering some of the stone was well manicured. Perfect. That's how it looked. Like a painting.

Waving the driver on to the stables, she gathered up her skirts and lifted her chin. She grasped hold of a new, highly polished door knocker and banged. How surprised Hobbs, their dear old butler, would be when he saw her. She had an eerie feeling that this wasn't her home any longer, but she pushed it aside and smiled as broadly as her nervous stomach would allow.

Instead of Hobbs a reed-thin man with a long nose answered the door. He appeared affronted by the task. "Yes?" he drawled while looking down his nose.

"Is Hobbs dead?" Kendra blurted out in

her shock.

"Hobbs?" The man blinked but remained so stoic he could have been a statue.

"Forgive me. I'm Kendra Col, uh, Townsend, the earl's niece, and I expected Hobbs, the butler who has been employed here for years, to answer the door. Has he passed on?" While she spoke she moved toward the dome-like foyer with the distinct impression that she would have to force her way in.

"I was recently employed. I don't know anything about Hobbs."

Drawing herself up and taking on her most intimidating posture, she stared daggers at the man and frowned. "You may call me Lady Townsend. Is my uncle at home? I would like to see him immediately."

"I suppose I can see if he will see you."

Kendra clamped her mouth down before she said something she regretted. "Thank you." She forced out.

After he left, Kendra was struck by her surroundings. New, thick rugs warmed the floors. Large, dark lacquered urns that looked to be from Japan held tall, potted plants overflowing the corners with leaves. She walked through the door to her right, into the front salon, and gasped in disbelief. The room was more beautiful than it had ever been. New drapes in a honey and cream-colored velvet hung over the windows, complementing upholstered chairs and sofas in a deep orange and gold. A purple chaise sat in one grouping with dark satinwood tables loaded down with painted porcelain statuettes and pretty vases and gilt-covered boxes. Across from those pieces against a wall was the loveliest desk she'd ever seen with delicate carved legs, and a gleaming turquoise inlaid top. Kendra turned round and round in a slow circle, taking it all in. New lamps and branches of candelabra lit the room, a rich painting graced one wall that must have been six feet tall. A glittering chandelier hung above her head. She felt numb. Unable to think why . . . how. The last time she'd seen this room there had been only a few worn pieces of furniture left from the sale of all their belongings. How could this be? Where had Uncle Andrew gotten the money for all of this? It was impossible that he could have earned it in the short time she had been away.

"You'll find the rest of the rooms refurbished as well," the soft voice spoke from the doorway. Whirling, she turned to see her uncle.

"It was about time, too. The place was looking shabby under your father's care, I must say."

There was a sneer in his voice that made the hair rise on the back of her neck.

"Please, my dear, come into my library. We have much to discuss."

Motioning for Kendra to precede him, she started to speak and then acquiesced, walking down the long hall, the back of her neck crawling with fear.

She walked into the dim library and sat in the chair Andrew motioned toward. He came around the desk that used to be her father's and sat across from her.

"When my butler told me you were here, I must say I was very, very angry. You have always done your best to make my well-laid plans go awry. But after considering it, I'm glad you're here. I should have done the job myself in the first place and saved myself the hassles of those bumbling colonial relatives of yours." He shrugged, his lips curving into a ghastly smile. "You know what they say, if you want a job done right . . . do it yourself," his arm waved in the air as his voice trailed off into a chuckle.

Kendra pressed her back into the chair shaking her head back and forth. Panic rose to her throat making her want to gag.

"I can see understanding is slow to dawn so I will have to explain. Such the pity." But he looked delighted to explain. *Dear God, help. He looks stark-raving mad!*

"You see, I've been a cheated man. I was the firstborn twin, not your father. But that unfortunate midwife tied a ribbon to his foot and they all insisted he was first." His eyes took on a glazed appearance and he looked to be in a trance as he continued, "She was my first kill. Strangulation. Fought rather hard but I was strong for my age."

"Age?" The question slipped out.

"Ah. Fourteen. Mother knew I deserved the title, but father loved Edward, so I became the second son." Andrew walked over and grasped Kendra around the neck. Standing over her he looked down into her wild eyes. "I couldn't just let him have it, you know. I vowed long ago that it would all be mine, including that paltry dowry your grandmother set up for you."

Kendra gasped for air. He let go and shoved her against the back of the chair. His movements were slow, casual, as he walked to the liquor decanter, pouring a long draught. After swallowing the contents, he smacked his lips together and continued. Kendra tried not to moan aloud with fear. "They all thought me such a spoiled dandy. No head for business. Couldn't handle my money." He laughed, a low and menacing sound that sent prickles of panic over Kendra's skin. "Fools — the lot of them. Especially Edward. All along I was making my fortune, more money than your father had ever dreamed of having."

Kendra shook her head and gasped out, "But you lost everything to that company . . ."

"The Brougham Company?" Andrew threw back his head and laughed again, this time loud and boisterous. Then he abruptly stopped and stared at Kendra — waiting, waiting, like a snake about to strike, he waited for her to see it.

"The Brougham Company. It wasn't bankrupt like you told my father. The ships that failed . . . they didn't fail, did they? It was all lies. Is that how you gained all this wealth?"

"I see that full understanding is beyond your reach, my dear. And it is such a brilliant plan. I wouldn't want you to miss a single nuance of it." His eyes lit up with glee. "Come now, you must see the irony soon. It's so delightful. The ships in my company are divided into two fleets. Half are legitimate merchant ships and the other half" — he grinned, his eyes feverish — "are pirate ships. You have even met with one of them! I hire my men from Newgate to work for me. Ex-prisoners, they're cheap labor and have the black hearts that I need. It's brilliant, really." His chest filled out with pride. "I send out two ships on each excursion. The pirate ship steals the cargo from other vessels then meets up with the merchant ship, where the stolen goods are then transported to the legitimate ship. My merchant ship forges papers documenting the sales history of the cargo and then sails to ports to carry out honest trade. You see, pirates have long had the problem of being able to sell what they steal. To appear more legitimate and sell my merchandise, I use the appearance of the Brougham Company as a front and the legal merchants don't know they're buying stolen goods. Genius, isn't it?"

Kendra was too stunned to answer. After a moment she spoke out in horror, "So you tricked my father into giving you everything he owned and left us practically penniless. But why?"

"But that's not all! I tricked him into giving me his wealth, but I still needed the title, and as you know, there was only one way to get that." Andrew raised his brows in expectation.

"You killed my father," Kendra whispered in horror. "You murdered your own brother for the title."

"Kill number two, I'm afraid. It *was* rightfully mine." Andrew's face reddened. "It was *mine!*"

"But if you were going to kill him, why bother stripping us of everything? It would all be yours after . . . after he died."

Andrew stepped closer, got in her face. "I wanted him to suffer as I had suffered. I wanted him to feel what it was like to lose everything."

"But he still had me, didn't he? We weren't as miserable as you had planned because all that really mattered was that we had each other."

Andrew turned his head away, white lines of anger on either side of his clenched mouth. "Yes, well, we can't have everything we want, can we? Looking back, I should have had you in the carriage accident. That would have destroyed him." He swung away from her, agitated.

Kendra could barely manage to get the words past the terror in her constricted throat. "No, it wouldn't have. My father looked to God for his strength. You couldn't take that away from him."

Andrew shot her a dark look. "Perhaps. And what shall I do with you now?" He tapped his bottom lip with one finger.

"Since those bumbling colonials couldn't finish you off, I will have to do it myself. It's too bad though, no one would have missed you in America. You've no doubt made your presence known across the countryside. I'll have to think of some accident for you. A fire, perhaps?" He mused with brows raised and a cruel twist to his lips. "Burning flesh, melting off your bones." He shuddered as if appalled by the thought.

Kendra could barely hear him above the roar of her heartbeat as he came nearer. The room grew dark around her. She fought for consciousness. She lost.

Kendra woke to utter darkness and a damp, musty smell. Struggling to rise off the dirt floor, she stood up, one arm curled protectively around her stomach. *Andrew killed my father.* The memory of what she had discovered hammered against her mind and caused her stomach to twist with nausea. She had known Andrew to be selfish and lazy, but never in her wildest dreams had she thought him capable of something so horrid. The man had murdered her father, his own brother, and was planning to kill her if she didn't find a way out of here. Panic rose in a bubble in her throat. She had to escape!

"Hello! Anybody here?"

Thrusting out her hands, she edged forward, afraid of what she might step on, until she felt a wall. Where had he put her? She turned in one direction and felt along the wall, easing herself around the room. A piece of furniture banged onto her thigh, making her cry out. It was a table. Feeling along the top, she found a lantern and a tinderbox. Thank God, Andrew hadn't left her without light. With trembling fingers she struck the tinder to the flint several times until she had a wavering flame. Careful not to extinguish it, she lifted the glass globe on the lantern and lit the wick. Turning around with the lantern held high, she studied her surroundings. The old abandoned cellar. There were sagging, half-rotted wooden shelves against one wall which held some dust-coated jars. The rest of the room was bare except for the crude table she was standing beside. Terror rose back up inside her throat. Would Andrew bring her food? Water? Or did he plan to leave her down here to die? She took a breath of the damp, cool air and walked to the shelves. If she got desperate enough she would open a jar and see if there was anything edible inside. She swallowed a wave of nausea. *Please God, don't let it come to that. Help me find a way out.*

Looking up over her head, she could just make out the outline of the door. It was a good fifteen feet above her head. She noticed that the wooden steps had been removed and wondered how she had gotten down to the floor. Andrew had probably just dropped her into the hole. The walls were bumpy dirt, but not anything she could climb. If only she had some kind of tool, she could dig out steps in the wall, but there was nothing. She could only hope that if she waited, there would be a moment when she could escape. She had to believe that. She just needed a chance.

CHAPTER TWENTY-SIX

Dorian lifted his spyglass to one eye and peered toward the eastern horizon. Never had a journey seemed to drag by as this one had. Never had time seemed to stand so still. Two, maybe three more days, and they would reach the London harbor. Glancing up at the dark clouds hovering near, he clamped his teeth together, suppressing a snarl. The weather had been clear up to now; cold, but clear. If this storm held off it would mean the difference between three days or as much as five. He didn't want to wait that long. He didn't want to wait another five minutes to get his wife back. But, of course, he had no choice. With balled fists, he turned away from the endless waves and scanned the deck for John. It had been a good thing John was along. His friend had kept him from killing members of his crew with his demand for speed more than once on this voyage; he'd kept him sane.

Dorian found John on the foredeck and walked over.

"You think we'll outpace the storm?" John asked the same question on his mind.

"It'll be close. I want to check those gaffs and that mainsail that was giving us trouble one more time, then I'll meet you in my cabin for some dinner."

"You know we've checked everything three times already today." John raised a brow at him, a look of concern in his brown eyes.

Dorian ran his hand through his hair, turned his head away, and sighed. "I know. It's just that I need something to do. This waiting is killing me."

John gave him a pat on the shoulder. "You are driving yourself crazy with this."

Dorian took a deep breath and let it slowly out. "I'm going to need a miracle to win her back."

"Good thing we know the Author of those."

The squeaking of hinges brought Kendra out of her sleepy haze where she had been curled up on the table, well away from the dirt floor where she imagined spiders and rats might live. Bolting upright, she saw daylight above her and a cloth bundle being lowered by a rope.

"Andrew?" she shouted. "Please, Andrew, let me out of here. I won't tell anyone what you have done. I'll go back to America and disappear."

A snorting laugh was her response. "You'll not get anything from him, Lady Kendra." It was the butler. "I'm surprised he is not letting you starve to death."

Kendra scrambled off the table and ran to the swinging bundle. She hurried to untie it and grasped it to her while the rope was pulled back up and the door slammed shut.

Taking the food to the table, Kendra unwrapped it to find half a loaf of bread, a small piece of cheese, some salt pork, and a canteen of water. Opening the canteen first, she took a long swallow. She wanted to gobble down the food as fast as possible, but she made herself eat slowly. Still hungry when the last crumb was gone, Kendra went over to the dirty jars. Taking the hem of her dress, she attempted to clean them enough to see what was inside. It looked to be fruit preserves, maybe sweet potatoes in another. After several attempts to pry open one of the jars, Kendra fell back against the table in frustration. The lid wouldn't budge. As she looked at the jar, an idea came to her. She could break it open and use the broken glass to dig grooves into the wall. If she dug them out in such a way that there were handholds, she might be able to climb up to the door. Taking up the largest jar, Kendra walked to the table. The corner was sharp. Raising the jar above her head, Kendra crashed it down on the corner of the table. The table wobbled and moved along the wall. She dropped the broken jar as it fell to the floor. Bending down, she picked up the largest piece of glass and put it on the table. It was sharp and would cut her hand if she used it like a knife. What she needed was some sort of handle. Lifting the hem of her dress, she reached for her petticoat and ripped off the flounced edge. There. That would do. Wrapping it around the end of the glass, she set to work.

Sitting on the floor, she began to make her first groove at knee level. The walls were hard-packed earth, making the process slower than she'd hoped. Within an hour, droplets of sweat dripped from her brow, but she kept going. Now and then she would take a short break and take a small drink of precious water, but only when she had to. Her hands ached and cramped, causing her to stop to massage or stretch them, and then she would start again. After four steps were made, Kendra crawled back up onto the table. The room flooded with darkness as she extinguished the lantern, but she was too tired to feel afraid. Closing her eyes, she was instantly asleep.

She woke with a start, terror gripping her. Her mind began to clear of the nightmare she had dreamed. Andrew . . . coming at her with his hands outstretched . . . as if to strangle her. He laughed in an evil roar while she cried out for her baby's life.

It was just a dream.

Just a dream.

Rubbing her hands up and down her arms, she tried to shake it off. Tears threatened to overwhelm her but she shook her head against them. There was no time to cry. She had to escape. She looked down at her hands, dirt-encrusted fingernails, swollen and aching. They looked like they had been beaten. Massaging them to work out the stiffness, Kendra picked up the glass and climbed up to the second groove, hanging onto the third groove with her free hand, she reached as high as she could and began to dig. Only three more grooves and she would be able to reach the door. The thought that the door might be locked kept trying to creep out of her subconscious and into conscious thought, but Kendra wouldn't let herself dwell on it. There was no reason for them to lock it, as they would think she could never reach it.

A creaking warned her that the door was being opened, so she jumped down to sit on the ground, the broken glass hidden under her skirts. The butler peered down into the hole. "I see you made it through the night," he yelled down, scowling. "I would have thought the rats had done you in by now."

Kendra hadn't seen any rats but she wasn't about to tell him that. The old man would probably find some to join her. Peering through the bright light, Kendra saw a similar bundle being lowered. Her stomach growled in anticipation. "Please, can you tell me what day it is? How long have I been here?"

"Time won't mean much to you before long. Lord Townsend is busy working out the details of your demise. But if you say pretty please, I might tell you."

Anger welled up inside Kendra, but the desire to know the day was greater. "Please," she muttered between gritted teeth.

The old man cackled with glee. "You've been in that hole for three days, and it's

399

Tuesday, about noon. I'm to bring you food once a day around noon." With that, he slammed the door closed and darkness engulfed the room once again. Three days! She'd been here three days, and if what he said was true, it didn't sound like Andrew would keep her here much longer. Grabbing up the bundle, Kendra ate the bread and the tiny piece of meat as fast as she could and took a small drink of water from the canteen. The last canteen had not lasted very long, and Kendra had to fight the urge to drink her fill of the new one. Wiping her dirty hands on her skirt, Kendra once again climbed up to the step she was working on and began again. If she worked hard, she might be able to escape by tomorrow night.

As soon as the *Angelina* docked, Dorian set his plans into action. He and John would go to the Arundel estate while the rest of the crew stocked up on supplies and waited for their return on board the ship. He sent John to buy the best horses he could find and get directions. If they rode fast and had decent horses, they might make it by tomorrow night.

Kendra looked up from the dirt floor at the eight grooves in the wall. She was ready to make her escape. She guessed that the butler had brought her food twelve hours ago. That would make it right around midnight, if her calculations were correct. She waited a little longer in case she was wrong. It must be dark when she made her escape and the later the hour the better. Her only chance was if no one was guarding the door, and if the door was not locked from the outside. She had gently pressed on it after she had carved out the last step and it seemed to give, but she remembered the squeaky hinges and didn't want to press her luck in broad daylight. Any number of people could be milling about the area and hear her.

What she would do once she gained freedom, she wasn't sure. She was hoping that she would be able to find one of the old servants she knew to help her. If not, she would just have to take a horse and get away as fast as possible. London. Back to London. It was the only place where she might find help in exposing all Andrew had done. What she really needed was proof. Documents that told of the schemes, the fake company, cargo records, letters, something. The obvious place to look would be Andrew's desk in the library. The likelihood that Kendra could get into the house and down to his room unnoticed was slim, but if she couldn't find anyone to help her, she would have to take that chance.

Looking down at her filthy hands, Kendra cringed. She had worked all day to finish the steps, and there was barely any feeling left in them. Using some of the precious water, she dampened a piece of cloth from her ripped petticoat and attempted to clean them as best she could. They were getting so dirty that she had hardly been able to bend her fingers enough to hold the glass, but her hands weren't the only casualties. Her whole body felt like it had been beaten, and she was covered with dirt from head to toe. She knew that even if she did see a servant, he or she would be hard pressed to even recognize her. With that thought, Kendra took a clean corner of the cloth and wet it. Using the cloth to wipe her face, she breathed a sigh of relief. She would never waste water again, should she get out of this mess. Taking the pins out of her hair, Kendra shook the mass out and ran her fingers through it to bring it to some sort of order. The effort was almost too much for her tired arms. Taking a fortifying breath, Kendra braided it into one fat braid down her back. She then paced in the small cell, trying to stay awake. It was tempting to sleep for a few hours, but she didn't dare, as tired as she was she wouldn't wake up until morning. The thought of spending one more night here was more that she could bear.

After what Kendra hoped was an hour, she prepared to make her move. Taking a clean piece of cloth, she wrapped it around the jagged glass. The glass had served her well as a shovel and now it would act as a weapon too. Next, she tucked her skirts up into the neckline of her dress to free her feet to climb and snuffed out the light. She wished she could have kept the light on, but she didn't want to risk someone seeing it when she opened the door.

Taking a determined breath, Kendra began to climb the grooves in the wall. Reaching the sixth step with her feet, she clung to the eighth step with one hand while stretching her other arm upward until she felt the door. She pushed on it while saying a silent prayer. Joy burst through her. It wasn't locked. They never dreamed she'd find a way out. Her relief was so great she almost lost her footing and fell to the floor. Catching herself, she pushed up on the door, letting in a cool shaft of moonlight. She climbed higher and flung the door open, it landing on the ground with a soft thud. Everything in her stilled as she waited for the hue and cry, but nothing but moonlight and the chill of the night air greeted her. Scrambling up the last groove, she pulled herself up and out of the opening, landing on the ground beside the hole. Her gaze darted around the moonlit grounds, seeing the kitchen garden and back of the kitchen building. She stood and lowered the door back into place. No one seemed to be around. Crouching low to the ground, Kendra tiptoed to the kitchen and then stood on tiptoe to peer through a window. Empty, dark, and quiet. Perfect. She crept to the door and opened it. Going inside, she washed her hands in a basin of clean water, packed a bundle of food — eating while she packed — and filled her canteen from a covered bucket of fresh water, drinking her fill first. She decided she better not carry her supplies with her to Andrew's library, so she hid them among some bushes just outside the door before making her way to the main quarters of the castle. Silently, she crept down the dark hall, feeling her way with one hand skimming the wall, toward Andrew's library. The door was shut. She took a deep breath, reached out, and pressed on the latch. It creaked a little as she pushed the door open. She stood still, not daring to breathe. Fright washed over her like a bucket of cold water splashed into her face. *Do it. You have to do it.* Stepping into the room, she closed the door behind her.

She was in the room. Her heart pounded in the silent room as she felt around for a light and found a branch of candles. She lit them from the tinderbox in her pocket and made her way to the desk. An overwhelming sadness took hold of her as she ran her fingertips along the gleaming top. This had been her father's desk. She remembered all the times she had sat next to him while he worked. How patient he had been with all her questions and interruptions. He always stopped his work to answer her or show interest in her ideas and solutions to problems. Once, when she had been sitting next to him, she noticed that he seemed troubled. "What's the matter, Papa?" she had asked in her eleven-year-old voice.

He had turned and looked at her with such love. "Nothing, my sweet. I was just missing your mother."

Kendra's heart broke at the pain in his eyes. She knew she missed having a mother, but she didn't really miss her mother because she had never known her.

"What was she like?" Kendra asked in a soft voice.

Her father's eyes became misty as he gazed in the distance. "She was wonderful. She loved life so much, Kendra. She was kind and thoughtful of others. She appreciated the small things in life and was not caught up in all this," he said with a wave. Turning to Kendra, he clasped her small hand in his and said with emotion clogging his throat, "She loved you very much. We wanted a child for a long time and then you finally came. Her last words were about you."

"What did she say?"

"She said that you were very special. That you were a gift from God and that we should all take very good care of you. And something else. Something I've not told you about yet."

Kendra cocked her head to one side. "What is it?"

"I was waiting until you were older, but the time seems right." He gave her a tight squeeze. "She made me promise that you should pick your own husband some day and that I shouldn't pick him for you."

Kendra didn't know what to say, and was a little embarrassed to be talking about someday getting married.

Her father chuckled and pulled her in for another hug. "Don't worry, sweetheart. I will be there to help you decide."

But he wasn't here. And she had picked the wrong man. A big tear dropped down Kendra's cheek. "I miss you so much," she whispered into the darkness.

Taking a deep breath, Kendra pulled herself from her thoughts. She had to find documents, something to prove Andrew's guilt. Opening drawers and sifting through papers, Kendra searched the desk. There. In the bottom, left-hand drawer, she found what she was looking for. All the paid receipts from the supposed debt to the Brougham Company, and underneath it the real ledger for the Brougham Company. Glancing through it Kendra could see that the company was making a profit, the kind of profit that came from stolen goods. Then a name, a familiar name, shot out at her. It was a cargo list from a ship . . . a ship named the *Angelina*. Her breath whooshed out with the revelation. Andrew had been behind the pirates that had attacked Dorian's ship. The pieces snapped together with sudden clarity. Andrew had sent those pirates to try and finish her off before she ever made it to America, on board a rich cargo ship, two birds with one stone. Oh, she felt sick. Would there be no end to what he had done to them?

"Find what you were looking for?" a sneering voice asked from the doorway.

Kendra's head snapped up, her heart in her throat. Andrew. *No, please God, don't let this be happening.*

Kendra stood up and started to back toward the window while Andrew advanced on her.

"I should have known you would try something like this. You've been nothing but trouble. Getting in the way of my well-laid plans! And you almost succeeded, didn't you." He was within inches of her now. So busy with his tirade, Andrew must not have heard the sound of horses riding up into the courtyard, but Kendra did. Her gaze flicked toward the window, but it was too dark to see anything.

His voice rose to a shout, "What did you think you were going to do with these?" He reached over and ripped the papers from her hands. "You'll need more proof than this, you know. I have many *friends* in the courts. No one can touch me. No amount of proof will destroy me!" His eyes bulged and his face turned red with rage. His voice rose even higher as he reached over and took a small gun from a drawer in the desk. Aiming it at Kendra's chest, he gloated, "You will never stop me, not when I nearly have it all. Your dowry was the only thing left, the last piece, and now I'll have that too."

Kendra knew she had to act — now. It was her only chance. Taking the jagged piece of glass from her pocket, she brought it in an upward sweep toward the hand holding the gun. Andrew screamed as it sliced into his forearm and then dropped the gun. Kendra scrambled to the floor for it, but Andrew was too fast for her. Picking up the gun, Andrew lifted her off her feet with one hand wrapped around the collar of her dress. With his other hand, he slapped her hard across the face, snapping her neck back. He arm rose back to smack her again when they heard a menacing voice from the doorway.

"Release her or you're a dead man."

Dorian and John stood there, rifles aimed at Andrew's back, certain death in their eyes.

"Dorian, you came," Kendra whispered through her bleeding mouth.

Sweat beaded on Andrew's upper lip as he turned Kendra and held her back against his chest, the gun aimed at her head. "If you want your wife alive, I wouldn't make any sudden moves."

Kendra tried not to whimper in pain as his arm cut off her breath.

"Drop your guns or I will put a bullet

right through her pretty head." Andrew rammed the pistol further into Kendra's temple. Dorian and John lowered their guns to the floor.

Suddenly, a loud boom went off from one of their guns. Smoke filled the room as a bullet whizzed toward the ceiling. All eyes saw it strike the chandelier above Andrew and Kendra, breaking the glass into a thousand falling pieces before they could react. The massive silver arms came plunging down toward Andrew, Kendra still within his grasp.

Dorian dove forward, plowing into Kendra, while Andrew's attention was riveted above his head. It all happened so fast. The chandelier hit Andrew first, pushing them down to the floor. Dorian reached them just as they hit the floor and pulled Kendra away. One of the broad arms of the chandelier caught her leg and she yelped in pain, but the sudden scream from Andrew said he took the brunt of it.

Dorian pulled Kendra close as the chandelier clattered to the floor around Andrew's head and shoulders. They all watched, immobilized, as the massive silver arms pinned him to the floor. Andrew lay on the floor, his face frozen in shock, his eyes wide open. There was a huge gash, bursting with blood, on his head. Kendra wailed and turned into Dorian's shoulder, gripping his coat with her hands.

The room grew quiet. The candles flickered as if a soft wind had blown by. John stepped over and picked up Andrew's arm, checking for a pulse at his wrist. He nodded to Dorian. "He's dead."

Dorian hugged Kendra tight to him, smoothing loose hair from her face. "I almost lost you. He almost killed you. Don't ever think of leaving me again."

The streaks of morning had just begun to color the bedchamber with rosy light when Kendra began to stir. Dorian had sat up all night, watching her sleep; thanking God she was still alive.

She opened her violet eyes and blinked up at him. A small smile, and then a wince crossed her face. "I must look a disaster." She frowned and looked away uncertainly, shy.

"You look beautiful." Dorian raised his hand to her cheek and gently stroked it with his thumb.

"I'm filthy and bruised from head to toe."

"You're alive."

She locked gazes with him, her eyes filling with tears. "You came for me. Why?"

Dorian reached around to the bedside table and grasped the tiny garment. "Recognize this?" His voice was sober, serious.

Kendra bit her lower lip. "The christening gown. I left it under the bed, didn't I?"

Dorian nodded. "Does it mean what I think it does? Kendra . . . are you expecting a child? Our child?"

Kendra looked away and nodded.

Clasping her chin, Dorian turned her face to look into her eyes. His heart pounded as he asked the question he had come thousands of miles to ask, "Why Kendra, why did you leave? Why would you not tell me about our child?"

Kendra's chin quivered as she burst out the story. "I overheard you talking to John, at your birthday party. You said that you wished you hadn't married me and, and that you would have to tell me . . . that, that our marriage would be over soon. I realized that you married me only to protect me and I-I couldn't bear the thought of your not loving me, so I left."

Dorian's emotions swung from confusion to anger to pain. He racked his memory for this supposed conversation. Suddenly, it struck him. He'd been telling John about Molly, and how he would have to tell Kendra about her. "Kendra, we weren't discussing you, love."

Kendra's gaze turned toward him with a snap. "But then, who?"

"I was married once before. We were discussing her."

Kendra gasped and pushed away from him. "You were married? When? To whom?"

"Her name was Molly. She tricked me into marrying her. She insisted she was pregnant but we found out later that she wasn't. I was eighteen. I made a mistake and then paid a very great cost for it."

"But what happened to her?"

"She died a couple of years after we were married. I was . . . relieved, and hated myself for it. I should have told you about her. I'm sorry. When you walked into my life" — he paused, leaning his head back, gazing at the ceiling with a sigh — "I didn't want to feel what you made me feel. I didn't ever want to be married again. Those years with Molly, it was the worst time of my life. I swore I would never remarry. But then you came into my life and I knew I would be lost without you. I love you, Kendra. I have never loved anyone until you. Can you ever forgive me?"

"What a fool I've been. Can you ever forgive me? I should have trusted in our love, but I've lost so many people that I was afraid you would leave me too." Looking up into his eyes, she whispered, "Can we make it right?"

Dorian pulled her closer into his arms and kissed her, branding her forever his. Lifting his head, his throat clogged with joy, he said, "It already is, my love. It already is."

Dorian swept her up into his arms and then pulled back with raised brows and a wicked-looking smile.

"What are you thinking, my black-hearted knave?" Kendra giggled.

"Ah, the name-calling begins. I've missed it so."

"You haven't answered me. Don't dodge the question."

"I was thinking that a bath would be next in order. And then I was imagining how we could both fit in the tub and how I would —"

Kendra stopped him with a kiss. "Scandalous . . . American . . . pirate of my heart," she murmured against his lips with a smile.

"Aye, my lady. Always your pirate," he agreed, forgetting all about the bath.

Dear Reader,

Have you ever tried really hard to be a good Christian? You're reading your Bible, praying, controlling your flesh, and following after Him. And it feels great! You might even feel justified, sanctified, worthy by your actions. And then BAM. Something (or someone) happens that throws you into a tailspin and reveals how weak and helpless you really are. You fail. You feel bad about yourself. And you might even hide from God, distancing yourself in shame instead of running to Him for help.

In my latest book, *Pirate of my Heart*, Lady Kendra Townsend finds out that she isn't nearly as good as she would like to be and that the American sea captain she falls in love with challenges all of her good intentions. Captain Dorian Colburn has a lesson in store too. It is easy to forget about God when life is going along perfectly. Oh sure, he goes to church and goes through the motions of being a Christian, but it takes a violet-eyed Englishwoman to knock the wind out of his sails and send his perfect life sinking faster than a flaming pirate ship. If they can just get through the struggles, there is real treasure to be found at the end.

It is such a relief to finally give all of our

being over to Christ Jesus, admit defeat, and ask for help. That's where the peace is. That's where the joy lies. In Him is our treasure. I hope you enjoy Dorian and Kendra's love story. It was great fun to watch the sparks fly between these two characters and see them find treasure in God and in each other.

Jamie

DISCUSSION QUESTIONS

1. Kendra's father and uncle are twins and the sibling rivalry is exacerbated by the elder earl's favoritism and training of the eldest son. Let's discuss sibling rivalry and parental favoritism. Read about Joseph's life in Genesis chapters 37–39 and compare his experience with his siblings to your experience as a child. What experiences have you had with this issue as a child, parent, or even in the workplace?

2. Kendra's mother died giving birth to her and her father becomes her whole world. When he dies, she is devastated. What were your relationships like with your parents? If you are a parent or would like to be in the future, what would you do differently? The same?

3. Dorian is happy with his life and has no desire to change it. He doesn't draw

close to God because he doesn't really feel that he needs Him. Have you ever fallen into this trap when life is coasting along fine? What happened and what did you learn from that time?

4. For the first time in her life, Kendra finds herself highly attracted to a man. She is confused — afraid and excited at the same time. What was your first crush like? What happened and what did you learn from it?

5. Love and infatuation can cause many emotions to surface such as jealousy and desire. The Bible has a lot to say about desire along the lines of James 1:15, "Then, after desire has conceived, it gives birth to sin; and sin, when it is full-grown, gives birth to death." What do you think about the emotional traps involved with falling in love? Is there a "best" way to go about it? Any other Scriptures come to mind?

6. Kendra's relatives in America have been disillusioned by life's hardships, making them cold and bitter. But Kendra's giving nature brings light and joy to their lives again even though their situation remains the same. It amazes me how much one

person can influence a household for good or evil. What impact do you have on your household and/or the people in your life? Is there something you would like to change?

7. How can you bring the love of Jesus into the lives of others? What practical steps can you take?

8. Angelene is determined to have Dorian as her husband. Dorian's mother tells her that God has the perfect mate for her, like Eve for Adam, and not to force a relationship. Have you ever forced a relationship? What happened?

9. Kendra overhears a conversation and jumps to the wrong conclusion. The Bible says in Matthew 5:37 to "let your 'Yes' be 'Yes,' and your 'No,' 'No'." What do you think this means? How has miscommunication affected you?

10. Even though Dorian loves Kendra he has a hard time saying it. How often do you tell people you love them? Is it easy or difficult to say? Were you raised in a family that was demonstrative in their love for you? How has that impacted you?